poisons
the soul…

— THE HIGHLAND LEGACY SERIES BOOK 2 —

BETRAYAL'S

Legacy

RENÉE
GALLANT

Betrayal's Legacy (The Highland Legacy Series Book 2)

Castle & Quill Press
http://www.reneegallant.com

Ordering Information:

Quantity sales. Special discounts are available on quantity purchases by corporations, associations, and others. Orders by U.S. trade bookstores and wholesalers. For details, contact the publisher at the address above.

Editing by The Pro Book Editor
Interior and Cover Design by IAPS.rocks

ISBN: 978-1-7340666-3-0

1. Main category—Fiction/Sagas
2. Other category—Fiction/Romance/Historical/Scottish

First Edition

Also By Renée Gallant

Novels
Whispers of Deception (The Highland Legacy Series Book 1)

Short Stories
A Finger for Each Cigarette
With Words We Weave – A Celebration of the Past
With Words We Weave: Texas High Plains Writers 2020 Anthology

To Vickie!
Thank You for
Your Support! It means the world
Renée Gallant

For my uncle Ho-*Beau*-ken
One of the greatest gifts
God has ever blessed me with.
I will love you always.

Chapter One

ELAINA PULLED HER COAT UP over her ears, shrinking farther into its warmth to escape the fog's icy grip around her throat. She didn't know if her companions had grown silent or if the mist had swallowed their words. Even the sound of Laoch's hooves striking the rocky ground beneath her took on a hollow timbre.

Although the hindquarters of the horse in front of her were but a smoky blur, she felt naked and vulnerable, as if the hidden forest surrounding her had eyes of its own and whispered her secret to the wind. At any moment she expected Robert Campbell to snatch her from the back of her stallion and steal her off through the woods, her disguise not hindering his recognition in the least.

She gripped the reins tighter and stretched her neck, trying to relax her jaw and unclench her teeth as she fought to calm her wits at that horrid image. The frigid Scotland air burned as she sucked it in through her nose and then it twisted and danced its way out of her mouth. Her eyes stung from lack of sleep due to the night terrors that woke her more often than not. She feared the only thing that would free her from this living nightmare clawing at her soul was the death of Robert Campbell.

While the image of her former coachman clouded her mind, a dark form began to take shape in front of her. It grew, taking on an ominous appearance. Elaina stifled the urge to make the sign of the cross. Instead, her hand slid to the hilt of the broadsword fastened around her waist. Her grip tightened, and she eased the weapon from its sheath. The tip of her sword met the air as her husband's features appeared, and she exhaled the breath she hadn't realized she was holding.

"Are ye goin' to take my head?" Calum asked, his words floating out on a cloud of smoke. The smile he gave her exposed the dimple in his left cheek that shone rosy with the cold.

"If you were Rabbie, yes," she answered, spitting her ex-coachman's more familiar moniker from her tongue like filth. It was only after her arrest for treason that she'd learned the truth of who and what he was.

"Is that where your mind is, *mo chridhe*? Worryin' yerself half-crazed over that man? I'll be glad when we can catch up to him and put him out of our lives forever."

"From your mouth to God's ear. What are you doing?" she said, sliding her sword back into its home as he swung his horse around to ride beside her.

"Countin'. Auld Ruadh is at the front of the line, and I'll bring up the rear. We dinna want anyone gettin' lost. 'Tis creepy, is it not?" His gaze roamed over what would have been the woods lining both sides of the road if one could see past the swirling gray smoke.

"Yes, it is."

"Well, dinna fash about it. 'Twill lift by mid-day. Meanwhile," his voice dropped to an ominous tone that sent chills down her back. "Dinna let ole Sawney get ye."

She snatched her hat from her head and swatted it at him as he turned back toward the end of the line of ten clansmen and two women.

His malevolent laugh trailed behind him as he evaporated into the churning mist.

Elaina had no idea who ole Sawney was, but she considered thrashing her husband whenever they stopped for a rest. All she needed was another creepy thing to invade her already ample imagination.

The final words Rabbie spoke to her before he had disappeared flitted through her mind. *"Remember, I love ye. I'll see ye again soon."* His face had been inches from her own, his green eyes piercing and almost full of adoration, but the smile on his lips before he shoved her to the ground, leaving her lying breathless from the pain, had been anything but affectionate.

That evil smirk would invade her dreams, waking her with a scream lodged in her throat and her body soaked in a cold sweat. Her mother would have called the man "tetched." Elaina considered him insane and evil beyond measure. His favorite pastime seemed to be confessing his undying love to her moments before he attempted to take her life or inflict horrendous acts of violence upon her. She shivered at the images her mind conjured and clutched the reins tighter again, praying the fog would lift soon.

Another more frightening thought struck Elaina. Calum was counting heads to make sure all were accounted for. Who was to count his head?

She swung Laoch around and headed to the back of the line to find her husband, her anchor in the tumultuous sea that was now her life.

⚬

True to Calum's prediction, the fog lifted by mid-day, gradually exposing the group of riders. The more that the surrounding landscape exposed itself, the more comfortable Elaina's breathing became. When the sun reached its peak in the sky, they stopped beside a small burn to water the horses and feed themselves.

Elaina groaned as her feet hit the ground. She loved horses and riding them, but it had been hours since they left the protective walls of Castle Balquhidder and months since she had ridden for this long, and her bum ached in protest.

"Let me have that demon ye call a horse, mistress," Ainsley said, taking the reins from her.

Laoch voiced his protest and yanked against Ainsley's hold.

"I dinna ken why ye ever wanted to bring this bloody poor excuse for a ride. Ye will never sneak up on Campbell on the back of this *glaikit* thing."

"*Glaikit?*"

"Stupid."

Elaina laughed, and Laoch's ears laid back against his head as the stallion bared its teeth. She'd have sworn he understood Ainsley's insult.

"Ye bite me, ye bloody bastard, and I'll give ye a skelpin' like ye've nay had before." Ainsley tightened his hold on the stomping, snorting horse. "Now, get ye a rest, mistress. I'll see to Laoch."

"You can call me Elaina," she told the lad for the hundredth time.

"Ye ken well enough I cannae do that."

Ainsley had gotten rather bossy for someone who, out of respect, could not call his former employer by her given name, but the sound of pounding horse's hooves stopped her from stating just that.

The rider barreled toward them from the direction they had been headed, parting the clansmen like the Red Sea. He pulled his steed to an abrupt halt before sliding to the ground, breathing near as hard as his horse.

3

Ainsley cast Elaina a questioning glance that she could only answer with a shrug.

"Settle yerself," Caitir said, handing the rider a flask of whiskey.

Elaina thought the boy could not have been much older than seventeen and recognized him as one of the scouts sent ahead days earlier. His pale skin was flushed pink with the cold and possibly the excitement of the news he carried. Perhaps he had spied Campbell.

The rider accepted the drink offered as he struggled to catch his breath.

"Now, then." Calum clamped a large hand upon the boy's shoulder. "Speak yer piece."

"There is a regiment of redcoats two towns over." The boy gasped, quivering out of either excitement or fear. His hands fluttered like a flight of birds as he explained the number of soldiers and their location. "But that's not all." The lad searched the faces of his captive audience, his gaze stopping on Elaina. "They carried this and were showing it to the townspeople."

"This" was a broadsheet with Elaina's likeness easily recognizable upon it and a reward of fifteen pounds sterling offered for her capture—alive. That one word alone made her want to cast up her accounts. She would much rather be taken dead.

"We will need to find another route." Auld Ruadh turned to the men who were eyeing the broadsheet. They mumbled and nodded their agreement.

"Wait," the lad interrupted as the Highlanders began to discuss alternate paths. "There is more."

"Aye?" Calum asked.

"Lieutenant William Edward Spencer leads the patrol."

The words hung on the air like the dense fog that had encompassed them earlier. No one moved or made a sound for several seconds.

Elaina broke the silence. "I must talk to him."

"Ye cannae do that, lass. They will arrest ye for sure if they lay eyes on ye." Calum took her by the arms and stared down into her face.

His eyes told her how foolish her words sounded. "I have to," she pleaded. "I can tell him what happened. He might get me pardoned."

"He might arrest ye," Calum said, his fingers digging into her arms and giving her a firm shake as she opened her mouth to protest. "Or ye might get *him* killed."

Her mouth snapped shut.

"This is a test, Elaina, to see if his loyalty lies with the King of England. They ken ye are his sister, and mayhap about the Jacobite money yer mother sent. We have no way to ken if that was a secret between Captain Cummings and Robert Campbell or if the whole of the British military holds that knowledge. What they wadna ken is how much yer brother is involved. Does he no have a stellar military career?"

Elaina nodded.

"That is the only reason, more than likely, that they are giving him the benefit of the doubt. Otherwise, he would be dead already."

Elaina's legs tried to collapse underneath her. Calum grabbed her up and seated her on the back of the supply wagon they'd hauled with them. She sat holding her head in her hands for several minutes, trying to sort through her husband's words while the surrounding men murmured about towns and paths. There had to be a way she could get to William. She must tell him the soldier she had killed was responsible for the murder of Ainsley's ten-year-old brother, Angus. She had to warn him that Rabbie MacLeod, their former coachman, was none other than Robert Campbell—the man they had hunted for their parents' murders. Worst of all was the news that she was not his sister after all.

"I have to speak to him." She raised her head, seeking Calum's gaze. "They don't have to see us…me."

"All right," Calum crossed his arms. "Say William doesnae arrest ye on the spot. What if the other soldiers spy ye? Yon wee lad had nay trouble pickin' ye out, breeks or no breeks." Calum's neck turned bright pink as he spoke, his temper on display.

"But he knew I would be dressed as a man. The troops are looking for a woman."

Calum scowled at her.

"I need to disguise my face, then."

"And how do ye propose to do that? Ye cannae magically sprout whiskers."

Elaina returned his glare. Jumping down from the wagon, she stormed off toward the creek.

"Where do ye think ye're goin'?" he called after her.

"To clear my head," she yelled over her shoulder at the nosy…bossy…unreasonable Scot. "Are you coming?" she snapped at Caitir.

"Aye, if only to see if yer hair catches fire." Smothering a laugh, Elaina's friend hurried to catch up with her as she stomped her way toward the burn.

Chapter Two

"**I** CANNAE BELIEVE YE!" CALUM FUMED yet again.

Elaina would have rolled her eyes if he hadn't been glaring at her and Erroll had not been holding a cold rag to her other rapidly swelling orb.

"Ye have to hand it to her. 'Tis a creative way to hide her identity," Erroll said, dabbing the cloth on Elaina's bleeding mouth.

"I dinna have to do anythin'," Calum growled, turning on Caitir. "How dare ye?"

"She begged me to. I refused until she called it payback for our escapade in Edinburgh the night the two of ye first met. What a romantic evenin'." Sarcasm dripped from Caitir's voice.

Elaina choked down a snicker.

"Rammin' yer fist into her face is outsteppin' yer bounds for a drunken night on the town." Calum bent down and studied Elaina's eye, pressing his cold fingers against the swelling tissue.

"She got me into a fight," Caitir snapped back at her cousin. "I had to care for her retchin' and stinkin' self all night. I had to bathe the shite off of her. Worst of all was the kiss in the middle of the damn street."

"You kissed her?" Calum's eyebrows shot up to his hairline as the surrounding men snorted with laughter.

"I saved her job," Elaina replied.

"Ye saved yer own arse," Caitir mumbled.

Elaina cast Caitir a sideways grin. "That was only a bonus. I did it all for you, love."

Calum threw his hands in the air. "What the hell do ye find so funny about all of this?" he growled at his men.

Elaina laid her hand upon his arm. When she'd concocted her grand scheme, she had not thought his reaction would be so visceral. "Calum," she said. "It's not their fault. Leave them be. Your anger is with me, although, you are being a bit dramatic about the whole thing."

"A bit dramatic?" He ran a hand over his face before planting them on the wagon on either side of her, penning her in place. He closed his eyes as he exhaled a huff of air against her mouth. "I never wanted to see ye like this again, *mo chridhe*," he whispered, looking away.

The pain that etched his gaze when he once again looked at her took her breath.

"What Rabbie and Cummings did to ye...the violence they exacted upon yer person...upon the woman that I love. I cannae bear it."

"I am so sorry. I-I didn't thin—"

Calum's mouth captured the remainder of her apology as he lay his lips against hers, soft as a feather. He wrapped his arms around her, drawing her close. "I am sorry, hen. I shouldna yell at ye so. It... I... It caught me off guard is all."

"You needn't apologize, Calum. It is I who should be sorry."

"Well, why don't the two of ye sit there tossin' apologies into the air like yer sprinklin' faery dust while the rest of us plan what to do about the British bein' on our arses," Auld Ruadh grumbled from behind Calum.

"Go on, ye old goat. Just because ye dinna have a bonnie lass to snuggle up to is no reason to be a heetherin'."

"Ye'll see heetherin', nephew, if I have to kill any redcoats because ye're too busy makin' nice with yer wife to bother with workin' out a plan."

Calum sighed and pecked Elaina on top of the head. "Duty calls." Then turning to Erroll, he asked, "Take care of her?"

Erroll answered with a nod.

Elaina watched her husband cross the clearing and join his fellow clansmen in a few long strides.

"The lass has a feisty punch to her," the short, older clansman said as he once again dabbed at Elaina's bloody lip with a wet rag.

"That she does." Elaina winced. "I'm almost sad she didn't break my nose again and straighten it up."

7

Erroll barked out a laugh. "There," he said, stepping back. "Ye'll do."

"Did it change my looks enough that they will not recognize me?" she asked, wishing she had a looking glass. If any of the soldiers recognized her, it would be all over. Although, Calum still had not given his blessing on the matter.

"It will come nightfall. Yer eye is changing color by the minute."

"Thank you, Erroll, for everything. Not just this." Elaina motioned to her face that he had tended. "I know all of you have put yourselves at risk for me, and I am humbled by it."

"Yer father was a generous and just Laird. Ye have his brown eyes, ye ken? Eyes like a stag, wise and sympathetic. Although, ye are the spittin' image of yer mother, temper and all." Erroll laughed when she smacked his arm with the back of her hand. "Even if Rabbie cut off yer lovely chestnut locks, ye could still be mistaken for yer ma. What happened to yer parents was unforgivable. Yer arrival and Robert Campbell's mistreatment of ye is more than enough to light a fire under our arses and revenge is sweet, lass. I've been itchin' to draw Campbell blood for twenty-plus years now. Ye gave us a good excuse, is all."

His soft amber eyes sparkled with the excitement of a coming war, and Elaina believed it would be a war. The two clans had been at odds for decades if not a century or more.

"Tell me about my father?" Elaina whispered, looking past the man's shoulder at Calum and Auld Ruadh squatting with their heads bent close to each other.

Calum's uncle had stick in his hand and was drawing in the dirt. Caitir and Ainsley had set about building a fire in the small clearing. The remaining clansmen either stood around whooping at two of the younger men sparring or busied themselves cleaning the hares they had trapped for supper. They would stay at this camp through the night, still unsure of their next step.

"Well." Erroll hitched himself up onto the wagon beside her, his eyes also traveling to the demonstration taking place. "What do ye want to hear? He was not an overly tall man, not like yon Calum, but he was a large man, in the physical sense and demeanor. He commanded attention and respect, and we gave it willingly. Yer da was a fair man—a man who would do anythin' for his clan. So much so, he gave his life for them." The last part came out in a hushed whisper.

Elaina did not turn her gaze from the display in front of them, but let the man gather himself before he continued.

"Yer father was so proud of ye. He carried ye with him everywhere. Ye were but a few weeks old when he loaded ye upon his horse with him and took ye from home to home, farm to farm, to show ye off to all of his clan. Yer mother wa' nay so happy about it." Erroll chuckled. "She had to follow along, ye ken, because… Well, because ye needed to eat and she refused to use a wet nurse. I thought for sure she would brain yer da. She was a braw lass," he continued. "She could hold her own against most men. Oh, she was bonnie. Ye look like her. Ye did, anyway." Erroll studied her face. "She had a mind of her own as well, and she gave yer da holy hell more than once."

"Chip off the old block," Elaina said with a laugh as she struggled to imagine these strangers he spoke of, her adoptive parents having raised her in the Royal Colonies—William's parents. Her eyes traveled over their small group of men, attempting to envision a warrior who commanded such loyalty as to have transcended over twenty years of being nothing but a memory. Impossible.

Calum approached the two still perched on the back of the wagon. "Come, Elaina. Let us see if yer new eye has hindered yer vision."

She accepted his hand and let him help her down. The light had begun to fade from the sky as the two of them walked out into the circle formed by the tramping of feet in combat.

"What are we doing?" Elaina blinked at her husband, trying to see how far she could open her eye. Not much at all.

"I want ye to block me."

Elaina nodded, noticing Calum did not have a weapon.

His right hand darted out, and she caught just before he struck the left side of her face. The corner of his mouth turned up as he nodded to his wife. "Good reflexes."

"Thank you," she said, catching his right foot with her left. Then she landed with a teeth-jarring thud, flat on her back, and lay there for a moment, dazed.

Calum took her hand, pulling her up, and she dusted off the seat of her breeks. She shook her hands at her side, changing her stance slightly. She nodded at him when she was ready, and he immediately cuffed her on her left ear.

"Ye cannae see out of that eye," he said. "I will have yer right side. No harm shall come to ye whilst I am there."

Elaina didn't argue. It eased her mind knowing that her husband would be standing beside her.

The pair strolled with their arms linked to join the men and Caitir beside the fire. Elaina caught a movement just outside the perimeter of the camp.

Guards. Calum and Auld Ruadh had set up guards to keep watch through the night. She wrapped her plaid around her, feeling safer, and accepted the whiskey jug from one of the men.

"If it makes ye feel any better," Caitir said, taking a seat next to Elaina. "I do feel a wee bit sorry for messin' up yer face, what when ye just got it back to normal."

"Oh, I am sure you do." Elaina grinned sideways at her before taking a long draw of whiskey and wincing as the spirits burned her raw lip. "You never told me you could hit like that."

Caitir shrugged her shoulders as she accepted the flask. "I would be a poor excuse for a Highlander if I couldnae."

The group broke bread, drank, and told tales of goblins and sea witches well into the night. Elaina learned what, or rather who, Ole Sawney was and thanked Calum for not telling her while they'd ridden cloaked in the fog. The thought that there had been a family of actual cannibals hidden in the caves of Scotland who had murdered and partially eaten thousands of unsuspecting travelers made her skin crawl, no matter how long ago it had been. She leaned back against Calum's legs, watching the fire crackle and listening to Erroll's wild tales. Her body seemed so alive out in the wilds with nothing but the woods surrounding them. This place felt like home. A feeling she had not felt for some time. Her thoughts turned to William and the news that she had to tell him if she could get close enough. It would not be easy for either of them. She didn't know if she could find the words to explain that he had now lost a sister. Of course, he may have already felt that way. He hunted her, after all, with a regiment of British soldiers and planned to arrest her for murder. Perhaps the news of her true identity could relieve a small portion of his burden. He was his father's son, ever the loyal British soldier. She supposed she was her father's daughter, the hot-headed rebel Scot. But she loved William. He was her brother, blood or no blood. He had cared for and protected her his entire life. She loved him even if he had orders to arrest her. "King and country first," their father had drilled into them at an early age.

"What is it, hen?" Calum leaned his chin upon her head.

"I don't know. Maybe I am tired is all." The statement held a morsel of truth. Her spirit had grown heavy, and tomorrow promised to be an even more vexing day if she had her way.

"Let us go to bed, then." Calum rose from his place on the log, pulling Elaina to her feet.

They said their good-nights and strolled hand in hand into the frigid darkness, where Calum had made them a bed of their coats with a cushion of leaves to lay upon. They snuggled down under their plaids, and Calum drew her into the curve of his body.

"Ye are worried about seein' William?" he whispered, stroking her hair.

Does that mean he will let me approach my brother? She snuggled closer to his warmth, trying not to get her hopes up. "How do you read my mind so well all the time?"

"I dinna ken if it is readin' the mind or only that I ken how I would feel if it were me."

"Well, yes, I am worried about what I would say to William, if you were to allow it. I don't want to break his heart. I don't know how to tell him I am not his sister." Her heart clenched with sorrow.

"Kin is no determined by blood alone. He is still yer brother and ye his sister. It is how ye were raised. It is like the clan, ye ken? We are no all related by blood, but by who we were raised up with and who has stood beside us when our enemies would like nothin' more than to destroy us. We are joined by a common bond, our beliefs, and our loyalties."

Elaina propped herself up on one elbow and tried to make out Calum's features in the dark. "He is ordered to arrest me. If he does not bring me in, what will happen to him? Will they hang him? Will they think him a traitor to the crown?"

"Perhaps."

"We can't let that happen. William is innocent."

"We cannae let him take ye in either. Ye will surely hang, if no worse. Especially, if Robert Campbell has anythin' to do with it."

"Well, we will have to come up with something, but for now, it is cold and I want you to warm me." Elaina squirmed against his side.

"Aye? And how do ye propose me to accomplish that feat?"

"Like this," Elaina whispered against his ear and wiggled out of her breeks. She slid her tunic over her head, pressing her naked flesh against her husband's body.

"It's like that is it?" Calum's voiced had dropped an octave. "I dinna see how less clothin' will make ye warmer," he teased, the leaves of their makeshift bed rustling as he removed his own clothing.

She wrapped her arms around him, curving herself into the nooks and crannies of his body and relishing the heat and intimacy of skin against skin. Her mouth grazed the little spot on his neck where his pulse pounded as his hand ran the length of her, the callouses on his palm rough and springing her body to life.

"Ye feel so small in my arms." He curled his fingers in her hair, his nails grazing her scalp as her mouth made its way down his chest. "Mmmm," he hummed in the back of his throat, gripping her tighter.

The vibrations of the noise against her lips sent tingles down her spine. She glanced in the direction of the campfire. Its sparks flickered into the black sky, the floating embers burning like stars until they dissolved into the expanse of darkness. The muted rumble of the men's voices drifted across the cold distance. They were too wrapped up in their tall tales to pay attention to two lovers in the night.

"I dinna care who—" Calum sucked air between his teeth in a hiss and his back arched against Elaina's touch.

Her fingers charted a course across the sculpted lines of his bare stomach while her lips blazed their own trail. Elaina cherished their moments of passion—the strength of their union seemed unbreakable because their souls as well as their bodies intertwined.

"Are ye tryin' to kill me?" Calum hissed, pulling Elaina up on his chest. He kissed her swollen eye, then grazed across the crooked bridge of her nose with his lips and followed it down until they came to rest on her mouth. His tongue flicked across the split, and he crushed her to him, rousing her hunger to a level of desperation.

"Calum." She squirmed in his arms. "I can't breathe."

"This"—his fingers found the end of the muslin wrapping that held her breasts flat to her chest—"must go." He pulled the muslin around her in an agonizingly slow circle until the cold of the night air caressed her bare skin. "Much better," he whispered, cupping one taut breast, his other hand moving in a different direction. His hands set firm upon her hips, guiding, controlling. Their rhythm matched the beats of their hearts as if their lovemaking could drive away all the evil that threatened to tear them apart.

"I want to protect ye always, Elaina. I cannae bear the wounds ye carry on the outside nor the inside. I want to heal them all."

The pain that draped his words blurred her eyes with tears. "You cannot protect me from everything, Calum," she kissed his neck, the salt of his sweat even in the frigid night air stinging her lip. "Your love alone is enough to sustain me through it all."

"Ye are so poetic," he whispered into her ear with a chuckle.

Her skin prickled with gooseflesh, and she shivered and bit his earlobe in response, causing him to laugh harder.

"I must no be doin' it right if ye can still find yer voice," he growled in her ear.

He flipped her over, making her squeak with surprise. Hovering above her with his curls falling in ringlets around his face and the backdrop of a million burning stars, he erased her thoughts and fears and silenced her voice.

Chapter Three

"I NEED TO STOP TAKING THIS thing off," Elaina mumbled, her chin pressed to her chest as she watched Calum bind her flat again.

"I dinna mind, *mo chridhe.*" He cocked a crooked grin at her. "I rather enjoy this view every mornin'." His hair was a tangled mess and lines etched the side of his face, deposited there by his makeshift pillow. She wasn't positive he was entirely awake, his eyes heavy-lidded.

"I'm sure you do." She leaned forward and kissed him as he tucked in the loose end of his wrapping. "Did you sleep at all?" she asked as he yawned so big she could see the back of his throat.

"No all that much." He raked his fingers through his hair.

The sky behind him was pink, fading into orange as the sun made its morning creep up to the horizon. The camp stirred with the sounds of men's voices husky with sleep. Her stomach growled, and she laughed as she covered it with her hand, trying to shush it.

"Hungry are y—"

"What in the bloody name of all things unholy do we have here?" A man's voice boomed, sending Elaina's heart into her throat.

Calum shoved her, sending her sprawling behind him with one hand and snatched up his dirk with the other as he sprang into a protective crouch between her and the imposing stranger. Where were the guards?

"Aron? Ye rotten bastard!" Calum leaped at the man. "What are ye doin' here?" He wrapped his arm around him, slapping him on the back.

Elaina eased into a sitting position, pulling her tunic to her chest to cover herself.

"I heard tell there was a crew of MacGregors out for Campbell blood, and ye ken I love a good fight. I came as fast as I could. I couldnae let my wee brother have all the fun." Even talker than Calum, Aron's guttural laugh boomed from his belly.

Elaina wasn't sure if his straight hair pulled taut in a binding was darker than Calum's or if the speckles of gray showing through only contrasted with the rest, making it seem that way. His broad shoulders and towering height gave her pause. The man was a giant. She sat unable to move as she watched the brothers exchange insults on the other's appearance. The two men hugged again, and Aron's gaze caught Elaina as she slipped her tunic over her head.

"What do we have here?" he asked, pushing his brother to the side.

Elaina stared at him out of her good eye as she raked her fingers through her hair and clubbed it at her neck.

"This is my wife, Elaina. Elaina, my brother Aron."

"I gathered," Elaina said with an edge to her voice. Her brother-in-law's open ogling was about to get him kicked in his stones.

"Yer wife?" Aron gaped at Calum. "Yer wife?"

Perhaps the man was simple. He seemed to have a hard time grasping the concept of marriage.

He looked Elaina over with what she took to be an air of disdain. "Ma is goin' to brain ye. Why is she dressed like that, and what happened to her face? Ye—"

"No!" Calum exclaimed. "I would never!" He then gave Aron a devilish smile. "It was Caitir."

"Caitir?" Aron turned and stared at his brother. "They were fightin'?" His voice dropped to a conspiratorial whisper and he leaned closer to Calum. "What does Caitir look like? Is the lass a scrapper, then?" He cocked his head toward Elaina.

"No. I mean, aye, she is a scrapper, but no, they were no in a fight. It is part of her disguise. She asked Caitir to do it."

"She wanted her to hit her?" Aron gaped at Elaina. "Why is she hidin' her identity?"

"Bloody hell," Elaina said. "I am right here. You two can stop talking as if I'm not, and I am not some oddity for you to gawk at, Aron." She glared at him as best she could with one eye.

"If that's what ye think," Aron replied.

There was a moment of tense silence as Elaina tried to decide if she wanted to stab him or not.

Quick as a fox, Aron lunged at her, scooping her up in his arms and hugging her tight. "Haha. Ma is goin' to brain ye for sure, but I kinda like the wee *Sassenach*."

"As far as *Sassenach* goes...," Calum said as Aron deposited Elaina on her feet. He proceeded to inform his brother on the happenings of the last several months.

Elaina took the opportunity to tuck in her shirt and slide her boots on. She was buttoning her vest when their attention turned back to her.

"That's...?!" Aron stared at her. "*That's* the outlaw? I've seen her likeness displayed over most of the Highlands. That's the woman on the broadsheet? The lass they beat and nearly burned alive?"

Elaina shivered at his words. "The one and only," she said with a bow.

"Why, she looks nothin' like her broadsheet." Aron bent down and studied Elaina's face.

"Thank you," she said. "And you are doing it again."

"What?" he asked.

"Speaking like I am not here."

"Ye married a wanted woman?" Aron barked out a laugh. "I cannae wait 'til ye tell ma. Promise me ye'll let me be there."

"You are making it difficult for me to look forward to meeting your mother." Elaina glared at the giant oaf, trying to decide if she liked him or not.

"Aye? Good," he replied. "Ye need to be prepared."

Elaina looked at Calum for reassurance. "You said she would love me."

"She will." Calum took her hand and shrugged. "Eventually."

Aron threw his head back and roared with laughter.

Elaina glared at Calum before turning her back on the brothers with a huff while she tied her sword and dirk around her waist.

"There is something else ye need to ken," Calum said. "Elaina is the missin' daughter of Laird Thamas and Mairi MacGregor."

Elaina turned in time to catch Aron's startled glance at her.

"But she's dead," he whispered. "Aunt Malina said the Campbells had thrown her into the Loch."

"Caitir's mother lied. She had taken the wee bairn to an earl's wife in Edinburgh. They took the bairn in and moved to the colonies first chance they got."

"In all my days…" Aron stood staring at Elaina. "Are ye certain?"

"I'm famished," Elaina said, interrupting the agonizing conversation. "If you would like to catch your brother up on the local gossip and proceedings of the day, I am going to see if there is anything left to eat. Aron." Elaina gave the enormous Scot a slight bow before she squeezed between the two men and trudged off muttering obscenities under her breath. She plopped herself beside Caitir on a log close to the fire.

"So, ye met Aron, then?" Caitir asked as she handed Elaina a slice of dried venison.

"Unfortunately so."

"Ah, he's no that bad once ye get used to him. He's loud and obnoxious, but he's got a good heart."

"He said their mother is going to hate me." Elaina turned her head to see Caitir better.

"He said that?"

"Not in those exact terms. I believe his words were 'Ma is goin' to brain ye.'" Elaina gave her best imitation of the annoying the man. "Three times over."

Caitir laughed, slapping her knee.

"I'm glad all of you think it is so funny."

"Eh, 'tis no goin' to be all that bad. Calum will protect ye." Caitir snorted.

"Why didn't you make this known before I married him?" Elaina elbowed the still giggling Caitir.

"But then ye would no have married the poor lout. I couldnae break his heart like that."

"His heart versus my neck?"

"The heart wins every time, my love."

Chapter Four

"**H**AVE THE THREE OF YE lost yer bloody minds?" Calum growled, looking from Elaina to Aron to Erroll and back.

Elaina laid a hand on her husband's arm. "It may be the only way to keep William from being charged with treason."

"I dinna think I understand this preposterous proposal correctly. Ye want me to let my own brother turn my wife over to the enemy? Just like that." Calum turned his glare to his older brother, who'd been standing with his arms crossed while Elaina explained. "Was this your plan?"

"Partly. 'Twas a group venture, ye could say. Erroll mentioned the idea, and we elaborated upon it. She didna need much coaxing." Aron cast a sideways glance down at his brother's wife. "But she is right. If he doesnae arrest her, he may verra well hang from the gallows himself. Besides"—Aron slapped Calum on the back—"a thievin' band of Highlanders will steal her out of their grasp before they can get to Fort William."

"Ye? Are ye in leagues with the enemy now, Erroll?" Calum asked the clansman.

"Nay, Calum. Ye ken my loyalties lie with the MacGregors and always have. It was only a thought. The lass needs to speak with her brother and could save his life at the same time."

"And what if it goes wrong? What if she is killed? What if they dinna take her to Fort William, but string her up on the spot?"

"They willnae do that. Her brother willnae allow it. It truly is the only way, *mo bhráthair*," Aron said with a sigh.

"And what of our task at hand? Campbell? Did ye forget him?" Calum said, fishing for excuses to not let her walk right into the hands of the redcoats.

"No, I haven't forgotten him. That will never be possible, but I love William and we may never have this opportunity again. I don't want to see him at the end of a rope nor in front of a firing squad." Chills gripped Elaina's spine, and she shivered, wrapping her arms around herself. "I might be able to garner a bit of information on Robert's whereabouts from William and the other soldiers. Consider it an intelligence mission."

Calum mumbled something under his breath that resembled "pure stupidity," then waved a hand at Elaina's bruised and swollen face. "So, all that was for naught?"

"Well, not *all* for naught. Caitir got her revenge for me getting her into a fight and kissing her on the street in Edinburgh."

"*Kissin'* her? What?!"

Elaina spun on her heel, leaving Aron staring after her with his mouth gaped open.

Let Calum explain that one.

Chapter Five

CALUM, AULD RUADH, AND ARON surrounded Elaina on the day's ride to locate her brother and his troops. The remaining men and Caitir waited at camp. The last thing they needed was someone in the regiment being curious about a group of Highlanders following them. Once Aron turned Elaina over to the British, the clansmen had estimated the trip to Fort William to take about four days. They planned to give the troops a day or two on the road with their captive before stealing her back. Aron would be the one to deliver her into the army's hands. William had never laid eyes on him before, so there was no danger of recognition nor giving the entire plot away.

They found the troops within the hour, the sound of their horses reaching the four of them before they caught sight of the regiment.

My god. How many are there? Elaina's palms grew sweaty, and she gripped her reins tighter. *What if William is no longer with them or the messenger was mistaken about the identity of the commanding officer?* Her stomach twisted itself into knots, her breakfast weighing heavy as a rock.

Aron leaned across his horse, passing Elaina a flask. "Here, lass. Ye look as if ye need it."

She downed three swift gulps and passed it back. Her voice hoarse from the burn of the whiskey, she whispered, "Thank you."

In the lead, Calum held his hand up, and the trio behind him reined in their horses. They slid off their mounts and belly crawled toward an outcropping that offered a glimpse of the road below. Spotting flashes of red through the trees, Elaina's stomach sunk to her feet. Forty or more soldiers. Some mounted, others afoot. She leaned out, trying to catch sight of their leader as they made their way down the road. She glimpsed him astride a black gelding as he disappeared around a curve. She would know that tall stature and square shoulders anywhere. Her heart leaped into her throat and tears threatened to show themselves. She choked them down before scooting her way back from the ledge, then leaned against a tree with her eyes closed.

"Ye dinna have to do this," Calum whispered in her ear. He plopped down beside her before scooping her up and depositing her on his lap.

She wrapped her arms around his neck and laid her forehead on his. "I know no other way. I have to do what I can to save his life. He would do the same for me."

"But?"

"There are so many of them and so few of you." Elaina raised her head and searched his eyes for reassurance. "How will you save me?" She knew her voice had given away how much fear she harbored on the subject.

"I will send Auld Ruadh now to gather more of the clan, and we will put together a large enough group. Dinna fash yerself, lass. We Highlanders love a good raid." He grinned at her. Although his mouth held a smile, concern creased his brow and his eyes remained clouded with apprehension.

"Are you worried that you won't be able to get me back?"

No." The word punctuated itself against her mouth. "I will move heaven and earth to get ye back, but I dinna want ye to go in the first place. I dinna want ye out of my sight."

"I don't want to leave you either." Elaina laid her head upon his shoulder, inhaling to imprint the scent of him in her mind—wood smoke, the aroma of dirt and leaves from the earth he had laid upon, and underneath, the scent that was Calum. Beneath it all lay the faint scent of their lovemaking from the night before. She slid her hands to his face and pulled his mouth to hers in a desperate kiss.

Someone cleared their throat behind her. "I dinna wish to interrupt, but if we are to meet them in the next town, we need to get on with it," Aron whispered.

Husband and wife sighed at the same time.

"Are ye sure?" Calum's eyes searched hers.

She nodded, fearing that to open her mouth would reveal the turmoil that churned and twisted through her at the thought of being without her husband, her protector and calming force. They had not been separated since her time in the gaol. She cringed at the thought of it, and the acrid taste of panic rose in her throat. She swallowed hard and pushed herself to her feet.

Auld Ruadh turned his horse back west, in the direction in which they had come. Elaina, Calum, and Aron headed east, into the still-rising sun. Elaina closed her eyes and tilted her head back, letting her mare follow Calum's horse, as she drank in the warmth of the mid-morning sun flickering down through the bare limbs of the trees. She struggled to control her nerves. After all, they would deliver her into the hands of her brother—a man who loved her dearly. By God's grace, Calum would set her free in a day or two. She dreaded telling William the truth about her identity and the difference it would make in their relationship. She supposed she had already damaged it almost beyond repair by killing a guard at the gaol and the part she played in the accidental death of Alex Campbell. Could they even have a relationship after all of that? He held to the strictest of standards. That was why he hunted her now. Duty first.

Elaina stifled a small yelp as a hand gripped her shoulder.

Aron touched his finger to his lips.

Her eyes traveled in the direction of his nod.

Jutting up through the trees rose the chimney of a house or an inn. The sounds of horses stamping and snorting floated on the morning air, and she glimpsed bits of red here and there through the gnarled brush. The trio slid out of their saddles. For a moment they stood awkwardly staring at each other, none willing to make the first move.

Elaina squared her shoulders and drew herself up. If she showed any fear, she knew Calum would not let her go. Instead, she nodded to Aron, who produced a length of rope and began to pull her arms behind her back.

Calum nudged his brother out of the way. Taking Elaina's hands, he kissed them one at a time and then brought them behind her and secured a knot around her wrists. He turned her to face him, but his eyes held too much concern for her to look into them. She might change her mind if she stared up at them too long, so she focused on the bob of his Adam's apple as he swallowed hard. With a gentle finger, Calum lifted her chin until he forced her eyes to meet his. The rough pad of his thumb ever-so-softly slid across the split in her lip. He leaned down and, with a feather's touch, kissed it. Cold fingers traveled to her injured eye, which he kissed as well. His lips moved to the spot in the center of her forehead, and he lingered there for a long moment.

Elaina felt him swallow and his jaw work as he gathered himself before he looked her in the eyes again.

"I will come for ye," he whispered, studying her face for understanding.

Elaina nodded.

"I promise."

She rose on her toes and kissed him.

He wrapped her in his arms until his brother tapped him on the shoulder and nodded that it was time.

"Two days," Calum whispered.

"I love you." Elaina's sentiment was barely audible.

"And I, you." His voice came hoarse and strained.

She spun away before the tears bubbled to the surface.

Aron lifted her onto his horse and climbed up in the saddle behind her.

The two brothers nodded at each other, and Aron turned his gelding through the trees, to the road that led to the regiment's resting place. His arm wrapped around her waist to hold her in the saddle.

Elaina wondered if he felt the fear that twisted through her belly and the wild beating of her heart. She wouldn't have to pretend to be scared.

Chapter Six

S HE COUNTED TWENTY HORSES. TWENTY soldiers, not including the other fifteen to twenty on foot. Thirty-five to forty muskets, sabers, bayonets, and who knew what else.

Elaina hoped against hope that her rescuers could gather enough clansmen to overpower the redcoats and rescue her. If not, she felt certain there would be no way to break her out of Fort William.

"I can't do this," she hissed to Aron just before they broke through the trees overhanging the trail and out into the blinding sunlight fifty feet from the inn.

"Too late now, sweetheart," Aron growled in her ear and nudged their horse forward even though it would have been just as easy to turn back. He slid from the back of the horse and dragged Elaina roughly to the ground though none of the men had yet alerted to their presence.

"What the hell, Aron?" she struggled to yank her arm from his clutches.

Gripping her tighter, he dragged her through the middle of a group of four soldiers and handed his reins to one of them. "Hold this for me, boy. Won't be but a minute." He shoved her toward the door of the building, nearly taking her feet from under her. He ignored the glare of the soldiers he elbowed out of the way.

Elaina assumed his size was all that kept the man alive at this point.

He kicked open the door and bellowed into the dim interior, "Lieutenant Spencer?"

"Here," a familiar voice called out.

Elaina dropped her head. What had she been thinking? She couldn't go through with this. The thought of the disappointment she would see in her brother's eyes was almost more than her heart could bear.

A pair of dusty boots appeared in her line of vision, nearly toe to toe with Aron's. "How may I be of service?" William asked.

"'Tis what I can do for you." Aron grabbed Elaina by her short queue, yanking her head back.

Elaina's gaze traveled up until she stared into William's vivid blue eyes.

Recognition and panic flicked across his face for but an instant before he collected himself. His gaze roved over her battered face without emotion. "What have you here?" he asked.

Aron ripped a broadsheet from his pocket. "Why it's the traitorous *Sassenach* whore ye call yer sister. Do ye no recognize yer own kin?" Aron pulled harder on Elaina's hair, bringing tears to her eyes.

She looked at him, their eyes meeting, and Elaina saw no friendliness nor reassurance in them. "Fifteen pounds sterling I believe is the reward, is it no? And ye can see she is alive." He stared coldly down at her with a rancid sneer.

Had he duped them all? Had this been Aron's plan all along? This bastard had lied to his own brother and her.

"Did you do this to her?" William's voice remained low and guarded.

"What if I did? It didna say she had to be in pristine order. Only alive." Aron challenged William, daring him to take the matter further.

William looked from Aron to Elaina and back.

"Anyway, no I didna hit her. I found her this way."

"Is it true?" William asked her.

She gave as much of a nod as she could with Aron's fist still buried in her hair.

"I'll take her," William reached out to take Elaina's arm, but Aron yanked her out of his grasp.

Aron wagged his finger at William. "Uh uh uh. The reward for the lady, if you can claim her to be one." He looked down with disapproval at Elaina's clothing.

"If you would follow us to Fort William, we can give you the reward when we arrive," William snapped.

"Dinna be offended, sir, if I say I dinna trust the English, but I dinna trust the English, so hand it over now or the lass goes with me and I will deposit her myself at Fort William…eventually."

Elaina's eyes pled with William. She didn't doubt Aron would haul her straight to the gallows if necessary.

"Applegate," William called over his shoulder. "Give this gentleman his compensation for delivering the traitor." His gaze never left hers.

Elaina could feel the heat rising in her face. She closed her eyes to escape his cold stare. The clinking of coins rang out as Applegate, she supposed, delivered Aron's handsome ransom. It had all been for the money. He had talked her into this now absurd scheme, betraying his brother, his brother's wife, and the clan all for a handful of silver coins.

Aron finally released his death grip on her hair as her brother's hand took its place on her arm, not nearly as rough as Aron's had been but not anywhere close to being gentle. She winced as all the blood in her body rushed to her feet. She tried to stop the trembling but couldn't.

Aron wished them all a good day and the door slammed, floating through her consciousness like the swirling fog they had traveled through the day before.

"She's going down," someone said as Elaina's knees buckled underneath her.

Chapter Seven

A TEPID, DAMP RAG SWEPT ACROSS her face and down her neck.
Calum.
Then the swirling thoughts in her brain collided, and she scrambled to get away from whoever it was.

"It's me," William barked.

Elaina opened her eyes to find him seated beside her on a rickety wooden chair. Someone had untied her hands from behind her only to chain them in front. Her gaze darted around the sparsely furnished room. A small table in the corner, a lone window with a piece of muslin as a curtain. The perimeter of the fabric was a milky white while the center, the part that caught the sunlight, had morphed into a dingy urine color. She lay on a lumpy bed that smelled like used hay. *The hay.* She scrambled off of it, catching William off guard and knocking his chair over, him with it. She stumbled for the door, frantic to escape, her shackled hands fumbling with the latch.

"Calm down, Elaina. It's locked from the outside. You cannot get out."

She turned toward the window in her desperation.

William grabbed her, pinning her arms to her side, and held her unfazed by her heels attacking his shins. Experience kept his nose and chin out of reach of the back of her flailing head. He had saved her from her own temper more than once. His grip remained firm, and his patience intact until she could not fight any longer and collapsed in his arms, sobs rending from her body in waves.

"No! Not the bed." She began to struggle again as he made a move to deposit her on the wretched thing.

"All right. Not the bed." William sounded puzzled by her words, but he deposited her in the wooden chair he righted with his foot and took her previous seat across from her.

"It…it smells like the gaol at Balquhidder," Elaina explained in a whisper between her tears, her face pointed at her lap. She could not look at him.

"I see."

The lock clicked on the door and it creaked open, a young soldier poking his head through. "Are things in hand, sir?" he asked.

Elaina watched him from the corner of her eye. His gaze passed over her with obvious curiosity before moving on to his commanding officer.

"Fine. The prisoner is awake."

Why William felt the need to state the obvious was beyond her. Perhaps his nerves were as rattled as hers.

"Do you need—"

"No. Wait," William said as the door began to ease closed. "Ale and food."

"Aye, Lieutenant," the man replied in the clipped tones of a lesser soldier addressing his superior before he closed and locked the door once more.

They sat in silence until the food and drink arrived and they were once more locked in the room together.

"Are you hungry?" William asked her.

Elaina shrugged without looking up. She sniffled, and he handed her his handkerchief. The manacles on her arms felt so heavy that her head had to meet her hands halfway.

William poured her a drink in a small pewter mug.

"Can you?" she whispered, shaking her chains at him.

"No. I cannot."

She sighed and once more bent to meet her shaking hands, draining her mug.

He filled her cup again. "What happened?" he asked.

"I don't know."

"You don't know? You don't know how you attacked a British soldier and slit his throat?" William's voice grew louder with each syllable.

"I don't know how I came to be there in the first place, but that is the only good thing that came out of that fortress of hell. That and Lachlan." Elaina raised her head, her eyes blazing with anger.

"Who is Lachlan?"

"A priest. They tortured and starved him before throwing him out to be eaten alive by wolves. That is how your army treats its prisoners. He lived, however, and sent help. He saved me." Her voice caught on the last sentence. She'd chosen to leave out the part about him having baptized her as a babe.

"Why did you do it?" He stood beside the small table and picked at a roasted chicken, awaiting her answer.

The words didn't want to leave her mouth. "He-he had killed Angus…shot him…and that boy…my precious boy died in my arms, terrified and wanting his mother." Tears fell again as the memory of the terror in his eyes overwhelmed her.

"I am sorry about Angus." William turned to her. "But you should have turned the soldier in if it was as you say, not murder the man in cold blood."

Elaina stared at her brother. "Turn him in to whom? I was a prisoner. Captain Cummings had made clear the code of ethics he lived by, and I knew he would laugh in my face. I exacted my own justice. At least I didn't torture him beforehand."

"I see you haven't changed," William said, returning to his seat in front of her. "Hot-headed and impetuous."

"I have changed more than you could ever know," Elaina whispered.

"Is that why you killed Alex Campbell and Captain Cummings?"

"Alex Campbell was an accident, and who told you I killed Cummings? I did no such thing!"

"Did you not?" William raised his brow at her. Word came through the men at the battle that Elaina Spencer shot the captain between the eyes. We all know what a good shot you are."

Elaina stared at him. "Did they tell you that Rabbie MacLeod is none other than Robert Campbell?" she asked as she tried to comprehend the information he had just thrown at her. Rabbie's cunning arse had pinned the captain's murder on her. Why did that not surprise her?

"I have learned that, yes."

"Did they tell you he starved me and beat me? He broke my nose and tried to kill me. Cummings tried to rape me. They wanted to burn me alive, William."

He looked away, a shudder traveling across his shoulders. "I am sorry for what he did to you. I berate myself daily for not discovering it sooner and for leaving you in his company. I wish I could take it back a hundred times over. We will deal him with when we find him."

"Hopefully, he will be dead long before you lay eyes on him." She leaned forward, elbows on her knees, daring him to look her in the eye.

"What has gotten into you?" he snapped. "What has made you this blood-thirsty creature dressed in…in… I don't know what." He waved a hand at her. "And what happened to your hair? Is it part of your disguise? Did you truly think cutting it would keep us from finding you?"

"Rabbie did it, you bloody idiot! He cut it before he whipped me with a cat-o'-nine-tails. Do you want to see the scars? He also stabbed me in the side. Would you like to see that scar as well? Look at my crooked nose. Rabbie. Then there are the scars you *can't* see. The ones that wake me screaming in the dark. I want him to die, and I want to be the one to administer that justice."

Looking uncomfortable in his skin, William gave the slightest of shrugs underneath his uniform as if it were weighed down by her words.

"And he killed our parents. He beat your mother to death after he let her watch him kill your father. You should be just as angry as I."

"I am angry, Elaina, but I have to do things by the book. There are laws to follow."

"You, apparently, are the only British soldier in all of Scotland who believes that to be true. Why must you always be so damned honorable?"

"That is how Papa raised us. Do you not remember? He would roll over in his grave—"

"To hell with Papa and his rules!"

"How dare you say that?" William hissed.

Elaina's heart pounded in her head. Standing up, she crossed to the window and pulled back the muslin curtain. This time he did not stop her. They were on the second floor. Even if she went out the window, she could not get down. There was nothing to hold on to. Well, it was now or never.

She took a deep breath. "He is not my father," she stated, turning to face him.

William's face showed abject horror at his sister's words.

"He was not my father. Mama was not my mother, and you"—her voice choked as the tears fell—"you are not my brother." She couldn't breathe. Spots danced in the corner of her vision, and she crossed back to William, flopping down in the chair and dropping her head between her knees.

William's hand appeared, shoving another mug of ale at her. "Drink."

She wished it were whiskey. "Is that all you have to say?" She wiped her eyes on her sleeve. "You don't want to know what that means?"

"I know," he whispered.

"You know what?"

"I know what that means, Elaina. I know how you came to be with us."

"You *what*?" The mug started to slip from her grasp, but she caught it and stared at him, unbelieving. "How long have you known? Our entire lives?"

"No." He scuffed the toe of his boot against a burn mark on the floor where a careless previous tenant must have dropped a candle. His eyes remained on the mark as if he couldn't bear to look at her. "The Duke of Newcastle told me when I went to Newcastle on that emergency trip. I had found the discrepancies in the books and threatened to have him hung from the gallows. That is when he confessed it all—Mama's actions and why she'd made them."

"You didn't feel that I deserved to know the truth?"

"What would have been the point, Elaina? You are my sister. Our parents are dead. Your birth parents are dead. What was I to do?"

"You were to tell me the bloody truth, is what!"

He glanced at her and then back to the spot. "And say what? Sorry, sister, but your parents were not your parents?"

"Yes. That would have been a start."

"You are impossible. I could not do that. I didn't think you would ever find out…" He stared at her now, his teeth working the side of his cheek. "How did you learn the truth?"

"After Rabbie tortured me and nearly killed me, Calum and Caitir and a band of Highlanders saved me. They put the pieces together while I lay near death. Between a birthmark on the back of my leg and a crystal that Ma—your mother gave me before we set sail for England, a pendant that my birth parents sent with me before the Campbells murdered them."

"The Campbells? What a coincidence," William mumbled. "I am sorry that you found out."

"You are sorry I found out? You are not sorry for *how* I learned this little tidbit of information? Being blindsided in front of people I barely knew? My brother could not tell me the truth? I had to learn it from strangers?" Elaina was screaming, her insides shaking nearly as violently as her hands.

"Calm down." William laid a gentle hand upon her shoulder.

Elaina jerked out of his grasp. "I will not bloody calm down!"

"I love you, Elaina. I didn't want to hurt you."

She opened her mouth to yell at him, but nothing came out. He'd known for months and never told her. Her heart felt like it had shattered inside her chest. Her voice dropped to a choked whisper. "You didn't want to hurt me and yet here I sit in shackles on my way to prison for murder, where I will be hung."

"This you did to yourself. You can't kill two members of the British army in cold blood and not expect them to punish you for it. I can plead for leniency, but it will be the garrison commander's decision. If they convict you, which I am sure they will, I could plead to get your sentence reduced to prison instead of death."

"Oh, now you want to do me favors." Sarcasm dripped from Elaina's tongue. "Don't bother. I would rather die." She turned away from him so she wouldn't have to see the hurt in his eyes. "I will not reside in a British prison again. All I ask is that you relinquish my body to my husband so he may bury me properly. I have seen how your army disposes of deceased prisoners."

William's words came slowly. "Your *husband?*"

"Yes." Elaina swirled around to face him. "It seems I have a secret of my own. Calum and I are married."

"When? You can't do that without my permission!"

"You are not my brother, remember. I do not need your consent for anything. As for when, after he saved me. He risked his life and the lives of his friends to free me from monsters you call brothers in arms." She could tell her words cut like a knife but was beyond caring.

"I am sorry about Robert Campbell. We are hunting for him."

"He killed Cummings. I did not kill him."

William studied her, confused. "That is not the information we received."

"Who told you? The men who were there? They were with Rabbie and Cummings. Rabbie shot the captain, not I. My shoulder was out of joint. I couldn't lift my arm, let alone shoot a gun."

William stood and began pacing the floor, rubbing his chin, and mumbling under his breath.

"What is it?"

"This is all my fault."

"What is your fault?"

He paused mid-stride, turning to face her. "Captain Cummings called me for a meeting after I arrived at Fort William. He asked about the rumors of suspicious activities involving the glass company. I told him about Mama. He wanted to know who the company belonged to now that she was gone. I told him."

"Y-y-you did this to me?" Elaina stammered. This time she got her arms up enough to hurl her cup at William's head.

He ducked and it crashed out of the window, ripping down the muslin fabric with it.

"I told him I had stopped the money. I didn't do anything to you, Elaina. This"—he gestured at her manacles—"this you did to yourself."

"Your words put me in prison with the man who killed Angus. Your words did this…" She furiously worked to get her tunic over her head.

"Stop it, Elaina." William struggled to pull her shirt back down.

"No. I want you to see what Rabbie and Cummings did to me. My breasts are covered. Look." Elaina turned her back to him, revealing a delicate crisscross of pink scars laced across it. If it hadn't been for Calum and Caitir and their clans, Rabbie would have continued his horrible actions.

William's cold fingers traced a mark from her shoulder to where it disappeared under her wrappings.

"And here." She turned to the side, showing him the two-inch-long scar on her side. She pulled her shirt down, turning to look at the man who had been her greatest supporter her entire life and her pillar of strength through the last year. Now, all she could see was a British soldier who had betrayed her. "I hold you responsible. You and your secrets and your lies."

The sorrow that filled his eyes made her turn away toward the window. She would not have sympathy for the man who had started her down this horrid path.

"I will have someone come and fix that," he mumbled. After a tense moment of silence, he said, "Elaina, I—"

"Leave." She no longer cared to hear his excuses.

"I just—"

"Get out." She turned on him, eyes blazing. "I can't look at you. I don't want to be in the same room as you."

His gaze locked with hers for the span of a heartbeat before he offered a stiff bow and rapped on the door to be let out.

A prisoner once again, Elaina collapsed onto the bed only to scramble off it. She dragged the blanket to the floor and curled herself into a ball on the wood planks, wrapping herself in the thread bare fabric. She had no tears, only a deep and churning anger roiling in her belly. Two days. Two days, and her husband would rescue her and take her far away from all of this. She could count on him.

The door opened, but she refused to roll over and acknowledge her visitor. The sound of boots crossed the room and hammering began. They were boarding the window closed.

That blasted man. He didn't want her to have a chance at escape. Always determined to do his duty to his bloody army and his almighty king. King George was not her king. The British thought her a Jacobite traitor, so she may as well be one. She had been the rebellious one, pushing her parents to the edge. William remained the obedient officer and loyal son who followed Papa's order to the letter. She would fight for Scotland, she vowed, lying there on the freezing floor and listening to the pounding of hammers. She owed it to her husband and her clan.

Chapter Eight

THEY STAYED AT THE INN the remainder of the day, Elaina locked in the room and William doing who knew what. Soldiers brought her food, drink, and an oil lamp. None of them spoke. She kept her back to them to discourage it and to not have to look upon the faces of those she now considered her enemies. Sleep eluded her most of the night as she lay wrapped in her coat on the hard planks of the floor.

A knock on the door the following morning announced one of the guards coming to fetch her. She refused his hand to help her up even though her bones protested the action, stiff with the cold, then trudged down the stairs to find only a small number of soldiers remained in the building. Her escort motioned to a seat close to the hearth. A pair of dry, cracked hands placed a bowl of parritch on the craggy, pitted table-top worn by years of Scotts stopping in for a rest.

Had my father sat in this very seat? Elaina glanced up into the face belonging to the overworked hands. Hands that labored at more than delivering a bowl of grains to a Scottish prisoner. The elderly woman's wary gaze rested on the remaining soldiers as she lingered at the table.

"Have you something to say?" A red-coat barked at her.

The woman shook her head so that it made the loose, wrinkled skin on her neck jiggle. She cast Elaina a sympathetic look and a nod before scrambling away into a back room, reaffirming Elaina's decision of the night before. Scotland was her home.

She relished her short time in front of the hearth before they led her outside into the cold where her breath hung frosty and thick on the morning air. The horses stamped and shook themselves, ready to be on their way.

One of the men loaded her onto a gray gelding tethered to another soldier's mare.

"This is dangerous," she announced to the soldier as he turned to leave.

"What?" he asked over his shoulder.

"If his horse should be startled and break, it will take mine with it. This situation is a hazard to horse and rider alike."

"Nothing I can do about it. Lieutenant's orders." The man cocked his head at William's form at the start of the procession before he turned and mounted a steed of his own.

William didn't cast her a glance as he ordered his men about, taking the lead on the long line of horses and men as they departed for Fort William.

She hoped that it would, in fact, be a four-day ride to the fort and the clansmen were not mistaken about the distance. She prayed that the troops, with herself in tow, didn't reach their destination before her rescuers found her.

The frigid, overcast morning gave way to an equally dismal afternoon as the group trekked down what someone might consider a road. Elaina took pity on whoever attempted to drive a wagon down the rutted and rocky trail. They passed a few locals on the way who studied the prisoner with curiosity. She searched each face for familiarity, thinking maybe her family had sent a scout to watch out for her. She recognized none. They stopped mid-afternoon for a brief chance to relieve themselves before continuing their journey.

Elaina wondered why William seemed to feel a push to reach Fort William in short order? Did he have suspicions of the upcoming rescue?

About an hour before nightfall, the troops stopped to make camp while there remained enough daylight to do so. They planted her on a rock and posted two guards to stand watch. The remaining soldiers started several small, roaring fires and prepared the clearing to bed down for the night.

The group had not tarried all day, and Elaina had been horsebound for the past several hours. "I've got to go," she said to a soldier standing watch beside her.

He looked down at her with a quizzical look pasted across his face, likely because she hadn't spoken a word all day.

"I need to take a piss."

The poor young soldier's face turned as red as his uniform. "Well…hold on." He left the one guard with her and went to find his fearless leader.

Her gaze followed the soldier's progress a short distance away. Seeing the exasperated look on William's face, she tried not to laugh.

"Well, take her then," she read from his lips.

She shrugged off her great-coat that they had wrapped around her shoulders so as not to have to unshackle her every time she had to relieve herself.

William glanced her way, and they locked eyes before he turned his back on her.

"Come along…Miss?" the soldier said, unsure of how to address her. He grabbed her under one arm and helped her to her feet.

Elaina and her two companions trudged into the surrounding woods to find a decent tree for her to duck behind. From the corner of her eye, she thought she saw a flash of something, but when she looked again, it was nothing but the sunlight showing itself for a moment at the end of the day. Its dwindling light danced off the frozen limb of a tree. She would be glad when she could be in a dress again. No wonder women wore them, and men wore breeks. It was a terrible hassle to relieve herself.

She had gotten the breeks back up and proceeded to tie them off when she saw him—a Highlander peeking over a dead gorse bush with his bonnet pulled low and a rag tied across his nose, hiding most of his face. She glanced around and spied several more. They moved cat-like through the brush without a sound. They were a day early, and Elaina could not be more grateful.

"Are you finished, madam?" A soldier barked around the tree.

A clansman held a finger up to what would have been his mouth, all of them hiding their identity behind rags.

Elaina nodded her understanding.

The leader gave a silent signal, and the men rushed her guards while another grabbed Elaina around the waist and hoisted her over his shoulder like she weighed nothing. As he turned to run through the trees, she looked up to see the falling bodies of the two soldiers—their heads nearly severed from their bodies. Two Highlanders wiped their bloody dirks on the dead mens' coats. Guilt churned through her belly, and she might have tossed up her accounts if there had been anything in her stomach. Her guards had been respectful toward her, and now they were dead because of her. They didn't have to kill them. Her rescuers could not be identified, although William would have a good idea who had taken her.

Her rescuer flung her onto a horse and climbed up behind her as they heard the shouts of the alerted soldiers. The group raced off through the trees in the failing light. Galloping through the underbrush, the horses picking their way, the Highlanders were quickly out of earshot and sight of the redcoats. The group rode for what had to have been an hour. Darkness had come upon them, and they picked their way by what moonlight there was. The glow of a small fire appeared in the distance, and Elaina gave thanks that their journey would end for the night. She was starving, cold, and just wanted to be in her husband's arms again.

Reaching the campsite, the men slid from their mounts as the other's gathered around, slapping each other on the back and speaking Gaelic—she supposed congratulating each other on their successful raid. She searched for Calum, seeking out his broad shoulders and dark curly hair.

Her head jerked forward as someone shoved her to the ground. "What the bloody hell?" She landed beside a figure lying curled up into a ball, shivering.

Flames from the fire flickered their light across the trembling body.

Elaina wasn't sure if it was the firelight or her eyes playing tricks on her. The person's hair looked almost red. Almost like... Elaina stretched out a shaky hand, gently touching the form.

The person scrambled away from her, swirling around in a crouched position. She clenched the rope that held her tethered to the tree in each trembling fist, daring her attacker to come at her.

"Caitir?" Elaina said in a barely audible whisper.

Caitir's terrified gaze met Elaina's, and the woman sat down hard on the ground, her eyes filling with tears. "Oh, God," she moaned. A purple bruise colored an entire side of her face, and the corner of her mouth was caked with dried blood.

"What's—"

A shadow fell over the two women, and Elaina scrambled to place herself between the visitor and Caitir.

"Well, well, well." The man squatted in front of her. "Looks like someone has already had the honor of decorating that pretty little face of yours." He reached out a hand, taking Elaina's chin and turning her face side to side.

She jerked away from him and backed up closer to Caitir, who grabbed Elaina's tunic.

"Who are you?" Elaina asked, though she knew damned well who crouched before her. Shuffling her knees, she tried to hide the fact that she was gathering the chains of her shackles in her hands.

"I am truly hurt that ye dinna ken me, my lady." The man placed a hand upon his chest, feigning offense. "After all the time we spent together."

He reached up and pulled down his mask, revealing the grinning face of Robert Campbell.

Elaina swung the chains with all her might at his head. The impact knocked him off his haunches, but swift as a snake, he turned back and struck her.

Chapter Nine

A LOW RUMBLE LIKE DISTANT THUNDER made its way through the fog of Elaina's brain. After a moment, she recognized it as the voices of men speaking Gaelic. She stifled a groan. Her head pounded from the impact of Rabbie's fist. She took a quiet inventory of her body. The shackles remained around her wrists and a rope bound her ankles. Something or someone lay at her back, and she fought through the haze to remember what had happened. *Caitir.* Now she heard the sniffles being buried in her plaid and wanted to comfort her, to reach out and take her in her arms, but didn't dare move until she had a better sense of what was going on. The ground was cold beneath her, and a rock dug uncomfortably into her side. She focused on the pain from that and the one bouncing around in her skull to bring her into her senses.

Peeking out from under her lashes at the men surrounding the fire—Campbell men, she counted eleven... No, wait. Two more guarded the perimeter of the camp—thirteen Campbell's armed to the teeth. If they were like their leader, they were capable of anything.

One man rose, made his way over to the women, and nudged Elaina with the toe of his boot. She considered kicking his legs out from under him, but it would do neither her nor Caitir any favors, so she only stirred instead, moaning. She felt like her head might crack clean open as he called back over his shoulder.

Another form rose from his place by the fire, and Elaina could tell by his stride that it was Robert. The name came easy to her mind, 'Rabbie' suddenly seeming too familiar. She could no longer think of him as the man he once pretended to be—her protector and her friend. This man was a letch and a snake. She wondered how he could fake a friendship so well when he was truly an evil, sadistic creature. She felt the tears welling up but choked them back as he squatted in front of her, his handsome face studying her. Sitting up, she once again took a protective position in front of Caitir.

"Ever the mother hen," Robert said.

"Ever the insufferable arse," she returned.

He grinned down at her. "I'll take it." He rocked back on his haunches. "My father has called me worse. Ye'll get to meet him soon, my lady. What a surprise ye will be for him."

"Don't call me that."

"Dinna call ye what? My lady? What shall I call ye then? Friend? Foe? Whore? Traitor? I could call you lover." The side of his mouth turned up.

"What happened to you?" she asked, tilting her head to study him. "Where did your life go so wrong that you would take a path that tortures women? You can't compete with other men, is that it? You can't hold your own, so you must lower yourself to demeaning women to make you feel like a man? Who leads these men?" Elaina glanced around at the other Highlanders, some still around the fire, but a few had gathered behind Rabbie. "It cannot be you. There is no way that you could command a group of men to follow you. Is it your father? They are doing all of this for your dear old da?"

Rabbie's smile froze.

"Your father must exact the revenge of your brother's death himself because his wayward son cannot live up to his expectations, is that it? You let a woman escape."

He grabbed a handful of her hair, wrenching her face close to his so that their noses touched. "Ye dinna fear me? Ye dinna remember our time at the gaol. If it hadnae been for the MacGregors, I would have burned ye alive. Must I remind ye of this?" His hand found the tender place on Elaina's flank and punched it, sharp and swift, taking her breath away.

The tears now came unwittingly.

"There, there. Cry it out," he teased. The rough pad of his thumb swiped the tear from her cheek and deposited it on his tongue.

She tried to wrench herself away while struggling to breathe.

Rabbie wrapped his hand around her throat, cutting off the remainder of her air. "I command these men. My father is their laird, and you will rue the day ye ever thought to cross either of us. 'Tis such a shame ye are a traitor to yer king, although I could have overlooked that less than finer attribute. 'Tis the murder of my brother I cannae abide. Ye should've been more honorable, like William. We might have been something, you and I."

He kissed her rough and passionate, her shackled hands pushing against his chest to no avail. Spots formed in her eyes, and at that moment, she thought he would kill her. Strangle her to death with his mouth locked on her own. As she was losing consciousness, he shoved her backward against Caitir.

"Ye better get some rest, my lady," he sneered. "We've a long road to travel on the morrow."

Elaina scooted herself backward, and Caitir wrapped her arms around her. The woman who had always been her champion and nurse laid her head against Elaina's back and wept.

"What happened?" Elaina whispered over her shoulder. "How did you come to be here?"

Caitir's voice came muffled in a hoarse whisper. "They arrived at the camp just after you left in search of William. They killed everyone—all of them." Her sobs began again, her body shaking against Elaina's back. "They tortured... Oh, God—"

"It's all right." Elaina rolled over, sliding her shackled arms around her friend, and held her as she wept into her chest. Her head rested atop Caitir's, the smell of wood-smoke and the salt of her tears filling Elaina's nostrils.

"Ainsley?"

Caitir shook her head.

"Mother Mary." Elaina made a small sign of the cross. She sat in shock at the death of her young friend. Both brothers were gone—murdered. She could never face their parents again. She could only pray that it had been swift and merciful, but knowing the Campbells...

"They kidnapped me and are using me to draw the MacKinnons in so they can slaughter them."

"I don't understand," Elaina managed to choke out through her own tears. "Why? Why not just kill me? I am the one who took Alex's life."

"It is a feud between the clans, and Rabbie believes the MacKinnons have access to the Jacobite funds."

"That's nonsense." *Isn't it?* Her husband could not have kept that from her. He wouldn't.

"They also want revenge for the attack at the gaol. Laird Campbell has a hate for the MacGregors and MacKinnons that has run through his clan for as long as I can remember. There are always clashes, but none so bad as what I believe is coming."

"I have to tell them who I am. Maybe that will end it. If the Campbells can exact their revenge on the daughter of their enemy—"

Caitir increased her grip around Elaina's waist. "Ye must never reveal that ye are the missing MacGregor babe. Please. They will still follow through with their plan, even if they kill you. I would be here alone."

"What have they done to you?" Elaina whispered, looking down into her friend's bruised face hardly visible in the glow from the fire, too far away to be of any use for warmth.

"Rabbie did this." Caitir waved a hand at her face. "But another… I fought him off once. I dinna ken if I can do it again."

Elaina followed her gaze toward the distant group.

"And who kens how many it will be the next time. Swear to me that ye willnae tell them and ye willnae leave me."

"All right. I promise." Elaina squeezed her friend tighter.

Long after Caitir had collapsed into a troubled sleep, Elaina sat awake watching the dwindling fire and the men around it as they communicated in hushed tones. Not that it mattered—she spoke no Gaelic. They drew with sticks in the dirt, gesturing and discussing. From time to time, one would steal a glance at her and Caitir. Elaina imagined they were planning their ruse to lure the MacGregors and their allies to their deaths.

She rested her head on her knees, the helplessness of the situation washing over her. There was no way to warn Calum. William had confiscated her dirk and her sword upon her arrest. Her only form of defense were the shackles she wore. She studied the shape of them in the darkness. As she traced their black shadow against her pale wrists, an idea struck her. It might never work. There was nothing to say that Calum would ever discover this campsite, but just in case, she eased herself down to the ground, lying with her back to the campfire. As quietly as she could with the hinge of one of her manacles, she carved one word into a protruding root of the Rowan tree they lay under. It took her until nearly dawn to finish her task and, as she eventually drifted off to sleep, she prayed that her family would find the message.

Chapter Ten

ELAINA AWOKE THE NEXT MORNING half-frozen and curled around the sleeping form of Caitir. A ripple of excitement ran through the camp and pierced the frigid air. She struggled to sit up and discover the cause of the palpable anxiety of the men.

Caitir stirred, rubbing her eyes. She froze when her gaze fell upon a tall figure seated straight and rigid on the back of a great white gelding. The horse and rider circled what remained of the fire, staring with open disdain at the clansmen who had gathered before it and taken a knee, all heads bowed.

Elaina studied the man as he wound his way around the group. A black leather thong secured his silver hair at the nape of his neck—hair nearly the color of his horse. The black of the saddle and tack stood in stark contrast against the white of the steed. A large golden boar's head decorated both sides of the harness, and a touch of flowing tartan of vivid blues and greens peeked out from under the man's black fur coat.

He surveyed the camp, his gaze searching. A look of utter contempt twisted his features as he found whom he searched for—Robert Campbell kneeling, his head bowed in subservience. Her attention darted back with surprise at the rider. He had to be Laird Campbell, Robert's father. The man sat still upon his horse, leaning his forearm on the pommel of the saddle as he studied his son.

"Get up, you fool," he barked at Rabbie. "If I had been a MacKinnon, you would all be dead. Why have you no guards posted?"

"I do— I did, Father," Rabbie said, rising and looking around the camp. He spotted the two men who had been ordered to guard the group. They were kneeling with a jug lying on its side between them, condemning their actions.

Laird Campbell followed his son's gaze. "These men? This is how you command your men? Let them drink themselves into oblivion while everyone sleeps?" He huffed out a sigh. "Kill them," he ordered as he swung himself gracefully from his horse.

The defunct guards were dragged into the woods by their comrades without a struggle nor begging for their lives.

Chills crawled across Elaina's skin at the realization that this must be a punishment the clan was well accustomed to. She tried to ignore the sickening thuds as their bodies hit the earth. Fear rippled amongst the once cocky men, and she and Caitir attempted to make themselves as small and scarce as possible.

Laird Campbell clasped his arms behind his back after handing off his reins, then paced a line before his kneeling clansmen. "So." He stopped in front of Robert. "What have you accomplished since last I saw you?"

"I have the girl." Robert raised his chin with prideful defiance.

"Congratulations. You have captured a woman." His father leered at him.

Elaina could see the redness creeping up Rabbie's neck.

"Where is she?" Laird Campbell glanced around, his eyes coming to rest on the two women.

The laird strode across the circle and squatted in front of them. The authority he commanded by his mere presence unsettled Eliana. He did not smile or blink, just crouched and stared. One eye was the piercing green of his son's, and the other a milky gray with a jagged scar that traveled from the bottom of his eye, down his face, and disappeared under the black silk cravat tied about his neck.

"Impressive, is it not?" he said as he watched her study his disfigurement.

She cleared her throat. "It is."

"An old foe did me the honor. In turn, I let his wife watch while I took his head."

She tried her best to hide her shock. Was it her birth parents he spoke of? Did he know the truth of her identity? She felt the color drain from her face.

"Aye. You should be afraid, Lady Elaina. MacKinnon, is it not? I've recent word that you have married into the clan. A worthless bunch of cowards," he scoffed, looking her over from head to toe.

After the laird's statement, she felt he did not know that she was the daughter of Laird Thamas MacGregor. There was no doubt that if he did, he would not hide this knowledge. She glanced at Robert over his father's shoulder. He talked in hushed tones to one of his men as he strolled in their direction, and Elaina wondered if he knew about her marriage.

Laird Campbell reached out a hand, shaking the chain on her fetters. "How did you come to be shackled so?"

She hesitated, looking from the laird to his son, who now stood behind his father.

"Answer me, girl."

Her eyes snapped back to his, and a chill crept down her spine. If she told him, would it mean danger for William?

"Speak." He leaned close, his face inches from hers and his voice low and eerily calm.

The man caused her skin to crawl, and she could almost imagine how Rabbie came to be a sadistic bastard. "The British, sir." She swallowed hard and straightened her spine.

"The British?" He sat back and studied her carefully, taking in her clothing for maybe the first time, truly seeing her. "This woman was a prisoner?" he asked Rabbie without turning his gaze from her.

"Yes," Rabbie responded with pride.

"Why? Where were you headed?" The laird directed his question at Elaina.

"They arrested me for the murder of two soldiers and a member of The Black Watch. Fort William was the destination." She left out the part about being in the custody of her brother.

"You daft idiot!" he roared, rising and striking his son.

Robert's head lurched sideways with the force of the blow, but his feet didn't budge. The impact seemed deafening in the silence that had descended around them.

"You took a murderess out from under the nose of the British army?"

"I thought ye would want yer revenge. She killed yer son." Robert stood chin to chin with his father, blood seeping from the corner of his mouth. He either didn't know or refused to wipe it away.

"My revenge?" The laird acted as if that were the most ignorant phrase ever spoken. "She would have been dead within the week and her blood would not be on our hands. Do you truly wish to draw the ire of the British army more than you already have? You are undermining all that I have worked to secure. We have an agreement with Cumberland, and you are dashing it all to hell!" the man bellowed. "Now, not only will we have the damned MacKinnons to attend to but also an enraged lobster-back regiment, you greedy bastard. First, you kill Cummings, and then you cannot leave the pleasure of killing this whore to the British. You want credit for her death as well."

"They dinna ken who took her, Father. They will think it the MacKinnons, and the British believe she killed the captain. His blood is on *her* hands."

"Do not speak to me like I am a fool. Gather the men. We must move out at once. Christ, I should have drowned you when you were a boy." Laird Campbell stormed off, leaving Robert standing and staring at Elaina and Caitir.

He squatted down and bent close to her, his teeth red with blood. "Make no doubt about it, I will have my revenge even if father doesnae. Alex was the only good in my life, and you took him from me."

She watched him stalk away and begin to ready the horses and the men for travel, her heart lodged in her throat. His words rang in her ears, and she almost took pity on the man. Almost. She now knew where his world had gone wrong and how close she had been to the truth of the matter. At this point, she might be glad to be back in the hands of the British. At least her brother would be there and could protect her until time for her to pay for her crimes.

"What are ye doin'?" Caitir hissed, looking down at the carved message on the tree root as she covered it discreetly with her legs.

"Leaving Calum a warning. Wipe that guilty look from your face before you raise suspicion."

Caitir buried her head in her arms.

"Was Laird Campbell talking about my father? His eye, did Thamas Mac-Gregor do that to him?" she asked her friend while watching the arrogant arse stride around the campsite barking at the men. He was single-handedly the most intimidating person she had ever met—a force unto himself.

"Aye. It was yer da who cast the blow," Caitir whispered.

Elaina stared at the man who had taken her birth parents' lives and started her off on this path of secrets and betrayals. Her gaze traveled to Robert. Like father, like son. Their stance was identical. Robert was responsible for making her an orphan a second time around. For the first time since being kidnapped from the British, she thought how fortunate she might be. Perhaps the Gods smiled on her after all. As she sat with her knees drawn up, the chain from her manacles draped across them, she watched the men prepare for travel. She fought to hide the smile that wanted to stretch her lips. The moment would come. She could not act in haste or without thought, for they were like a two-headed snake. You must take them both or risk the other striking before you had time to think. She looked up from Laird Campbell to catch Robert staring at her. He followed her gaze to where his father stood. Slowly, he turned back to Elaina and the corners of his mouth curved up. His eyes dared her to try something, anything. His right hand twitched on the hilt of his broadsword, and she raised an eyebrow at him in response, bowing her head and accepting his challenge.

"Get the prisoners," Laird Campbell barked, breaking the spell between them.

Robert strode to Elaina and squatted in front of her, cutting the ties around her ankles. "Ye may share a horse with me, my lady. We dinna want ye gettin' lonely or careless. Mistress Murray can travel with Ruske since they are already well acquainted."

Caitir's head snapped up, and Elaina didn't miss the look of fear that swept across the girl's face. She scrambled backward, her feet pedaling against the dry leaves and the hard dirt of the forest floor as she crouched in defiance. "I willnae ride with him."

Ruske gave a sickening laugh as he advanced on the women. "Oh, ye'll ride me alright," he growled. The bear of a man clenched and unclenched his fists, his eyes trained on Caitir. Greasy, dark locks hung in strings from his head and tangled in the sides of his long unkempt beard. Bloody scratches trailed from temple to beard, and Elaina found herself shocked that Caitir had managed to fend off this fiend.

Caitir raised herself in a crouched position under her newly freed legs as the oaf inched closer, she turned to run, but he caught her by her hair, dragging her back.

Elaina launched herself at the beast as he passed her. She bashed him in the side of the knee with her shoulder, sending him thudding to the ground like a felled tree. Elaina and Caitir tumbled head over heels with the man. He hit the forest floor with a loud "oof." Caitir kicked out, landing a strategically placed boot heel in his stones. While he clutched himself, howling and writhing, Elaina scrambled to her knees and slammed her iron manacles across the man's nose. She raised her hands to repeat the process, but someone caught her irons and yanked her flat on her back.

Robert stood with a boot upon her chest, pinning her down.

She didn't struggle but turned her head to keep from looking directly up his kilt. She felt sure it was not a coincidence that his foot placement put the opening in her line of sight. Instead, she watched Ruske roll around on the forest floor, blood pouring from his face and making sounds that seemed impossible for a man to make. He managed to right himself to all fours and then vomited.

Elaina smiled with satisfaction.

"Catch the girl before she draws the redcoats in our direction." Laird Campbell snapped his fingers at the men, and Elaina realized Caitir had bolted. "She will go with me." He cast a disapproving glance at Elaina and then at his son. "Can you handle the feral cat, or does she need to ride with me also? Am I the only capable man in this clan?" The last part he directed to all the men.

They dropped their eyes away from their laird.

All except Robert, who replied, "She's mine. I can handle her fine."

Elaina could see his jaw hard at work. His father knew how to twist the knife after ramming it home. If Laird Campbell was not careful, his son might do Elaina's job for her.

Robert pulled Elaina to her feet and dragged her across the rocky ground to his horse. "Why the hell do ye always insist on causin' trouble?" he growled at her as he checked the tack and saddle on his stamping steed.

Elaina reached out her manacled hands and spoke soothing words in French as she rubbed the horse's jaw, ignoring Robert's question. The black gelding snuffled at her, and she laid her forehead against his neck. She needed a plan. She wasn't certain what Laird Campbell had in mind. Caitir had said they were using her to lure in the MacKinnons. Laird Campbell had been surprised to find Elaina at the camp, but he knew of her marriage to Calum. Would he return her to the British to appease the Duke of Cumberland or use her as he was Caitir to lure the MacKinnons to their deaths? Whose plan was this? She had felt it to be Robert's, but now her suspicions headed in a different direction.

Without a word, Robert grabbed her by the arms and hoisted her up into the saddle. He climbed up behind her and turned their ride into line with his father and a satisfied looking Caitir.

Elaina glanced back over her shoulder as they left the clearing and caught a glimpse of the red and green fabric she had torn from her plaid and placed beside her warning etched into the root. She hoped it was enough to catch someone's eye. At this point, she didn't care if it was her husband or her brother.

She looked at Caitir, who raised her head and glanced sideways at Ruske and his bloody face. Her eyes cut over to Elaina and held her gaze for several seconds. Elaina nodded to her friend, and Caitir gave her a sly smile before she turned back around and dropped her head once more.

Elaina's stomach clenched in a knot as she studied the back of the hairy brute. The first chance she had, she would take his head. *Where are all these bloodthirsty thoughts coming from…taking someone's head and killing people? Have I become a monster? Am I no better than the man I'm riding with?* This side of her might have always been there, lurking in the recesses of her mind—a propensity for violence. Although, it was not as if she were wreaking havoc on unsuspecting innocents. They'd all been men who truly deserved what they got. She was administering God's justice. At that thought, she immediately recited a prayer of repentance, hoping she would have a chance at confession before she died. Could one beg forgiveness ahead of time for a sin you had yet to commit? Most likely not, but she did it anyway.

Robert tightened his grips on the reins as the ground took a steep downturn on the rocky hillside. Elaina leaned back against his chest to keep from toppling over the head of his horse. The gelding slipped and slid on the frozen terrain, following the other horses and riders concentrating on not tumbling down the side of the hill.

When they had leveled out again, she sat up away from him, then felt him inch slightly closer. His bare knees locked against her thighs, holding her in place.

"Where are we going?" Elaina asked.

"The castle."

"Where is it?"

"Ye ask a lot of questions. Haud ye wheesht or I'll stick a rag in yer mouth."

Elaina studied the terrain around them, realizing they were trailing down the middle of a long valley between two braes. She searched the hillsides for any sign of movement, red or otherwise. After a time, her attention turned to the skies, gray and heavy, holding a dampness that had not been there the day before, and she watched the clouds with a wary eye.

"There will be a storm soon. How far are we from the castle?" She wasn't worried about a snowstorm, thinking it might be to her advantage. She was more concerned about arriving at the Campbell stronghold before someone found them. Once inside the Campbell keep, it would take more than an army to rescue her and Caitir if the laird's stronghold was anything like the castle at Balquidder.

Robert tilted his head up and studied the swirling clouds, then kicked his horse and clicked his tongue, spurring them forward until he came even with his father. He spoke to him in Gaelic, and Laird Campbell glanced up and nodded. Then Robert called out to the men in their language. He fell back into the group who now watched the clouds as well.

The morning turned into afternoon, although the sun remained hidden behind the coming storm. The group did not stop. They passed cold oatcakes and dried venison between them and flasks of whiskey. Elaina's stomach rumbled. She could feel Robert's chest move as he chuckled.

"Here," he said, handing her some of the dried meat and alcohol. "Ye are no good to us if ye die of starvation."

She accepted the flask, the whiskey sending warmth to her belly and down her legs to her frozen feet. The air was growing colder, and the wind had begun to pick up. She wondered what Robert had told his men after he spoke to his father. She studied them and the weapons that they carried and began making plans in case the storm overtook them. The damned manacles were a hindrance—noisy and cumbersome. She discreetly took one of them in one hand and tried to slide the other out of it. Not possible. They were tight to her wrists. *Damn William.*

"Ye'll never get out of them, lass. Not even in yer death," Robert whispered in her ear.

A chill crawled along her skin, and she shivered.

He wrapped an arm around her waist and pulled her back into his chest. "Cold are ye, or did ye feel a rat run across yer grave?"

Elaina tried to squirm away from him, but he held her tight.

His hand inched its way up until it rested on her bound chest. "What's this?" he asked, picking at the muslin wrap that held her breasts flat.

She remained silent, reaching up and trying to pull his hand away.

He jerked it back, and it landed on the cairngorm pendant that she still wore under her tunic. "And what is this?" he asked, reaching down the neck of her tunic and extracting the chain that held the pendant. "Well, well, well, what a bonnie wee bauble." Robert fingered the delicate silver filigree. "Wherever did you find this fancy little relic?"

"It was a gift from my husband on our wedding night," Elaina lied.

"Yer husband? Ye...ye didna marry—"

"Calum. I am now Elaina MacKinnon." Elaina stiffened herself, awaiting his reaction.

He sat in silence for several seconds before throwing his head back and howling with laughter, causing the men to look their direction. "I'll be damned. I didn't think the lad had it in him. Took yer maidenhead, did he? Lucky bastard." Robert's hand crawled up her shirt as she struggled against him. He ripped the muslin from her breasts. "This is even better." He kept laughing as he groped the full roundness of her. "When he finds out that I have his wife, he will come, I have nay doubt, and then I will make ye a widow. I may let him watch me take ye before I end his miserable life."

With one of his hands on the reins and the other fondling her breasts, Elaina took the opportunity to throw all her weight to the side and send them tumbling off the horse, to the rocky ground. She landed flat on her back and lay stunned for a moment before scrambling to her knees and then to her feet. She darted past trees and bushes, trying desperately to catch her breath. The shouts of the men floated on the air as someone's footsteps followed close behind her. She tripped over a tree root and landed face first. A hand grabbed her foot and dragged her backward. She fought and kicked, but Robert took her by both of her legs and began to drag her back to the horses. The rocks and the roots from the trees scraped and dug into her bare skin as the tunic she wore rose up from the friction. At some point, her muslin wrapping came off completely. The uneven ground tore into her breasts as her hands drug helplessly above her, the manacles catching here and there and digging into her wrists. Robert only yanked harder. By the time they made it back to the horses, her arms and wrists were raw and she had scratches along her face. Her mouth was bleeding where a root had caught her even though she'd tried to keep her head out of danger.

Robert dropped her legs, thank God, stopping the torment, and Elaina dropped her cheek on the cold earth for a moment before she was wrenched over onto her back, the frosty air blasting across her bare chest. She lay with her plaid and tunic bunched under her chin, uncomfortably aware of the many sets of eyes on her exposed and bloodied breasts. She pulled her tunic down, covering herself. Miraculously her crystal still hung about her neck, but her MacGregor brooch was gone. Robert snarled down at her, a trickle of blood running down the side of his face where he must have hit his head on their tumble.

"Are ye quite finished, then?" he asked. "Or do I need to drag ye behind my horse to teach ye a lesson?"

Elaina shook her head as she caught Caitir's wide-eyed expression from where she sat still perched in front of an annoyed Laird Campbell. The laird's one piercing green eye studied her, his gaze coming to rest on the crystal about her neck. Something in his expression shifted, but then he turned to his son and admonished him for his carelessness, ranting on about if he could not control a single lass how did he expect to command an army against the enemy.

Robert yanked Elaina to her feet, pulling her close to him. "This is not finished, my lady," he sneered into her face.

His hand traveled down her back and cupped her buttock. He slid it farther under her, letting is touch linger, but she refused to react and give him the pleasure of seeing how uncomfortable he made her.

With an evil grin and a wink, he thrust her up onto his horse. He arranged himself behind her, and with a length of rope that appeared out of nowhere, he looped one end around her neck and the other about the pommel of the saddle.

"Now then," he whispered in her ear, his mouth trailing down the side of her throat. "If ye throw yerself again, ye will be doin' me a favor." He snatched her tight into his body and clicked his horse into a trot, following the other men already moving on without them.

Chapter Eleven

AS THE SUN, STILL HIDDEN by a sheet of clouds, began its descent behind the mountain range, Laird Campbell called over his shoulder in Gaelic. The group of men kicked their horses into a full gallop, turning up a dry ravine and trailing its progress up a craggy hillside.

Elaina looked around once again for signs of life but found none. The clansmen pushed their horses on until the laird took a sudden turn off the creek bed. She ducked the low-hanging branches as they picked their way through the dense forest.

Laird Campbell brought his horse to a stop and motioned a man forward. The clansman slid from his mount and disappeared behind a clump of trees and dry bushes, returning a short time later nodding his head. The laird barked an order for everyone to dismount.

Robert dragged her from the saddle and shoved her in step with Caitir. The two women huddled close together as he sent them stumbling behind the brush and into a hidden opening.

Elaina's pupils expanded as they struggled to soak in light, their destination black as pitch. She and Caitir stood with their hands clasped as the others fumbled around outside.

After a moment, a clansman appeared carrying a burning branch and traveled his way down the wall, lighting torches that hung at intervals. As the flames grew, they revealed what turned out to be a massive cave, and Elaina realized they stood in what must be a well-used stronghold for the Campbell Clan. The room was rather significant, and it was hard to determine if the hand of God crafted the cavernous room or if Campbell men deserved the credit. Six torches lined the walls, three on each side. Toward the back of the cavern, she could make out some barrels and a few crates. The place seemed to be well-stocked, possibly for moments just like this or for warfare when there was a clash with one of their rivals.

Someone shoved Elaina and Caitir down beside the wall as several of the group began building up a fire in a pit in the middle of the long room.

A moment later, Robert and three others accompanied the laird as he approached the women. One of the men grabbed a torch from its place on the wall and brought it over. With a flick of his hand, the laird ordered Robert and another man, and they snatched Elaina off the ground, one under each arm and dragged her to stand before their laird.

Robert ripped the plaid from around her shoulders and flung it to the side. Elaina was uncomfortably aware of her torn shirt, the soft mound of one scratched and bloodied breast partially bared, and the rope still hanging about her neck, irritating the exposed skin.

The laird reached out a hand and fingered the pendant that hung against her tattered clothing. "Where did you get this, lass?" he asked, his eyes turning toward hers.

"A gift from my husband," she repeated the lie she had told earlier.

Her head flung to the side, and the men's painful grasps on her arms kept her from collapsing to the ground. Her eyes watered from the impact of the laird's back-handed blow as she turned her face back to his.

"I'll ask you again. Where did you get this?"

Elaina stared at him.

He spoke in Gaelic to the men without turning his eyes from Elaina's.

"No!" Caitir yelled, scrambling to her feet.

The man holding the torch shoved her down.

Robert and the other clansman stripped Elaina of her breeks. She fought and kicked, earning her a swift punch to the kidney. They held her up as she gasped for air, her tunic hanging near to her knees and covering her most intimate parts. Robert twisted the rope around his hand, making spots dance in her eyes. Laird Campbell made a motion, and the two men spun her around, lifting the hem of her shirt. Elaina stood stark still, staring into Caitir's horrified eyes and clenching her teeth as an icy finger traced the outline of her birthmark.

"I will be damned," the laird whispered, his warm breath tickling her naked buttocks.

They twisted her back around, and she stared into the knowing eyes of the laird.

"Never in my life…" He seemed too stunned to speak as he turned her bloody and bruised face side to side. "Yes. I can see it now." He spoke again in his foreign tongue to the men.

For a moment, all was still in the cave.

Laird Campbell ripped the pendant from around her neck and shouted while holding the amulet high in the air, and a roar went up from the group.

Elaina knew at that instant that the danger she and Caitir were in had risen substantially.

Laird Campbell gathered Robert and several of the men together, and they whispered with their heads bowed close to each other.

Elaina seated herself beside Caitir, pulling her tunic over her knees and tucking it tight around feet to hold it in place. The two women held each other as best as they could with their hands still bound. Elaina defiantly met the eyes of some of the men as they stood ogling her, silently daring any of them to touch her. She would have their bollocks for dinner. *Damn the British army for making her remove her great coat.*

"What did he say to them?" Elaina whispered to Caitir.

"He told them they held the heiress to the MacGregor clan. The bairn of his enemy that had been missing for over twenty years. He plans to use you to draw out the MacGregors. Then he said he would have yer head on a pike for the all the Highlands to see, and his life's work will be done."

"Well, I am glad he has such lofty goals," Elaina mumbled, swallowing the bile rising in her throat. She watched the laird for a moment, then Robert and two of the others disappeared through the mouth of the cave. "I am truly sorry for all of this," she whispered to Caitir as she reached up and removed the rope from around her neck.

"'Tis not yer doin'," Caitir said, her gaze trained on the men milling about the cave.

Elaina watched Caitir's eyes warily following Ruske.

"If not for me, you would not have been at that campsite, the others would still be alive, and Calum would not be walking straight into a trap. I told Calum my life was cursed. He wanted to argue."

"Aye, well, that may be true," Caitir said. "Trouble finds ye like fleas to a hound, but ye hold no blame as far as I'm concerned. What has happened has happened, and what is meant to be is meant to be. Ye cannae give up now, though. The MacKinnons and the MacGregors are keen. They can smell a trap. They ken not to trust a Campbell. What we have to worry about is staying alive until they can get to us." Her gaze rested on the sizeable Scot as he sat by the fire, rubbing his battered nose. "Thank ye, by the way." Caitir nodded at the man.

"You needn't concern yourself with him," Elaina said. "He didn't…" She cut her eyes at Caitir.

"Nay, but he came damn close. Too close. See that man? The one that resembles a rat?"

Elaina followed the tilt of Caitir's head. "Yes."

"If not for him, I would be a ruined woman. I dinna ken why he stopped it, but he did."

The man stood slight of stature, and Elaina wasn't sure how he could stop someone the size of Ruske from doing anything. Her gaze moved to the beast and gave him a nod when he glanced in their direction. She had more in store for that man if she ever got the chance. There was a lot of revenge to exact standing in this one cave. It was almost as if she could feel the blood of her father pumping through her veins as she scoured the men's faces, trying to commit them to memory should the need arise. She stared at the scar on Laird Campbell's face—her father's handy work. Their eyes locked on each other, and her mouth turned up in a smile at the same time as the laird's.

Who would be the first to make a move—the captor or the captive? Elaina knew it did not matter who struck first. Only the final blow mattered, and she intended for it to be hers.

Chapter Twelve

THE TWO WOMEN HUDDLED TOGETHER against the wayward gusts from the winds howling outside the cave entrance. It whipped through the cavity, ebbing and flowing like waves in the ocean and sending Elaina into fits of violent tremors. Caitir spread her skirts over Elaina's nearly naked, bunched up form and wrapped her arms around her, pulling her close. They sat too far from the fire for them to feel any heat from it.

Robert and the other men had returned a short time ago, ice frozen in their hair and eyelashes. Of course, they stood by the flames and thawed themselves while discussing who knew what with the laird. When they cast a glance in Elaina's direction, she glared at them in return, refusing to be intimidated.

Laird Campbell spoke to Robert and nodded his head toward the women. Robert scowled but gave his father a curt nod. Lengthy, determined strides brought him to stand in front of the women. He paused long enough to scoop up Elaina's discarded plaid the men had taken from her when they'd stripped her half-naked.

"Ye're no good to us frozen to death," he said, tossing the plaid at her. "Come." He grabbed the women by the arms and yanked them to their feet, leading them to a small rock somewhat closer to the heat.

Elaina struggled to wrap her plaid around herself with Caitir's help, then fought to stop her teeth from chattering. Although they were now perched closer to the fire than the mouth of the cave, the air continued to whip about, buffeting the heat in a swirling dance. The moments it reached Elaina were heavenly but fleeting. She sat on the small rock for several minutes before her frustration took over and she grabbed Caitir's arm and drug her into the circle of men huddled up to the edge of the blazing logs.

Laird Campbell, along with the few henchmen standing with him, stared at the two women.

"If you want to talk in secret, you can go stand in the freezing wind. You are better dressed for the occasion," Elaina barked when the laird opened his mouth to speak. She looked him up and down with his fur cape and gloves as she stood there bare-legged in a thin tunic with nothing for warmth but the length of plaid she clutched around herself.

Laird Campbell glared at her for a moment, then lowered his voice and continued his talk in hushed tones that Elaina couldn't hear over the babbling of the men.

She plopped herself down on the ground as lady-like as she could manage in shirttails and manacles. Stretching her booted feet toward the heat, she supposed she should be grateful the bloody bastards had at least left her that comfort. After a good while, her teeth finally stopped clanking together.

The men laughed and spoke in Gaelic while exchanging a flask amongst each other. One of them started to pass it in front of the women but paused, eyeing both of them. "What will ye give me for it?" he asked, wiggling his eyebrows at them.

Elaina and Caitir shared a look before Elaina turned back to the man. "Why I'll give ye something," she whispered seductively, leaning toward him with her gaze trained on his mouth.

He leaned forward, licking his lips, until they were inches apart.

Elaina stared into his arrogant brown eyes. "I'll let you live." She snatched the flask from his hand. "Bloody cheeky bastard," she grumbled as she passed the whiskey to Caitir, giving her the first drink.

The man stared in disbelief at Elaina, then the flask, before his gaze darted to Ruske.

"That's right," Elaina said. "Take a hard look, because if you try anything, you will have more to worry about than a pair of sore bollocks and a mangled face."

With a huff, he turned back to the fire, and the men around it roared with laughter.

Elaina didn't have to speak Gaelic to know they needled the man. The redness in his face told it all. She and Caitir took their fill of the whiskey, letting it warm their bones.

Elaina returned the drink to the man with a polite smile. "Thank you," she said with a nod.

He paused for a moment, then gave her a nod in return.

"This is getting ridiculous," she whispered to Caitir. "I'll be right back."

"Where do ye think ye're goin'?" Caitir hissed at her trying to grab her as she struggled to her feet.

"I just need a word." She crossed the expanse of the cave, approaching Robert. "May I have my breeks back if I agree to play nice?"

"I'm no sure ye ken how." He folded his arms across his chest and gave her a raised brow.

"What am I going to do shackled and trapped in a cave with a gaggle of Campbell men surrounding me? Just give me my bloody breeches."

"Language, language," he said, clucking his tongue at her.

She thought about kicking him.

"I would, but I burned them in the fire." Robert jerked his chin toward the roaring pit.

"You didn't." Elaina whipped her head around to stare at the flames.

"Sorry, lass," Robert said with a chuckle.

If she had a knife, she would cut out his tongue and roast it on a spit. Instead, she closed her eyes, trying to control her temper. She could feel everyone staring her and wondered if she were to strike Robert down would the laird try to stop her or let her pummel him bloody. She stood for several moments with the flames from the pit dancing across her eyelids before casting Robert one last glare and striding back to the fire with his laughter following her. A thought struck her as she reached the group of Campbells, and she searched out the small rat-looking man and approached him. He prattled on in Gaelic to his friends until his attention was drawn to her by the curious looks of the other men. She gave a jerk of her chin, bidding him stand and speak with her.

"Will you help me?" she asked when he had made it to his feet.

He looked with uneasiness at the men.

Maybe he only spoke Gaelic and not the King's English?

He turned his questioning eyes back to her.

"Show me how to put this on like yours." Elaina held the plaid out in front of her. She needed to wear it as a kilt, for warmth and ease of movement and to keep her hands free.

The man stared at her, unblinking.

She was about to give up and ask someone else when he gave an almost imperceptible nod. He passed a nervous glance to Robert before they left the circle.

Robert paid them no mind. He and his father had moved closer to the mouth of the cave.

"What is your name?" Elaina asked the man as they walked to an open space with no men.

He was quiet as he spread the long piece of fabric on the ground. Finally, as he knelt to show her how to make the pleats in the material, he answered, "Rupert."

"Rupert, thank you for helping me. And thank you for saving my friend's virtue."

He paused mid-pleat. Without looking at Elaina, his nimble fingers went back to their task. "I dinna take wi' rape," he mumbled.

Elaina watched his deft hands and thought about all the times she had watched Calum do the same. It always amazed her how his thick fingers and large hands made for fighting, created beautiful pleats, every one of them sharp and clean, the same distance apart. She wished she had paid more attention at the time. Pain like a boulder lodged in the middle of her chest. She should have paid attention to a lot of things. He had begged her to disappear—to go to his family at Gleann Eader, but no, she had been hell-bent on revenge. She wanted to watch Robert die by her hand, avenging the torture he'd exacted upon her and set to right the wrong he had caused by murdering her parents. Why did she always have to try to be the heroine and save the day? Undoubtedly, her brother could have saved his career and his own neck. Her shackles now felt as if they weighed ten stone, and she sank to her knees beside Rupert, burying her head in her hands. Unable to keep them at bay, she wept silent tears at her own stupidity, hiding her moment of weakness as well as she could from the men behind her. If she gave the slightest impression of being broken, she had no doubt they would take advantage of the situation. Ruske had already tried once. A cave full of drunk Campbell clansmen on a freezing night with two restrained women was dangerous.

She fought to pull herself together. Wiping her face on the sleeve of her tunic, she looked up to find Rupert staring at her. "I-I'm sorry," she sniffled and cleared her throat.

"Nay worries, madam," he grumbled after a moment's hesitation. He reached beside her, grabbing the length of rope that Robert had tied around her neck, and worked it under the pleated fabric in lieu of a belt. "Now, if ye will lay down this way—I am sure ye have watched yer husband?" he asked, cocking his head to the kilt.

Of course she had. You had to lay on it and kind of roll yourself up in it. She wiped her nose again and took her place on the fabric, trying to make sure none of her extra bits hung out, top or bottom. "Do not get any ideas." She cocked an eyebrow at Rupert as she lay down.

"I wadna dream of it, madam. I would like to see my son and my wife again…with all my parts in workin' order." One side of his mouth turned up the slightest bit. After he had instructed her on how to roll herself up properly, he ordered her to stand up and tied her belt. "This part," he said, "the tail? Ye can draw it up over yer shoulders and head for warmth and protection from the rain and elements." He nodded toward the mouth of the cave where snow swirled in from the darkness outside. "Ye can cover yerself when hiding amongst the brush. 'Twill make it harder to find ye."

Elaina nodded her understanding at his odd choice of explanation. The plaid was one that she had borrowed from Ainsley. The thought of the slain young man brought a fresh sting of tears to her eyes. She attempted to blink them away, refusing to cry again. The plaid hung a little past where men's usually did, but that was fine with Elaina because it covered more of her legs. Rupert showed her a few more ways that she could wear the plaid before footsteps interrupted them.

"Getting' a wee bit fresh with the captive, are we, Rupert?" Robert's snide voice came from behind Elaina.

"Aye," Rupert replied without batting an eye. "She asked for help, and I thought it a good opportunity to see more of the landscape. Ye cannae blame a man." He reached out and fingered the tear in Elaina's shirt, grazing his knuckles along the bare skin beneath it.

She grabbed the length of her plaid and wrapped it around herself as best she could with her hands chained together. "Bastard," she spit at him.

He grinned and shrugged his shoulders.

Robert laughed. "Aye, ye cannae blame a man. I would tread carefully with this one if I were you. Keep a hand on yer dirk at all times." He slapped Elaina on her derriere and strode away.

Rupert locked eyes with her. "I may need to sleep with my hand on my dirk, but ye would do well to sleep with one eye open. Ye ken?"

She studied his face. Was the warning about him or the other men? "I ken," she managed to whisper.

They rejoined the circle of men, and Elaina settled herself once more beside Caitir.

"Ye look good in a kilt with yer short hair and yer black eye."

"Thank you. It's a good thing I have it because Robert burned my breeks."

"Wasn't that thoughtful of ye? Sacrificin' yer breeches so we can all stay warm."

"I'm nothing if not charitable. Where is Laird Campbell?" Elaina's gaze flickered to the mouth of the cave.

"I dinna ken. He left minutes ago with another man."

Elaina contemplated all the things the laird could be doing, but none of them made her feel any better about their situation.

The hour grew late and the torches were extinguished, leaving only the dwindling flames for light. However, most of the men were half-drunk and didn't seem to care. The ones who were not half-drunk were completely pished. After a while, Elaina found her head bobbing and had a time of holding her eyes open even with the unease in her gut about the men surrounding her. She and Caitir found a place a little out of the circle, yet still close enough for what remained of the fire to cast a bit of warmth. They lay down and curled up together, and Elaina eventually drifted off to sleep serenaded by a group of drunk Highlanders.

<hr/>

Something was not right. Indeed, something was terribly wrong. Elaina fought to come to her senses, her mind trapped between the moment when your brain still sleeps but your body is woken in a violent manner.

A sizeable, sweaty hand clamped itself upon her mouth as someone pinned her to the ground. Red-hot embers were all that remained of the fire, and the darkness in the cave hid her attacker's face. Scuffling noises behind her drew her attention, and she strained her neck to see the cause, but her head was trapped between her attacker's hand and the hard earth. She struggled in vain for several seconds before her shackled hands found their target, and she squeezed with all her might. The man howled, struggling to get away, but Elaina held a death grip and twisted her wrist. Once his body had fallen off of her, she let go and gave it a good swift punch for extra effort. She scrambled to her knees to find another man atop Caitir. The lass kicked and fought to no avail. Elaina lunged, landing on the assailant's back, and wrapped the short-chain on her manacles around his neck. Putting her knee in the center of his spine, she pushed against him while leaning into her stranglehold, the strength of it causing the shackles to cut into her wrists. He struggled first to get his hands on her, before clawing at the chain digging into his throat. Someone grabbed at Elaina, trying to pull her off of him, but she had a death hold. Caitir squirmed her way free, and moments later, the man's body fell slack against Elaina. The metallic scent of blood filled the black night where Caitir must have gotten to the man's knife and slit his throat.

Mass confusion reigned with one man lying on the ground screaming in pain and the other lying dead, his weight crushing her. The men scrambled and barked at each other in Gaelic, and someone shoved the man off Elaina and dragged her to the far wall of the cave. She could make out a few figures moving around in the dimness.

"Come," a man hissed in her ear before she was shoved into another figure who squeaked in surprise.

Caitir.

"If ye want to live, move yer arse," the man growled behind her.

He pushed their frozen feet into motion, and they wormed their way down the edge of the wall until the black mouth of the cave gaped before them. The wind whipped through the entrance, fluttering Elaina's kilt about her. Caitir grabbed Elaina's arm, pulling her to the ground, and they crawled on their elbows and bellies out of the cave and into the bitter winter storm. They scrambled to their feet and ran hand in hand, one manacled in chains and the other tied with a rope, but they had made their escape before the clansmen had a chance to re-light the torches.

The two women stumbled through the night, blinded by snow and darkness. Bushes and trees loomed everywhere, giving Elaina a start more than once as she thought Campbell's men were upon them. The branches and limbs tore at their clothes like demon fingers extending through the night. Fear pounded in Elaina's chest as shouts rose on the winds of the storm behind them. Elaina turned her head to look and saw a torch waving about. Wonderful. The men had light, and the women did not. The Campbells could follow their tracks in the snow… Unless…

She prayed the swirling wind and snow would cover their path, but just in case they needed to double back on themselves and possibly split up. Bile rose in her throat at the prospect of losing Caitir in the storm or if the Campbells recaptured them. There was no doubt in her mind that they would not be lenient in their punishment.

"We have to split up." She grabbed at Caitir's arm.

"What? No. We can't."

"We must. We stand more of a chance. You keep running in this way. I will double back on our tracks and hopefully throw them off."

"I willnae leave ye," Caitir hissed.

Elaina shoved Caitir in the direction they were headed and turned her head into the wind to double back. The time for talk had passed. If they were to avoid capture, it was the only way. Needles of sleet and blowing snow stung her face and bare legs as the abominable Scottish winds whipped her kilt about in a fury. The force of the howling gusts made it almost impossible to breathe, hitching gasps all she could manage. Tucking her chin to her chest, she pressed on, tripping over rocks and tangling herself in bushes. Someone grabbed her kilt, and with a surprised squeal she spun, arms swinging in a panic to escape. A nervous giggle escaped her throat when her hands met the dead branch of a tree.

Pull yourself together.

The admonishment fell short with a bone-jarring thud.

"Goin' somewhere, princess?" Robert growled in her ear, his knee embedded between her shoulder blades.

His fingers intertwined in her hair, and he yanked her to her feet, the force of it and the blinding wind sending tears down her cheeks. He dragged her along by the manacles, back to the hole in the mountain. Torches once again glowed in the Campbell stronghold. Her eyes flitted around the cave, searching for Caitir's pale red hair.

Two clansmen stumbled in behind her and Robert.

"We lost her," one of them panted.

"How in the hell did ye lose her?" Robert yelled.

"I dinna ken. She vanished is all," the other defended.

"Women dinna vanish, snowstorm or no. Get out. Ye find her or ye will pay the penalty."

The pair passed a glance between themselves and shuffled back out into the night.

Elaina prayed that Caitir had, in fact, vanished and would gather help and lead them to rescue her.

Chapter Thirteen

OUNTED ONCE AGAIN IN FRONT of Robert, Elaina closed her eyes to the blinding sunlight. The storm had eased just before daybreak, and the Campbells were once more on the move.

Robert had kept her close at hand the remainder of the evening, laying with one arm wrapped tightly around her waist.

Ruske and Rupert had dragged the lifeless body of the man Caitir killed from the cave. Elaina had hoped it had been Ruske himself, but they had not been that fortunate. The sound of wolves nearby gave her chills, and she tried to block the images swirling through her mind of the would-be rapist being torn apart by the scavenging beasts.

The two men searching for Caitir had returned an hour after daybreak empty-handed. There were no signs of her now either, as far as Elaina could tell. Her eyes searched the surroundings, but the only sights to see were brush put to bed for the winter and hills covered with a thick blanket of snow.

"Cold?" Robert's breath on her ear sent extra chills down her arms.

The chattering of her teeth and uncontrollable shivering was answer enough.

In an unusual show of consideration, Robert pulled his thick fur overcoat around Elaina, draping it over her legs, and drew her closer to him. She wanted to fight, but she was half-frozen and too exhausted. They had been riding the entire day with but two stops, and she hadn't slept a wink after her attempted escape.

As her body warmed, her eyelids grew heavy and her head bobbed. She fought to stay upright and vigilant, but before long, rocked by the gentle rhythm of the horse, she could do nothing but lay back against Robert to keep from falling over the front of their ride. She jerked awake, thinking she had dozed off for only a moment. Instead, she found that night was coming on as the horses topped a hill. The group trailed single file down a narrow road, toward a bridge, at the end of which jutted the rounded nose of a castle wall. The gray behemoth angled out from the pointed tip into what seemed to be a triangle shape, as much as she could tell. The walls went on forever, but worst of all, the castle sat like an island in the middle of a black moat—one road in, one road out.

They had arrived at the home of Laird Campbell without incident, and Elaina felt the strangling hand of panic squeezing her throat closed. There would be no way to break her free once she entered the stronghold. It was worse than she had imagined it could be. Her gaze darted frantically around for signs of her husband and her clan. The land around the stronghold had been cleared. Nary a bush or tree grew within one hundred yards of the castle on any side. An attack could be seen long before the combatants could ever reach their destination.

The horses' hooves echoing against the wood of the bridge were like hammers pounding her coffin closed, and she felt a tear run down her cheek. She dashed it away. Crying would not help her survive, nor would fighting or brute force. The only thing to save her now would be to bend to the will of her captors, to tamp down her hard-headed ego and play nice until she could come up with a plan. That was not her strong suit.

Not one bush nor a blade of grass inhabited the entrance to the stone walls of the keep. Robert slid from his horse and grabbed her about her waist, pulling her off after him and depositing her on the ground constructed of gray rock. Elaina watched as stable lads gathered the horses and led them away, other hands following behind sweeping up any excrements left behind. Her gaze traveled over the gray stone walls and outbuildings to the large, rectangular, drab stone castle. How fitting. The laird's home seemed to match his cold, dark heart.

She entered the castle ahead of Robert, his hand resting on the small of her back and guiding her inside. The interior appeared more elegant than the outside made it seem. Tapestries woven in subdued blues, browns, and golds decorated the hallways. The colors of the furnishings were all muted but refined. Servants skittered about taking cloaks and wiping footprints from the floors behind the few men following Robert and Elaina. The silence of the place rang in her ears. No one spoke. It was apparent the help was efficiently trained in their duties, and she held no doubts that punishment for failure to perform would be swift and merciless.

Laird Campbell appeared from around a corner. So, this was where he had disappeared to, having never returned to the cave. He had made it to the castle even through the blinding snow.

"We seem to be missing someone," he said. "Where is the Murray girl?"

"Ye ken well enough that we dinna have her. I ken that Rupert and Ruske have already informed ye of such," Robert replied, the square of his shoulders defiant, but he did not return his father's icy glare. Instead, his gaze rested on a tapestry beyond his baleful laird.

Laird Campbell sighed and gave Robert a look of absolute disdain as a severe-looking gray-haired woman appeared at the end of the hallway, her hands clasped before her and head dipped in servitude toward her master.

"Doireann, Mistress MacKinnon will stay with us for a time. See to her needs. She is a...guest." The word held a meaning other than a welcome friend arriving for a visit, and a chill crept across Elaina's skin. "You ken where to put her."

"Aye, my lord." Doireann gave the man a small curtsy before turning her emotionless eyes to Elaina. Her gaze halted on the shackles remaining around her wrists before she barked out her order. "Come."

With a deep breath and her head held high, Elaina followed the woman down another hallway, resisting the urge to glance behind her as Robert received an earful from his father. She could show no doubt. No fear. The deeper Doireann led her into the castle, the more bile rose in Elaina's throat as the words of the laird replayed in her mind. Where were they going to hold her? Panic surged in her wame as her thoughts drew her back to the cell at the gaol. It took every ounce of strength not to turn and run. By the time they had traversed up two flights of stairs and down numerous corridors, her knees were trembling so she didn't think she could stand for one more minute. Doireann stopped in front of a heavy wooden door, and Elaina tried not to let her anxiety overcome her.

With the click of a key, hung with various others from an iron ring tied at the woman's waist, the maid opened the door to the room. Once ushered inside, Elaina nearly toppled over in a faint. Instead of a rat-infested cell with a filthy pile of hay for a bed as her mind had conjured, the chamber was as elegant as the rest of the castle. A large four-poster bed stood draped in curtains of the deepest blue that were drawn back with gold chords. Magnificent paintings of rearing stallions were displayed in gilded frames along one wall, and the opposite wall was covered in tapestries of rich landscapes. She gave a start as servants brushed past her, carrying in a copper washtub. One stoked the fire as others began toting in buckets of steaming water.

Doireann grabbed the chain binding Elaina's wrists and jerked her around to face her. A searing pain shot up Elaina's arms, the shackles digging into the raw skin around her wrists where Robert had dragged her across the ground. She stared at the rigid woman while she tried key after key to unlock Elaina's bindings. Her gray hair pulled into a severe chignon made the woman's feature's sharper, more severe. Elaina didn't believe her to be the age of Laird Campbell, but she couldn't truly determine how old she might be. Somewhere between Robert and the Laird was the best she could estimate.

The restraint on Elaina's right hand broke free with a click of the lock, and she thought her arm would float up in the air after being weighed down by the irons for so many days.

Doireann glanced up at Elaina as she gathered the restraints into her hands. Her brow raised as if questioning Elaina's scrutiny. "Ye will bathe, and ye will dress. Ye will dine with the laird," she snapped before she turned and left the room.

All the attendants except for two left after having prepared her bath. Those remaining immediately undressed her. Without making eye contact, they helped Elaina into the wash tub, and she smothered a groan as her sore muscles slid down into the steaming bath. They made quick work of bathing her with lavender scented soap, one set of hands washing her body, the other her hair. Their hands gently glided over her wounds—her raw wrists, the bloody scratches across her breasts and her belly, the scars upon her back. Elaina sat with her eyes closed through it all. She didn't want to see their pity and didn't want them to witness her shame.

Far too soon they pulled her to her feet. The attendants had stoked the fire into a roaring blaze, but Elaina still shivered with the chill of the air as the women dried her and dressed her in silk stockings secured in place with emerald green ribbon, a silk chemise, and a velvet gown the same shade as her stocking ties and trimmed with gold lace. The garment was a snug fit, and Elaina hoped she would not burst a seam when she sat down.

The two girls bobbed a curtsy with their faces pointed at the floor as they backed from the room. They swung the heavy door shut behind them, and the lock clicked home. Though her treatment seemed a courteous offering extended to a guest, she was very much a prisoner and needn't forget it.

She glanced around her at her stylish surroundings. The laird presented himself as a rather regal man, but Elaina would never have believed his dreary stone castle would be furnished so lavishly. Crossing the room to one of the two slits someone might consider windows, she stared out at the night. Torches lighting the rock walls of the keep at precise intervals prevented Elaina from seeing the land past their flames. She could, however, see the servants as they scurried about performing their duties. If she were to break a window and by some unbelievable chance could squeeze her body through the slight space, there was no way for her to escape. She could never scale her way down the wall to the ground. Even if she could, the area was too filled with inhabitants of the hold, and then there was the greatest task of them all—the forty-foot shield wall separating the castle grounds from the black moat surrounding the entire keep.

Chapter Fourteen

IN A STONY SILENCE, DOIREANN led Elaina down the stairs and through the winding halls to a small dining hall. Robert and several of the men were assembled around a large rectangular table. Their muted whisperings stopped when Doireann entered the room with Elaina in tow. Robert stared at her momentarily with an odd look upon his face, then stood and rounded the table to lead her to an empty chair across from him. No sooner had he seated her and returned to his place than Laird Campbell emerged from another doorway. Everyone rose, their heads bowed, so Elaina followed suit. Crossing the room in four long determined strides, he took his place at the head of the table to Elaina's left. Once he sat, the men followed. Elaina sat, trying to breathe as best she could, but between her nerves and the snug gown she wore, the feat was much harder than usual.

"Ye look lovely…besides yer mangled face," the Laird said. "It will heal in a few days," he offered when she stared at him in silence. "Eat," he barked at her as servants placed a plate of roasted meat and root vegetables in front of her.

At the delivery of food, the surrounding men dug in and their talk turned to duties that needed doing since their return home. The laird remained silent, and Elaina could feel his watchful eyes upon her, so she placed a small piece of roast chicken in her mouth and fought to keep it down. She didn't know what she thought her time in the Campbell castle would be like, but dining with the laird at his table, dressed in finery, was not it.

Her gaze roamed the hall as she raised the goblet of Madeira to her lips, coming to rest on a portrait of a lovely woman hung in prominence over the massive fireplace. Her blonde hair draped her shoulders, her expression demure. Elaina had thought Robert resembled his father. They had the same eyes, but this young woman who could not have been over one and seven, was very much Robert's mother. The innocence portrayed was almost shocking. Elaina wondered what her life had been like here at the keep and took pity on the girl.

Feeling the laird's gaze upon her, she forked a bite of roasted turnip in her mouth before turning to look at him. His green eye glinted at her in the candlelight, his expression unreadable before he turned his attention to one of his henchmen asking about security.

The laird's intentions remained unclear as the dining hall rumbled with men's voices, and tableware clunked against itself in the frenzied feasting taking place under the portrait of Robert's dead mother staring down at them. A hint of fear seemed to linger behind her painted eyes. Had the laird ordered his wife painted in that fashion or had the artist seen deeper into the woman's soul and wanted to capture the essence of his subject? Elaina touched the fine boning in the stays that held her waist cinched tight. Did she wear her gown? Had Robert's mother been a willing participant in her own life or had she been a prisoner of an evil demented man? She tried to wash down the bite of food that felt impossible to swallow.

"Tell me, lass, I am curious, how did the daughter of the laird of the Mac-Gregor clan happen to be taken in by a British Earl and his wife?" Laird Campbell addressed her, causing her gut to clench.

"I'm not sure what you mean? I am the daughter of the late Edward and Diana Spencer." Her throat now squeezed as tight as the stays around her waist.

"Nay, lass. The pendant you had in your possession belonged to my dear friend Thamas. The birthmark you carry on your leg just below your dainty little buttock identifies you as his daughter. I ken the Murray girl translated my Gaelic for your British reared ears. What a pity you ken nothing of your homeland nor your family. Your father and I were close friends. I cannae understand why he would send you to the British and not to your dear ol' Uncle Oran." The laird leaned closer. "That would be me, you ken?"

"I gathered as much," Elaina replied. "I'm not simple, and I am sure that you ken the answer as well as I. You killed him. I find it hard to believe that Thamas MacGregor would have ever considered himself to be your friend or confidant."

A humored chuckle escaped the laird's throat. "It would surprise you all the things you dinna ken about your father, nor your mother and I."

"Why don't you tell me. I'm sure it is a delightful story."

"In time, my love. In time." The laird switched to Gaelic to address his men, no doubt giving them orders.

Elaina pretended not to care about what they spoke, but unease settled in her bones like a chilled wind as several sets of eyes flickered to her and back to the laird. The remainder of her meal she consumed in liquid form, the thought of food unappetizing. Raising a silent toast to Robert's dead mother, she prayed the woman may have escaped this world before too much harm had been inflicted upon her.

"Come." Laird Campbell motioned to her as he rose from the table. "I will give you the tour of your new home."

She stared at the muddled image of his hand, unsure of her ability to stand on her legs. The Madeira had worked to sooth the squeezing in her chest, but it had also clouded her reality.

The laird sighed and pulled her chair out for her.

With hesitation, she took the offered hand, stumbling into him upon rising as her blood rushed to her feet and the wine to her head. He linked her arm through his and turned her toward the door he had entered through. She glanced back over her shoulder at Robert before his father pulled her through it. He held his knife clenched in his hand, and his expression twisted in an odd mix of distrust, anger, and jealousy.

Elaina wished she had eaten more and drank less, her mind fuzzy as the laird ruminated about each room they passed. She hadn't the faculties to process any of it. The doorways and hallways continued on in a blur, and she found herself leaning more heavily upon the man's arm the farther they went.

"This, my dear, is my private study," Laird Campbell said leading her through a doorway.

Her soul seemed to scream at her to run, but her feet were impossible to control. The room was warm and cozy in muted tones of browns, mahoganies, and ambers. The fear inching up from her toes seemed a stark contrast to the charming room.

"Here, sit. There is something I want to show you." He seated her on a tan velvet sofa close to the fire and poured her a tumbler of amber liquid. She took it, but placed it on her lap instead of tasting it. She had had quite enough to drink.

Laird Campbell, holding his own tumbler, lowered himself beside her. "Let us drink," he said, his voice haunting and lilting. The waves of his words seemed to travel on the air.

Elaina closed her eyes against the swimming images in front of her.

"To family and heirlooms," the laird continued, his proposed toast bouncing off the backs of her eyelids.

She felt the glass of his tumbler clink against hers and raised hers to her lips out of habit, the whiskey smooth as the laird's voice traveled down her throat.

"Open yer eyes, Elaina," he whispered, his breath hot upon her ear. "I want you to see."

Her eyes obeyed, though she fought to keep them closed. She struggled to focus on the man staring back at her.

Several seconds passed in an odd silence as Laird Campbell studied her face. Elaina thought she raised an eyebrow in question but couldn't be sure.

"This is my grandfather two generations past." The laird waved his hand at a pair of portraits on the wall across from her.

One depicted a young man and a boy, so she forced her gaze to the other portrait of a sour looking man with gray hair. Elaina nodded, politely wondering why in the hell he was showing her a likeness of his ancestors. She was a prisoner, was she not? Shouldn't he lock her away in a tower, not force her to study images of his dead relatives? *Shut up, you bloody fool. Enjoy the damn portrait. Compliment him. Do you really want to be shut away in a tower, you bloody idiot?*

"Focus, Elaina." Her name rolled off his tongue like a silk ribbon.

She truly had imbibed too much.

"What do you see in the picture?"

"An old man," she replied before her brain could control her mouth.

The laird chuckled. "Very astute. Look closer."

Elaina glanced at Laird Campbell who sat entirely too close to her side. Huffing out a sigh, she rolled her eyes and returned her gaze to the portrait, taking in the gentleman's silver hair, the Campbell brooch, the Campbell coat of arms over his shoulder, his coat, the brooch on his jacket over his heart... Her eyes darted back to the brooch. The stone was markedly familiar, though no pine needles were etched upon its surface. The bell cap was not silver pinecones either. It was smooth silver. There were many Cairngorm stones in the Highlands. It was a common crystal, however the shape and size of this one was identical to the one Laird Campbell now held in his hand.

"You see, the stone you wore about your neck belongs to us. It belongs to

Clan Campbell, one of the greatest and most powerful fighting clans in all of Scotland. A lowly MacGregor stole it some one hundred fifty years ago when the laird of the clan killed this man you see here."

"What a pity. Doesn't that mean Clan Campbell is not near as fierce as you believe?"

Laird Campbell's hand was on her throat in an instant, squeezing until darkness danced before her eyes instead of firelight.

Damn my mouth.

"Mayhap then, but not now. Make no mistake about it, lass." He shoved her away, and she gasped for air, nearly dropping her tumbler. He took it from her before it hit the floor.

"Why am I here, if I may?" Elaina croaked after recovering her breath.

"You are here because I want you to be. I had planned to use you to bargain with the British, but now that I ken your true identity, I have many other things in mind.

"The British? What could you have possibly gained that would be of any value to you? Surely fifteen pounds would be nothing to a man like yourself?"

"You are correct," Laird Campbell leaned closer. "The money is nothin' to me. But my name is, and my son has sullied it by killing Captain Cummings. Eventually the British will learn that it was not you who fired the fateful shot, but that is no longer my concern. They can have Robert. I have you."

Her gaze darted back to the portrait of the young man and the boy. "I am to assume that is Alex by your side?" Her words slurred off her tongue and something akin to compassion crossed her heart as the meaning of the laird's words wormed their way into her brain. There was no portrait of Robert gracing the Laird's wall. "You would throw away your only surviving child?" Elaina asked thinking back to his open contempt for Robert.

"In a heartbeat to have what I now possess. I suppose I should thank him for it, even though the idiot has no clue what he has brought me."

She tried to focus her gaze on the weaving snake of a man beside her. "Why don't you let me in on your little secret?"

The laird leaned closer, gripping the back of Elaina's neck as she tried to move away from him.

"Get your hands off of me," she growled through her teeth, struggling to ease his bruising grip.

"Just like your mother. In so many ways." His eyes traveled over her face, pausing on her lips before continuing their trail down her décolletage. "So much like Mairi." He kissed her forehead, her nose, and then his mouth consumed hers as she fought to break free.

Chapter Fifteen

DOIREANN LED A TREMBLING ELAINA once again through the halls of the castle, this time with Laird Campbell's handkerchief stained with blood clutched in her hand. Her tongue traced the newly opened wound on her lip where his crushing kiss had split the healing skin. After his bruising attack, he had shoved her from him and called for his trusted servant.

Several servants passed them in the hallways, speaking in low tones. The castle crawled with Campbell men. She grew clammy at the thought of Calum and the MacGregors trying to raid the keep to retrieve her. It would be an unwise move. A familiar voice broke through her ruminations as two men passed her, and her gaze darted up and over her shoulder at the retreating figures.

Erroll's face peered back at her, his eyes wide. He held a finger to his lips before he turned back to the man he was walking with.

Elaina stared at his back as he continued down the hallway, her thoughts twisting in a whirlwind. A MacGregor in Laird Campbell's keep? Someone she had believed to be dead. She smacked into the back of Doireann, nearly taking both to the ground.

"You bloody fool," the servant woman barked at her.

"Apologies. I-I was lost in my thoughts," Elaina stammered. Looking back, she watched Erroll disappear around a corner.

"Well, learn to think and look at the same time." The irritated maid rattled the keys at her waist and unlocked the door. "Imbecile," she muttered, ushering Elaina inside. Doireann followed her, closing the door behind them. "Turn." The woman took Elaina's arm, twisting her around, and unlaced her dress.

Elaina stood naked in the middle of the room, shivering. Soft linen dyed the color of a fresh field of grass flowed over her head. The Laird seemed to have a penchant for green. "This is what I am to wear?" she asked, gazing down at the night dress. It was a lovely bit of fabric but illogical for the frigid winters in the Scottish Highlands. She would freeze to death.

"Yes." Doireann took the ends of the deep green satin ribbon that weaved its way through the creamy lace at the low, rounded neckline and tied them together, repeating the same at Elaina's wrists before she turned on her heel and left without another word.

This time she received the click of the lock with gratitude. At least if she were locked in her chamber, she was somewhat protected. It would also serve as a warning before Laird Campbell or his sinister son entered her chamber. Not to mention the ghost of Erroll. Where had he come from and what was he bloody doing in the enemy's midst? Snatching the cover to the gown from the bed, she shoved her arms through it. It didn't provide much more coverage than the original garment. She may as well be sleeping naked.

Dragging the heavy brocade blanket off also, she wrapped it around her and then crossed the room and stirred the fire, adding more peat. She pulled a chair closer to the hearth and curled herself into it, then poured a dram from the cut glass whiskey decanter they were so gracious as to provide her with. Between the whiskey, the flames, and the blanket, her shivering slowed. God how she wished it were Calum giving her warmth with his tall, sturdy form wrapped around her.

Tears slid down her cheeks as her resolve crumbled. There was no stopping them now that she was alone, locked safe inside her elegant prison. Where was he? She could not do this on her own. The fire blurred and sobs tore from her throat as the leaden hand of loss laid itself upon her soul.

Angrily wiping the tears from her face, she turned her thoughts from longing for her husband to how on earth she might escape. She could not rely on her husband and the MacGregors to save her this time. No plan that she could imagine seemed plausible for rescue from the outside world. Her freedom must come from inside the walls of the keep. Tomorrow, she vowed, she would not over imbibe and would pay attention to the layout of the castle and search for signs of weaknesses. The puzzle of Erroll's existence there would need to be worked out as well. His actions had told her not to alert the Campbell's to the fact that she knew him. That gave her hope that a comrade was with her. Tomorrow, she would hash out a strategy. Tonight, she would grieve and drink herself to sleep. Her shaking hand filled her glass, and then she raised it to toast the fire.

"To self-reliance and the power of a female mind," she whispered through her tears.

———————⊷⊷⊶———————

Doireann graced Elaina with her cheerful countenance yet again the following morning. She started awake to find the woman standing over her, hands on her hips as she gave her the most contemptuous glare. Unfolding her body from the chair elicited a loud groan from the prisoner whose tongue did not want to release itself from the roof of her mouth.

The horrid maid mumbled and grumbled under her breath as she set about returning the blanket to the bed, leaving Elaina huddled and shivering by the near dead fire. "I dare say ye need this." Doireann shoved tooth powder at Elaina. "Well, don't just stand there. Get to it," she barked at her hesitation.

Elaina could hardly perform her ablutions for the uncontrollable trembles. This had to be the coldest room she had ever occupied in her life. Two young girls had scurried into her chambers to stoke the fire none too soon and delivered a foul-smelling tray of food. She eyed the contents with apprehension until her gaze landed on a bannock. That seemed to be the safest thing to put on her stomach, so she nibbled on the bread until Doireann the Despicable returned with her two minions and a dress draped over her arm.

She cast a glance at the untouched meal before turning a glare on Elaina. "Starve if ye want," she grumbled while snapping the girls into motion.

"I think I am quite capable of deciding whether or not I wish to eat," Elaina spouted off, making Doireann's helpers cringe. She wondered how often they were beat for insubordination. Hopefully not much anymore. They seemed as well trained as the rest of the staff. They helped her out of her nightdress and changed the dressings on her war wounds. One emitted a small gasp as she rounded Elaina, and she didn't have to turn to know that the scars on her back had given the girl pause.

"They were a gift from Robert, the son of your master. I am no stranger to their evil acts. You need not fear m—"

"Shut up!" Doireann snapped, waving the girls from the room. She finished dressing Elaina herself, snatching and pulling.

Such a foul-tempered creature.

"I cannot do anything with that." She waved a hand at Elaina's hair.

"I quite understand," Elaina offered, picking up a brush. "It takes a good deal of effort and knowledge in the finer ways of life to know how to pull a brush through someone's hair. I wouldn't expect you to know of such, living here in the keep, watching over your lowly maids. As I can see they've entirely more knowledge than you about such things." Elaina gave the maid's coiffure a disparaging look.

"Ye are making no friends with that sharp tongue of yers," Doireann growled, taking a step toward Elaina.

"I am not meaning to. Your attitude leaves much to be desired, and I'll not be bullied by the likes of you." Elaina stood toe to toe with the hateful maid, the brush held in a death grip.

"Ah, we are awake and ready for our day." Laird Campbell strolled into the room. "Getting along marvelously too, I see." He cast an amused glance from his employee to his prisoner.

"Charmingly," Elaina responded with a broad smile.

Doireann stormed out of the room in a huff.

"Ye might want to tread lightly with her." The laird gave a nod after the maid. "She could make your life miserable."

"More wretched than you or your son have made it? That would be a difficult task to accomplish."

"Did your father not teach you to mind your manners when you are a guest in someone's house?" Laird Campbell hooked his arm through Elaina's and led her from her cold prison as if they were on a Sunday stroll.

"Yes, my father, the late Lord Spencer, brought me up well. But he is dead, and I am a prisoner. Manners and niceties can go to the devil, as may you, Laird Campbell. With all due respect, my laird." Elaina inclined her head in a polite bow with a disdainful smile plastered across her face.

He chuckled. "Just like your mother, God rest her soul. Come. My son tells me ye've a love for horses. I have a fine pair of Arabian stallions I believe you will appreciate."

"What of my mother? That is the second reference to her."

"In time, my dear. All things in due time."

Elaina let him lead her through the halls and out to the stables, taking mental note of every doorway and window along the way, as well as the guards posted across the tops of the stone walls at 300-foot increments. All stood statue-still, staring out across the moat and the expanse of grasslands toward the surrounding forests. It would take an army...

Chapter Sixteen

ELAINA DIDN'T WANT TO ADMIT it, but the laird's stables impressed her. The pair of Arabians pranced their way out of the stalls led by Rupert and Ruske, of all men.

"Gentlemen," she acknowledged as Ruske eyed her with wariness.

Turning her attention back to the horses, Elaina ran a hand along one's graceful brown neck and down its withers. The stallion stood approximately fifteen hands tall, its nose and tail pointed in the air as if standing before the king himself.

"Glorious," she whispered.

The second, whose ears had directed themselves toward the nearest stall, stomped and called to his prospective mate, who ignored his gesticulations and unsightly randiness.

"Isn't that just like a female?" Laird Campbell commented, eliciting a chuckle from the handlers. "Putting on as if she is too wrapped up in other matters to notice his obvious affections?"

"Isn't that just like a male?" Elaina challenged. "Acting as if prancing around like a cocksure is enough to impress a woman? It takes more than a flash of a member to secure one's affection."

"Touché, Mistress MacKinnon."

A lad of about fifteen appeared, interrupting their posturing. "M' laird, the messenger has returned."

"Excellent. You will excuse me? I've important matters to see to. Ruske shall attend to your needs."

Elaina nor Ruske bothered to mask their displeasure.

"Come, my man. Dinna be bashful. Give the lady a grand tour of the stables and the yards. Make her feel welcome to her new home."

Ruske glared at her as his laird followed the boy out of the building.

"May I?" Elaina waved a hand toward the walkway.

"Aye," he muttered, leading the stallion back to his pen.

Elaina meandered down the line of stalls, inspecting each horse. Fifteen horses lined one side of the walk while the same number stood across from them. When she reached the end, the corridor made a right turn where more horses held residence. These were older, though no less impressive. Ahead of her, Erroll worked forking hay into a stall. She wanted to run to him but resisted while pretending to take an interest in a bay mare until the lad tending a brown gelding disappeared around the corner, leaving her and Erroll to themselves.

"What the hell are you doing here?" she hissed at him.

The pitchfork in his hand clattered to the ground. He closed his eyes, one hand on his chest. "Dammit, lass. Warn an old man yer comin'."

"I thought you were dead!" she whispered with a glance over her shoulder to make sure they were still alone. "What are you doing here at the castle?"

"Keepin' an eye on ye. When I arrived at the campsite and everyone was dead and Caitir gone, I had a good mind who had taken her. I doubled back in time to see the Campbell's take ye from yer brother. That's when I volunteered my services as a groomsman. I figured they would bring ye here."

"So, you've no word from Calum?" Elaina wrung her hands.

"Nay, lass. Tomorrow a supply wagon will go out and another return. I had plans to be on it or at least get a message out somehow."

She nodded.

Erroll seized her arm. "Erase that ridiculous thought from yer mind. There would be no way. They inspect every cart comin' and goin'."

"I believe it's 'bout time to head back, mistress." Ruske's gravelly voice raked down her spine, and she turned to find him halfway down the aisle. His wary glance at her and then at Erroll sent chills across her flesh.

"Mayhap the laird would see fit to let ye take a round one afternoon when the sun is out," Erroll said loud enough for Ruske to hear. "I'll figure somethin' out," he whispered moments before Ruske snatched her up in a death grip.

"Get your hands off of me." Elaina yanked her arm but failed at dislodging it from his hold. "I did not give you leave to touch me."

He sneered at the two of them. "Do ye truly think I need yer permission?

Come." He gave her a jerk, almost taking her feet from under her. She had no choice but to stumble after him and fight to keep up with his lengthy stride. Once they exited the stables, he released her.

Heavy wet flakes of a dense snow landed with soft pats around them as they walked. She rubbed her throbbing arm while resisting the urge to kick his legs out from under him. "I see your nose is healing quite nice. What about the rest of you?" she asked with a smirk instead.

"Why? Are ye offerin' to check it for me? Could use a woman's touch." He cast a leer down at her.

Elaina brushed the snow from her hair as she chastised herself for her reckless comments.

"I thought that might shut yer blasted mouth. It's time to retire to yer room until the laird calls for ye." Ruske led her down the hallways without hesitation, and it made unease settle in Elaina's stomach to know that the man knew exactly where she was held. He snapped his fingers at a young girl who skittered down the hall and out of sight. "A word of warning," Ruske growled not looking at her. "Watch yer back, mistress."

"That was quite the waste of breath. I am the daughter of a MacGregor and the wife of a MacKinnon in the center of Campbell lands."

"Yes, well."

They turned the corner, and Elaina realized where the girl had disappeared to. Doireann stood beside her door with her damned keys awaiting their arrival. "Some residents of the keep are more dangerous than others." His lip curved in a taunting jeer. "If ye catch my meanin'?"

"As in you? I do not fear you, Ruske. You need to remember who delivered you that pretty little mark across your great beak."

"Revenge is sweet, mistress. Dinna forget that." His gaze traveled a burning path down her body and back up again. He licked his lips before handing her over with a nod to her jailer. He gave her a wink before he retreated the way they had come.

Doireann seemed as happy as ever to lock Elaina away, and Elaina's thoughts were so muddled, she was glad to return to captivity. She did not feel near as alone as before. Erroll was here. She had at least one ally. Two against probably hundreds.

Crossing the room to the narrow windows, she inspected the fields that now lay covered in a soft blanket of white. A few prints by the forest edge marred the pristine cover, but she was too far away to know what or who they might belong to. Then the massive stag that stepped out from between the trees dashed her hopes to hell. He nudged the snow from the winter grasses, foraging for a meal. A deer, and not a man. Not her husband.

Chapter Seventeen

ONFUSION DRIZZLED ITS WAY THROUGH her mind, and she stared dumbfounded at Robert.

"'Tis simple, Elaina. What can ye no understand? Ye have free rein of the keep except for one area, and ye needn't worry which one. The guards will make sure ye ken it well."

"I may roam...freely? You do not think I will escape?"

"Where are ye to go? It is an impenetrable fortress as ye can tell. There is no escape. Now, if you will excuse me, I've things to attend to. I bid ye good day."

Elaina watched Robert's long, lean back as he exited her room. Her feet remained planted in place, waiting for the door to slam closed and the lock to click into place. Only the sound of Robert's footsteps retreating down the hallway could be heard. She inched her way toward the open doorway and peered into the hall. Empty. With caution, she slid a foot out into the openness beyond her room. Giggling at her jitters, she stepped into the cool gray expanse. She felt very much like a deer must feel stepping from the woods during season and looked behind her for the hunter, for Doireann and her chatelaine, but found emptiness. Shrugging her shoulders, she ventured in the opposite direction of the path they usually took to dine.

The castle was a monstrous affair with innumerable twists and hallways. Nine floors of dreary stone hallways dotted with elegant drawing rooms, immense libraries, three ballrooms, innumerable bedchambers, two court yards, six dining halls, and three gardens. Raised beds dotted the stone surface with winter foliage peeking through the snow here and there. How the gardener grew anything in this unfriendly place was beyond her. She encountered many servants on her expedition. Most eyed her with wariness, and she wondered what they had been told about her. What she did not find, however, was a single portrait of Robert. She hadn't realized that she was looking for one until she came across the fourth portrait of Alex in a drawing room. He must have been about one and five, and it was easy to watch the transformation of a precocious young child into a serious young man by following the trail of likenesses throughout the castle.

Her nose and rumbling stomach drew her out of her woolgathering and into one of the two kitchens. Standing in the doorway, she closed her eyes and let the warmth from the ovens envelope her. Inhaling the mingling aromas brought memories of Mrs. Davies bustling around the kitchen at Duart Manor, barking orders at the other help. The pungent smell of onions and garlic...the comforting scent of baking bread...the clanging of pots and the distant buzz of someone receiving a dressing down made her think of the first time she had met Angus—the precocious stable lad who had stolen her heart. He had added a much-needed levity to the grief of the inconceivable act of having to bury her parents. She almost laughed out loud at the image of Mrs. Davies chasing him from the kitchen that afternoon. Sadly, it was his death—his murder—that had started her down this path. The remembrance of the ample cook stroking her hair while she wept on the kitchen floor for her lost ten-year-old boy, his blood soaked into her dress and its overwhelming scent wiping away all the comforting smells of a kitchen made her eyes snap open before the tears could fall. She steadied herself against the frame of the door before forcing herself to move farther into the bustling room, nodding at the many helping hands as she went.

"Mistress." A tall scarecrow of a man approached her. "What ye be needin'?"

"I thought I smelled soup. My empty belly led the way."

"Aye. We've soup. Cock a Leekie. If ye would like to return to yer room, I will have a meal delivered."

He knew who she was. Did they all know she was a captive or did they think her a visitor? "May I dine here?" she asked not wishing to return to the confines of her room so soon. She wanted to venture to the stables and see if Erroll had indeed made it out on the supply wagon.

"Ye cannae dine with us, 'Twould no be right," the man said.

"What would be wrong about it? You are a servant. I am a captive. I am of no worth, and it is warm and inviting in here." Softer she added. "It reminds me of home."

The man eyed her with caution. Releasing a small sigh, he resigned himself.

"Very well. I am Fredrick. Head cook. If ye need anythin', call for me. In the meantime… Bridgette," he called to a petite black-haired lass. "Serve Mistress MacKinnon at the north table."

"At the north table, sir?" The lass raised her brow, her gaze darting to Elaina and then back to Fredrick.

"Yes. The north table. Close to the ovens but with a view of the courtyard. 'Tis the best I can do down here, mistress." He bowed to Elaina and returned to his work overseeing the making of meals for the inhabitants of the keep.

"This way," Bridgette said with a bob of the head.

Elaina followed the servant girl around the bustling kitchen and to a small nook just to the left of the giant ovens. True to Fredrick's word, the table sat with a view of one of the courtyards. She let the warmth of the great ovens nearby envelop her in a comforting embrace as Bridgette placed before her a bowl of soup, a large crust of toasted bread, and a mug of mulled cider.

Several minutes later, Bridgette returned carrying another bowl of steaming soup. "Is it to yer liking, mistress?"

"Very much so. Thank you."

"May I join ye? 'Tis time for my break, and I do love the view from this table."

"I have no objections as long as Fredrick does not mind you consorting with the enemy."

Bridgette's laugh sounded like pebbles bouncing off a large rock.

Elaina smiled. She had not heard anyone truly laugh in she didn't know how long. What a magical sound.

"Ye are no the enemy, mistress. Ye are the lady of the castle. In truth, ye should no be dinin' down here in the kitchens with the help. Laird Campbell may not smile on the matter, if he kenned it."

The lady of the castle? Could it be far worse than she had imagined? For now, Elaina ignored the title and the girl's shocking news and bid her to sit with her. The raven-haired lass was the only friendly face, save Erroll's, that she had met, and she planned to enjoy her company as long as possible. Besides, she seemed to have a free tongue compared to the others. Perfect for garnering information about the laird's plans.

Bridgette slid onto the bench across from Elaina. For several minutes, neither spoke as they watched a red bird dip and dive after the female of his species, trying to entice her in a whirlwind of a dance.

"How did you come to work here at the keep?" Elaina asked, breaking the peaceful silence.

"My parents were killed in battle and the laird took me in. I was but ten and four. These people gave me a home and a purpose."

Her comment conflicted greatly with the image Elaina held of the Campbell men. "How kind." She mumbled as she tore off a piece of her bread and dunked it into her soup.

Bridgette giggled her tumbling laugh. "I've never seen a high-born lady dab her bread in her soup."

"This high-born lady, as you call me, was reared in the wilds of the mountains in the Royal Colonies. I am not normal high-born."

"Aye, that I can tell. Ye are dinin' in the kitchen with the help. Never in my life… Ye like the bread, then? I made it. I make all the bread," Bridgette offered at Elaina's nod around a mouthful of the item.

"'Tis very good," Elaina said.

Bridgette beamed. "I am blessed ye think so. I will try to assure ye have it at every meal. Now, I must get back. Are ye finished, then?" Bridgette offered to take Elaina's empty bowl.

"Aye. I've had my fill, and I thank you."

"I feel privileged to finally meet the lovely lass in the portrait. I have admired it for several years, and I must say, ye've no aged a minute."

"Wait," Elaina called as Bridgette turned to go. "The lass in the portrait? What portrait?"

"I-I am sorry I spoke of it. Please do not mention it to the laird."

"I promise I will not say a word, but where is it? I should very much like to see it." Elaina leaned toward Bridgette, whose lovely face held serious doubt. "It has been so long since I sat for it, I've quite forgotten what it looks like," she added for good measure.

The girl glanced around the kitchen, looking for listening ears. "I had taken the laird a meal. He was ill at the time, and it… Well, at the time, it had leaned against a wall in his chambers, but not long after, it disappeared and I wondered where it had gone. It was such a delightful portrait. I always wondered what the lass painted on the canvas was like. She seemed to be strong and full of life. Which ye are. Ye are very near everything I had imagined ye would be. Except that ye are a wee bit worse for the wear, beggin' yer pardon." The lass grimaced at her words.

"Yes, I imagine I am. No offense taken." Elaina's mind scurried and tumbled, wondering what a portrait of her mother would be doing in Laird Campbell's castle? "So, it is gone? You have no idea where it may be?"

"No. I ken well enough where it is now, castle gossip, ye ken? But it is where I have no privilege to go. There are parts of the West Tower that only a select few may enter, and I am nay one of them."

Elaina stared at her. The west tower? Was that where she was not allowed to venture? What secrets did the laird hide there besides a portrait of her dead mother. "Who told you the portrait was there?" And why was the help discussing it at all?

"That I cannae tell ye. I must return to work. Lovely dinin' with ye, mistress."

Elaina watched the maid scurry through the kitchen and then hurried out herself, her curiosity piqued.

Chapter Eighteen

ENTERING THE STABLES, ELAINA PAUSED to let her eyes adjust to the dimness. Curiosity had pulled her in two separate directions—here and the west tower. She had chosen the safer of the two options first. Her gaze roved over the horses and all the nooks and crannies in their stalls as she made her way through the building, searching for Erroll. Instead, she found Ruske.

"What do ye want?" He towered over her with a pitchfork clutched in his grasp.

"What does it matter?" Elaina said, running a hand down the nose of a roan mare.

"Because ye are in my stables." He took a threatening step toward her.

She refused to cower under his scornful glare. "That's funny. I thought they were the laird's stables, and I have been given leave to go anywhere I want within the keep. I came here. So, if you don't mind stepping out of my way, I will carry on. If you have any issues, take them up with the laird." Elaina brushed past him in a swish of skirts without looking back. *Insufferable horse's arse.*

After a thorough search, she decided Erroll was not present, but that did not mean he'd left with the supply wagon. He could be anywhere.

"Searchin' for someone?"

Elaina almost fell from the ladder she stood on, looking into the loft over the stables. Clearing her throat and climbing down as slowly as possible, her mind scrambled for a reasonable explanation to give the giant oaf who had caught her unawares. "Yes," she said staring up into Ruske's suspicious face. "I was searching for the man I spoke to the other day. He promised he would show me his favorite mare if I ever happened down this way again."

"His favorite mare? Why the bloody hell would ye care which was *his* favorite mare? Do ye ken the man?"

"No," Elaina answered too quickly. "I just…we were discussing horses is all. I told him I have a penchant for them, and he offered to show me around when you so rudely interrupted us." She stuck her nose in the air, trying to give the impression of aloofness and hide her lies. Erroll's words came back to her about the obviousness of her actions written upon her face.

"Well, yer little friend is no here," Ruske said. "But if yer interested, I could show ye my best stud."

"As pleasant an offer as that sounds, I must pass. If you will excuse me, I believe I have more enjoyable things to attend to…things like shoving sharp instruments under my fingernails and such." Elaina hurried from the stables and away from the horrid man.

She shuddered, trying to shake the chills from her skin. If she had the chance, he would be one of the first to die after the father and son duo who held her hostage in this cold horrid environment.

Her footsteps led her toward the outside of the west tower. She peered up at it, its stone façade broken by only four windows. One on each side, if one could say that a cylinder had sides, all on differing floors. What on earth could be housed there that was forbidden for her to see besides the portrait of her dead mother?

Two guards approached her, and she hurried on, nodding at them as they passed her. She made her way around the back of the keep and down the south side until she reached the east turret, which identically resembled the western one.

"There ye are, my love." Robert's voice startled her heart into her throat. "What are ye lookin' at?"

"I-I was admiring the workmanship is all," she stuttered.

"Aye? Well, enough admiring the construction of the keep. 'Tis time to ready for dinner. Ye shan't be late." He placed a hand on the small of her back, ushering her toward the front of the castle.

Elaina shrugged away from the familiar contact, causing him to chuckle. He reached out and took her arm, draping it over his.

"I would prefer it if you did not touch me."

"I would prefer it if ye would let me escort ye like a lady instead of ye always actin' like ye've no upbringin'. I ken yer father was a British officer, and I ken well enough he taught ye manners ye seem to have forgotten since ye married into that worthless clan."

"That worthless clan is my family, and I would thank you not to insult them."

"We are yer family now, Elaina. Ye must grow accustomed to it." Robert stroked her hand he had draped over his arm.

"The Campbells will never be my family, Robert." His false kindness prickled her skin and made her wonder just what exactly the Campbells were up to and what part she played in it?

As they rounded the entrance to the castle, two wagons rolled through the gate and stopped in front of a handful of guards who attacked them like ants to a crumb—lifting, searching, and counting. Erroll sat upon the seat of the first and gave Elaina the slightest of nods as Rabbie led her away from the wagons and through the yawning doorway of the castle.

The supply wagon had brought several dresses more in keeping with Elaina's size. She sat to the left of Laird Campbell more comfortably in her dress if not so much in her skin. Considerable amounts of Gaelic along with whiskey were being tossed about the hall this evening, leaving Elaina out of the conversations purposefully, it seemed. She pushed the food around on her plate while listening for any patterns she might pick up and learn. The guttural, lilting speech still evaded her. There were two words she understood, however—MacKinnon and British. One gave her hope, and the other sent chills racing down her spine.

"Are ye cold, my dear? Should I ask them to add more peat to the fire?" the laird asked leaning toward her.

Elaina's hands came to an abrupt halt where she was involuntarily attempting to rub away the gooseflesh that had risen on her arms at the mention of the British. She cleared her throat. "In all actuality, it helps me concentrate while I try to decipher your mysterious dialect. I too would like to be a part of the conversation," she said, trying to hide her unease.

"'Tis a pity your Scottish mother taught you no Gaelic, but then she was a Lowlander, no? Why would she ken the language of the Highlands?"

His question was simple enough. Why would her adoptive mother have knowledge of their language? But she had, and Laird Campbell knew it. Rabbie had found letters her mother had written to a Highlander discussing the Jacobite cause and sizeable sums of money given to it. The rumors of an uprising to overthrow King George II from the throne and return a Stuart king to power ran rampant throughout Scotland and England. Whether the speculations were true, she hadn't yet determined, but gossip alone had placed Elaina in the clutches of a Highland clan with a powerful alliance with the British.

"Here. Have more whiskey, love. Your color is fading. I would hate for you to catch the vapors and retire early." The laird filled her cup, but she didn't touch it.

Her thoughts returned to her first dinner at the keep and her over-indulgence. She couldn't repeat the same unwise actions. Pinching off a crust of bread and popping it in her mouth, Elaina studied her host...her captor. "I am wondering. What is my reason for being here?"

"To eat, of course," the laird answered.

Rabbie smirked at her from across the table.

She considered kicking him. "I mean here in the castle. Dining at your table. Wearing the clothes you give me. Walking your cold stone grounds. Held as your prisoner. What is your plan for me? Are you drawing in my family to kill them? Are you using me as a pawn between them, yourself, and the British Government? The highest payer wins, is that how it works?"

"A lass wise beyond her years." The laird raised his glass in salute. "Yes."

"Yes what?" Elaina placed her hands in her lap lest she take leave to strangle the bloody fool.

"Yes, to all the above and more. I shall hold a dinner party in your honor in a few weeks, and there you shall learn all you need to ken on the matter. Until then, eat, drink, and enjoy your freedom."

Chapter Nineteen

ELAINA MADE HER WAY PAST the opening of the west tower, taking stock of her surroundings. The two burly guards with their feet planted wide and their arms crossed eyed her with suspicion. Let them. Her intentions were not honorable. She wanted to see the portrait that rumor placed in the tower behind them and needed to work out a plan to find it. The problem was that she held no alliance with anyone at the keep except Erroll, and he remained in the stables until mealtimes. In case the rumors were wrong about where her mother's portrait rested, Elaina vowed to scour every inch of the castle. Besides, knowing the layout of the keep could be quite handy in the event anything ever happened, like an unexpected rescue.

Inside a salon on the third floor, a door opened to a small storage room of sorts. After inspecting the hallway for unwanted guests, she took up a candlestick and crept into the room, easing the door closed behind her. Leaned against the far wall stood several frames with their faces pointed to the wall. Rolled canvases graced both corners on either side of the door, leaning like sentries guarding the room, and a grouping of rugs also rolled into tubes had been piled along another wall.

Dust filtered through the candlelight as Elaina made her way to the row of portraits. A bit of daylight would have been nice, but no windows graced the room. The first two gilded frames she pulled away held images of landscapes of wooded glens and snowcapped mountains dotted with heather. As she took one away from the pile, she stacked it against the opposite wall so she could put them back in order when she finished. The third picture she uncovered brought her up short—a young Laird Campbell looked back at her with two vivid green eyes and hair the color of a new fawn falling loose about his shoulders. She hated to admit the image was striking. He had been quite handsome before her father scarred his face and blinded one eye. His scar did not make him unattractive, but it gave one pause at first sight of it. She carefully laid the portrait aside with the others. The next several paintings were more landscapes and people she did not recognize. From the style of their clothing, they must have been Campbell men from centuries ago.

Elaina stood straight and groaned as she stretched her back. Only a handful remained. Her hopes that the mystery portrait might be amongst the others dwindled along with the pile of frames. Returning to the task, she turned the next frame around and her heart melted in an unexpected flash of grief. Rabbie's mother sat with a tot of a boy beside her, their gazes on one another with adoration. The characteristics were the same as the portrait hanging over the mantle in the dining hall—the same artist capturing the profound love between a mother and a child.

Elaina sank to the floor in front of the picture and held the candle closer to see the details better. How old had Rabbie been when his mother died? Was it ten? He had to have been about seven when they sat for this portrait, his shaggy blond hair swept against his shoulders. But it was the love exuded in the mother's and son's eyes that caused a tear to slide down Elaina's cheek. Seeing Rabbie as a young boy set him in a different light. What a horrible life he must have lived, losing the person who meant the most to him at such a young age and being left in the hands of his cruel father who made quite clear he had no use for his own son. Fate and circumstance had twisted Rabbie into a hardened, cruel man.

"There ye are."

Elaina started, nearly dropping her candle. She wiped the tears from her cheeks before scrambling to her feet. She turned to face Rabbie with her heart lodged in her throat.

"Snoopin'?"

"You said I had free rein. Just curious is all." Elaina pushed herself to her feet, placing her full skirts in front of the portrait she had been studying.

"Aye. But I dinna ken if this is what my da had in mind, rummagin' through his belongin's. What makes ye want to gander at old pictures, anyway?" He took a step closer to her.

She fought not to take a step back. "Boredom." She hoped her face did not betray her. "I have explored this blasted place from one end to the other, except the west turret, of course. I was searching for painting or drawing supplies."

"Why did ye no just ask for them?" Rabbie took another step, his green eyes narrowing. "I've never known ye to sit behind an easel with a paint brush in yer hand." His words dripped with sarcasm.

Elaina took a tiny step backward, kicking the portrait she was attempting to hide.

Rabbie caught her by the elbows before she hit the ground.

"*Merde*! I've gotten wax all over my dress." The exclamation uttered a tad too shrill, trying to draw his attention away from the picture.

Rabbie stared at the image her clumsiness had uncovered. Sorrow tore across his face before he buried it behind a hardened stare. "So, this is where it has gone to," he whispered.

Elaina stood silent, letting him process his emotions.

He turned his burning gaze upon her. "How dare ye put yer nose where it doesnae belong," he growled, snatching her by the arm.

"Rabbie, it is alright to grieve for your mother. It is normal to miss someone who—"

"Shut up! Dinna speak of my mother. Yer pity is not needed. I buried all my sorrow with her the day we laid her beneath the ground." Rabbie dragged her from the storage in a swirl of dust.

Gritting her teeth, Elaina refused to utter even a slight whimper as his grip tightened and she thought he might twist her arm in two. He dragged her from the salon and down the chilled hallways, winding their way toward her room and leaving a trail of melted wax in their wake. Rabbie shoved her through the doorway to her chambers and slammed the door closed behind him, trapping them both inside.

Elaina crossed the room and placed her trembling hands flat upon the table, refusing to look at Rabbie until she had her emotions under control. She hoped he was gathering his as well. It was obvious Rabbie had not dealt with the death of his mother. He had not buried the memory of her in the grave with her but instead buried his sorrow and his anger deep within his soul. He was a broken man.

His boot heels clipped in a determined cadence as he crossed the room in her direction, and she stiffened in wait for the attack, but he stopped just behind her, his breath ragged from their hurried jaunt through the halls of the castle.

"I dinna expect ye to understand, Elaina. Ye had yer parents. I had a tyrant."

"You do not know what my childhood was like, Rabbie," Elaina whispered. "I might understand you more than you realize."

"Just because yer dear ol' da was not the man who sired ye, doesnae mean ye didna have a pampered childhood. I'd be willin' to bet he didna beat ye. That ye didna fear for yer life. There will be no more snoopin' through the castle and there will be no talk of my mother. Do ye ken what I'm sayin'?"

She gave him a small nod of understanding as his breath came hot upon the back of her head, his body too close to her own.

"With that agreement, I will see that ye have some canvases and paints sent up so that ye may entertain the artistic demon waitin' to emerge from yer fingertips," he said, the laughter in his voice clear without her having to see him.

Damn her poor choice of an excuse. She was an abysmal painter, and he knew it. Silence roared in her ears as she refused to respond.

After a moment, with a chuckle and a soft pat on her cheek, Rabbie quit the room and locked her inside. Her knees gave out, and she caught the edge of the chair before she dropped to the floor. She sat for several minutes with her face buried in her hands, grieving for the lost lad in the portrait.

Chapter Twenty

THE CAMPBELLS DID NOT CALL for Elaina that night, nor the next day—not even the day after that. She took her meals in her chambers with Doireann ignoring all her questions. On the third day, Elaina refused to eat anything except bread. Doireann simply scooped up the full tray and left. After two days with no change, Elaina could take no more of being a prisoner in her room and stood at the door with her arms folded as Doireann's key turned in the lock.

The evil hag stood with a waif of a girl by her side. The lass trembled so that the glassware clinked together like tinkling bells on the breakfast tray she held.

Elaina blocked their advancement. "You are not entering."

"I have orders." Doireann cast a withering glare.

"I believe you know what you can do with those orders. If I am to be a prisoner, so be it. 'Tis not the first time." Elaina snatched the hunk of bread off the tray and slammed the door in Doireann's face. She smiled to herself at the stream of probable Gaelic obscenities that poured from the woman's mouth.

Her regrets over her actions might be soon coming, but Laird Campbell would give her an answer as to why he felt the need to lock her in her room day and night when he had given her the grand tour himself and let her roam freely for nigh on a sennight. He may not care at all if she starved to death, but at the moment, she didn't either. Not used to being cooped up, she had had about all she could stand. The soft bread tore in her hand, and she stared at a bit of folded paper that dropped to the floor.

She snatched it up moments before the door flung open and Robert's form filled the opening with a derisive smile upon his face.

"Tsk, tsk, tsk. Treatin' the help poorly, I gather, and when she has been so good to ye?" He waved Doireann into the chamber where she deposited the tray on the table.

"When the lass has eaten a proper meal, ye may return to groom her." He waved the help from the room.

With her nose in the air, Doireann exited the room with a satisfied huff.

Elaina bit into the bread she held with one hand while she slid the folded note into her pocket with the other. "I am not a horse for her to groom, and your definition of 'good' is questionable."

Rabbie stepped into the room and closed the door behind him. The lock clicked into place.

A cold sweat broke out on her neck. "This is most indecent, me locked in a room with you."

"Dinna fash, lass. I willnae pounce on ye. We need ye to heal, and ye cannae do that without proper food. Sit."

"I believe I am doing just fine. I am almost back to normal." A light green bruise underneath her eye was all that remained of her injuries.

He planted himself on a chair by the table and motioned her into the other. When she had taken the seat, he examined the meal before them. "Now, what would ye like?" He inspected her face while waiting for her reply. A glint of something passed behind his eyes before he turned his attention to the tray in front of them.

"I would like to know why your father has locked me in this room for five days."

"He didn't. I did. Da is gone, and ye are a prisoner. I'm sorry, I thought ye kenned it well enough."

"Laird Campbell said I was a guest, and he allowed me to roam free throughout the castle. You said yourself there was no escape," Elaina countered.

"Guest...prisoner. 'Tis all the same. Ye'll learn with time, ye cannae trust him. He's a wee bit tetched." Rabbie tapped his temple as he crossed his legs. He popped a dry fig into his mouth, watching her.

"Like father, like son." She nibbled on the bread she held, her mind on the note in her pocket. Bridgette had told her she made all the bread. Had she hidden the message or was it from Erroll? Had he learned something? The possibility of Bridgette letting Erroll hide a note in her food seemed implausible, but she handled all the bread. Elaina glanced up to find Rabbie's green gaze roving over her face.

"If ye could have controlled yerself, ye may no be locked away. Yer eye is almost back to normal, and yer lip." His gaze lingered there, unsettling her before he turned his attention to pouring her a steaming cup of tea. "Ye should be back to yer pristine loveliness by the time our special occasion rolls around."

"What harm could come from me looking at a few paintings you stashed away for years, and what occasion?" The teacup served as both a way to hide her piqued curiosity and to warm her frozen hands. This room was always so blasted cold.

"A lovely dinner party we have planned. Ma may be long passed, but Da and Doireann can put together a fine fete on their own."

She arched an annoyed eyebrow at his flippant nature and his avoidance to discuss the portraits and her being locked in a room for days on end.

"Here. Eat. I'll not leave this room until ye have had a proper meal. Now, if ye would like me to remain and help ye with yer ablutions, then by all means, nibble on your bread, little mouse. I should be happy to lend a hand and share your bed when night falls."

Elaina glared at him before turning her attention to the feast in front of her. "Are you trying to fatten me up for slaughter? I cannot eat all of this nonsense."

"Aye, there's a thought. Slaughter. What a fine word. I do love a good slaughter."

The cold sweat that had beaded on her neck before now rolled down her back.

"But, never ye mind. I'm sure it's better for breedin', no slaughterin'."

A ragged cough ripped from her throat as she choked on the bit of bread she had tried to swallow.

"Oh, dear. Here, my love. Take a sip." He came around the table and knelt at her side, one hand giving her a gentle pat on the back and the other holding her teacup to her lips.

She gulped it down before coughing and gasping into her napkin.

"It shouldna come as a surprise. Ye ken I've been wantin' to bed ye since we first met. Now though, 'twould be but a bit of added assurance that we will get what we want."

"I will not—" another choking cough seized her.

"No, I expect ye willnae…willingly." He pushed her loose hair behind her ear, his finger grazing her cheek.

His words and his actions froze her to her spot. He would not, but she knew he could and given the opportunity he might. He could at this moment, if he so chose. Here they sat locked in her room together.

"Och, not now, my love. Ye can get that appalled, terrified look off yer face. Ye never could hide yer thoughts." He tapped her nose with his fingertip before rising to his feet and waving a hand at the tray of food. "Eat. I've things to do." He crossed the room and stirred the fire in the hearth. "It's bloody cold in here. How do ye stand it?" He shivered, and she considered bashing him over the head with the fire poker. "I will have extra peat brought in for ye, and I will deliver your meals from here on out since ye treat yer help like a cast out."

"That woman is a witch. Why can I not have the other girls as my help, or better yet, set me free and leave that woman to shovel shite or something more fitting?" Elaina slid a spoon of parritch into her mouth, attempting the difficult task of eating fast yet not drawing attention to herself. She needed him out of the room. The note in her pocket called out to her, and her virtue begged to be untainted. Neither were safe with Rabbie present.

"That is why ye may not have the younger girls. Do ye think any of these skittish lasses can endure yer foul tongue? I dare say not. It takes a witch to care for the likes of ye. That or a man. Finished? Excellent. I'll send up more peat and as a show of good faith, I will have Doireann find ye some warmer clothes." He shivered again as he gathered the empty tray before crossing the room and kicking the door three times.

"Thank god," she whispered as the lock clicked into place behind his retreating back.

The note ripped in half as she scrambled to unfold it before anyone returned with supplies for the fire. She laid the two pieces on the table in front of her.

"MacGregors coming."

MacGregors to my rescue? Her stomach clenched as she tried to figure out how. She sat in the middle of a bloody moat. Her gaze traveled out the window once more. It seemed all she did was stare out the window in a state of hopelessness. Just inside the tree line, across the expanse of the field, she thought she saw something move. Her heart leapt before she recalled the stag feeding on winter grass.

Pull yourself together. Your father raised you better than to stand around depending on others to defend you. Stop feeling sorry for yourself.

Her eyes stopped on a shadow under a massive dormant elm just beyond the bare brush at the edge of the field. Blast it, she was too far away to tell if a breeze through the bare limbs of the elm made the shadow seem to move or if it moved of its own free will. She could have sworn that the shadow turned, and she stepped closer toward the window to investigate. The lock clicked, and she snatched the two pieces of paper into her fist and braced herself upon the table. Remembering Rabbie's words, she tried to wipe all expression from her face. Ruske entered with the promised fuel. As big as he was, he brought enough for several days. He stacked it beside the hearth and raised to go. He held her gaze for a brief moment before he left with a sneer that warped his disheveled features.

As soon as she was alone, she rushed to the window. The shadow was gone. Had it been man or beast? Trying not to get her hopes up, she hurried to the fire and burned the note.

They are coming!

Chapter Twenty-One

ABBIE DELIVERED HER MEALS EACH day, leaving Doireann and the girls to bathe her as he so graciously stood guard on the other side of the screen in case should she attempt to drown one of the women in the copper tub. His daily visits unnerved her. After all, she had killed his brother and knew he had a vendetta. She also feared there would be another note secretly hidden somewhere in her food and her secret would be discovered.

She watched the forest for mysterious shadows, but several days passed with no changes. No notes, no Calum, and no MacGregors. Her hope dwindled more and more by the end of every day.

Doireann, Rabbie, and a seamstress arrived one blistering cold afternoon. It seemed no matter how much peat Elaina shoved in the hearth, the roaring flames could not chase away the chill.

"Stand," Rabbie ordered. "Ye will have a new frock for our dinner party."

She obeyed his command, leaving her post by the fire and shucking the blanket she wore around her shoulders. "And just when is this extravaganza?" she asked, holding her arms out while the seamstress measured them from armpit to wrist.

"Soon."

Rabbie seemed distracted. He was not his usual talkative, unnervingly nice self. He stared into the flames while the ladies finished the business at hand. "I will have tea brought up soon. Can ye behave yerself without me? I've things to do. If not, I can send Ruske to take my place."

"I swear I will give them no grief."

"That's an obedient lass." He patted her on the head like a dog, and the threesome took their leave.

A special made dress, an extravagant dinner, locked in her room for days on end, a distracted Rabbie, and the possibility of MacGregors arriving. A slow-moving dread rose from the pit of her stomach. All this time she had waited for her clan to break her free. The situation might turn out much different from how she imagined.

Doireann returned with a tray of tea and shortbread, depositing it and leaving without a word.

Elaina dropped herself into a chair by the table and stared at the tray with its fine bone china, the steam from the elegant teapot swirling in a gray ribbon into the chilly air of the room. The situation could be worse. The gaol at Balquhidder, for example, and she had survived that. She could survive this. Picking at the shortbread, she thought of Calum and his jovial smile. His dimple and sparkling hazel eyes. She closed hers and brought forth images of their times spent alone—the only thing that kept her going day after day. With another nibble, she imagined the feel of his rough hand caressing her cheek…his mouth trailing over her skin…her fingers wrapped in his soft cur—

Her eyes flew open as her fingers found the hidden note. How did Erroll know Rabbie would not be in her room today? Or did he only get lucky? She shivered at the thought, opening it as quick as she could with her trembling fingers.

"Two days."

Two days until freedom? My family is coming for me!

She scrambled to the fire. Tossing the paper inside, she watched as the color of the flames expanded to a bright glowing orange before returning to their more muted tones. With her mood lightened, she returned to the table and poured herself a cup of tea. She wrapped a shawl around her shoulders, moved to the window, and then leaned against the ledge and looked down at the men moving about the stone grounds of the keep. There seemed to be more activity than usual and more guards posted on the wall. She refused to let the sights on the ground below dampen her spirits. Her clan had saved her once without knowing who she was. Now that they knew she was the daughter of their laird, she had no doubt they would rally to the cause and set her free once again. When they did, she vowed to get as far away from Campbell lands as possible. If she could kill Rabbie in the process, all the better, but she would not linger to accomplish the task.

A flash of crimson caught her eye, and she turned to watch the red-bird circle about below. Instead, her blood turned to ice and the teacup crashed off the windowsill, shattering into hundreds of pieces and drenching the front of her dress with the steaming contents. Her attention remained on the trail of red down below as ten British soldiers on horseback meandered across the field, toward the single road leading into the keep. Elaina's knees gave out, and she sank into the space between her magnificent bed and the hard-stone wall of her prison. Never in her life did she think she would want to remain with the evil Laird Campbell and his demented son, but she thought it might be the better of the two options. As long as she was not hanging from the end of a rope, there was the possibility of rescue. Had the British outbid the MacGregors? Were they coming to take her away? Elaina drew up her knees and buried her face in her skirts.

Doireann came and went with an annoyed huff. Someone returned to clean up the broken china, but Elaina never raised her gaze. Instead, she prayed for God to have mercy on her. Hours later when Rabbie arrived with her dinner, he found her huddled in the corner and shuddering violently, her body too stiff to stand.

He lifted her with ease and laid her upon the bed, wrapping her in the blanket and calling for a hot bath and whiskey while he rubbed her arms and legs, speaking Gaelic in soft tones that scared Elaina more than they assuaged her fears.

Elaina lay buried under two blankets and a fur staring at the ceiling. Rabbie had told her the soldiers' visit the day before had nothing to do with her. They'd collected a bribe. She wanted to believe him, but his history of being less than truthful wouldn't let her.

His attentions the night before alarmed her in the light of day. The man was capable of anything and everything. He had massaged the warmth back into her body and nursed her until she came back to herself enough to push him away. She didn't want to admit that his actions had been soothing. Tears slid down her cheek as her eyes traced the square canopy above her bed over and over. She had taken comfort in Rabbie's presence.

I'm so sorry, Calum. Her chin quivered, and she buried her face in the pillow and wept.

"What is it, love?"

Scrambling away from the soft hand that lay upon her back, she stared into Rabbie's green eyes filled with…with what? Concern? Did the man even know the meaning of such an emotion?

"Did I scare ye," he said, his voice soft, almost kind. "I didna mean to. I have brought yer food, if ye feel up to eatin' somethin'."

Her stomach twisted in revolt. "Perhaps just tea," she whispered, clutching the fur coverlet he had brought her the evening before to help warm her.

Rabbie reached out a tentative hand to wipe a tear from her cheek, but she jerked away. He dropped his hand and gave her a slow nod. "Come then. I will pour ye a cup." He strolled to the table in long, easy steps and poured a cup of tea, dropping in the correct amount of sugar and a spot of milk. Just how she drank it every morning.

How long have I been here? She had lost count and was quickly losing hope. Her mind a muddled mess, she climbed from the bed wrapped in the fur and took her seat across from Rabbie. Their ritual was now her new normal, and it made her skin itch to think about it.

"How much longer until I can venture from this room?" she croaked over her teacup, her voice hoarse from the crying of the night before and the morning. She attempted to clear her throat.

Rabbie presented her with a handkerchief.

With a sigh, she took it and blew her nose.

"Tonight ye will dine with us in the main hall."

"Why now? You have locked me in this…in this…this prison for a sennight or more. What did I do wrong?" The damned tears were starting again, and she couldn't stop them.

"Ye musn't cry so much. Yer face will be puffy tonight for the guests when ye healed so beautifully."

"Why are you not answering my question?"

Rabbie studied her face. "Ye cannae seem to stay out of trouble, Elaina. I'm no sure why I ever thought ye could."

"I was exploring the blasted keep. Do you know how many times I have been around this bloody thing? There is only so much gray stone a woman can look at before losing her mind. It was a portrait, Rabbie. Nothing more. I was not in the West Tower."

Rabbie studied the tray of food in front of him, picking at a bit of cheese. "Well, we had much to discuss and prepare for and 'twas no for yer eyes nor yer ears. The dinner is tonight, love. We had much to accomplish for our celebration this evening and no one free to watch ye."

"To watch me what? Walk in circles around this stone city with its towering stone walls and guards everywhere? What am I going to do? Scale a smooth stone wall? There is no escape, Rabbie. You told me yourself and believe me, I've studied it."

His smile stretched across his mouth. "I ken well enough there is no escapin', my love. I also ken well enough my men, and they are a randy bunch. Just ask the lasses that work here. With no one to watch ye, I hate to imagine the things that could happen to ye."

Elaina's skin crawled at the thought that he'd locked her in here for her own safety and not as punishment. Had the timid girls who rode Doireann's skirt tails… She didn't dare let her mind go there. Instead, she picked up a scone and nibbled at it. "What are you afraid I will find? What are you hiding from me besides a portrait?" The portrait of her mother and not his was the one on her mind.

"Well, now. If I told ye, we wadna have to hide anythin'." When the only response he garnered was a heated glare, he continued. "Ye shall be free tonight. There will be a celebration in yer honor."

"Who are our esteemed guests this evening?"

"Our? Does that mean ye see how much a part of this family ye will be?"

The bite of scone she was attempting to swallow stuck in her throat like a boulder. "I say 'our' because I am a prisoner inside this castle. Do not read more into it than what there is. I am a MacGregor and now a MacKinnon. I will *never* be a Campbell."

"Yes, well. We shall see."

"I killed your brother, remember? I would think you wouldn't want me around."

"How can I forget?" His expression turned hard. "But, ye make a good bargaining item." He took a sip of tea, his expression softening once more. "Besides, I killed your mother and father. Perhaps we are even."

"Perhaps you are only biding your time. Playing with your prey before the kill?" Her mind told her not to believe a word that came from his mouth. He was a lying sick bastard who had been nothing but congenial for at least the past week, or however long they had locked her in this room. The days ran together.

Pushing back his chair, he stood. "I cannae linger this mornin'. I will leave ye the tea and scones, if ye like. Doireann will fetch ye in a bit. There is much to do to prepare for this day. No more tears," he said before he chucked her under the chin and took his leave.

She sat in stunned silence, unable to move until the maid came to fetch her, escorting her and her fur to an unfamiliar room on the first floor of the keep. A warmer room. Servants wandered in and out, bringing a copper wash tub, petticoats, and undergarments. Doireann remained with her the entire time. There was no chance for escape, and where in the bloody hell would she escape to? The rocky interior courtyard? No, she sat in a cushioned chair in the corner, her feet under her and the fur gripped snug around her body while the rest of the Campbells prepared for whatever horrid thing would happen this eve. She knew them too well to think it merely a celebration. Something was amiss.

"I am not wearing that." Elaina gawped at the custom-made gown Doireann carried through the doorway.

"I knew you would put up a resistance," Laird Campbell announced as he strolled through the door. "That is why I came to supervise. Now, shut your mouth like an obedient lass and let your humble servant do her job."

It was a good thing Laird Campbell's gaze was upon Elaina and he could not see the look of fire Doireann shot him at her description.

Laird Campbell stepped closer to Elaina, his gaze roving over her healed face. He reached out a hand to touch her, and she flinched away. Undaunted, he stepped closer and grabbed her chin, holding her still. "Incredible," he whispered as his gaze trailed across her forehead, down her nose, around her jawline, and came to rest on her mouth.

For one horrid moment, she thought he would kiss her again. His clouded eyes cleared, and Elaina sensed he had not been looking at her at all, but someone long past. Someone like her mother.

He took a step back, and Doireann advanced on her.

That the gown was green, as usual, did not bother Elaina. It was the drape of the full over-skirt that opened in the front to reveal the deep green of the petticoat itself and the bodice that were the problem. They were the rich blues, the midnight blacks, and the forest greens of Clan Campbell. Laird Campbell would announce her as his property to the attending guests.

Elaina closed her eyes in defeat. She had nothing left to fight with. Where were her bloody people? Why hadn't they come for her yet? Raising her chin, she gave the laird her best contemptuous look. "Fine. I will wear it, but I'll be damned if I let you watch them dress me. I am a lady, and you will treat me as such. You may leave, and I promise not to quarrel. It is merely fabric, after all. It means nothing." That was not what her heart was telling her, however. It felt like a betrayal to her family and her clan. Her people who had abandoned her. She had waited for them. Anticipated them. The note told her two days. It had been four at least. She might as well resign herself to the fact that they were not coming.

With a smug smile, the laird turned and stalked from the room, his actions setting the women in motion. Three of them stuffed her into the gown, one tying garters while another fastened stays. When they had her many layers of clothing applied, one of the girls even managed to pin her hair up into a semblance of a respectable style. Then they left and locked her again in a room. A much more comfortable space. It was warmer, having no windows. Shelves of books lined one wall from floor to ceiling. The ever-present tapestries draped the other walls along with a large clan crest. Chairs covered in deep cushion and fabric of opulent blue damask dotted the chamber accompanied by rich walnut hued tables. Elaina perused the spines of the books, not truly reading their titles. Her eyes glazed and unfocused, seeing colors only—browns, blues, blacks. This dinner…this *whatever* it was. What was the point of it? What did the laird think he would accomplish by dressing her in Campbell colors and parading her around in front of a group of guests? Unable to concentrate, Elaina flopped herself down on a luxurious chaise lounge close to the fire and closed her eyes. She rested her head on the back of the seat, not caring if she messed up her carefully crafted hair. It was not her trying to impress anyone.

"Get up. It is time."

Elaina seized the arm shaking her, jolted awake by Ruske's gravelly voice. Her mind swam in a disoriented mess filled with lingering images of fighting boars tearing each other to shreds and red birds plunging and diving through the surrounding sky.

"Up." Ruske grabbed her arm, dragging her to her feet.

"Let go of me." Elaina glared up at the giant.

He cast her a wicked grin but released her. "After you, Mistress MacKinnon." He gave her a bow and a sweeping arm, ushering her through the doorway and out into the corridor. "This way," he said and clomped off down the hall.

Elaina scurried to keep up with his long legs as she followed him into yet another wing of the castle. They stopped before a pair of closed double doors where the smell of roast lamb hit her nose and her stomach announced the fact that she had not eaten all day.

Ruske cast her an amused glance, which she returned with a scowl.

The rumble of male voices sounded from inside where heated words were being exchanged. Ruske pounded twice on the door. Moments later, they swung open and Ruske placed a firm hand on Elaina's back, shoving her into the massive dining hall.

She stumbled, nearly falling to her knees. Righting herself, she cast the giant a withering glance before taking a survey of the room. Scores of Campbell men lined the stone walls. The gaping mouth of an immense fireplace filled with the carcass of two lambs roasting on spits covered one wall. More Campbells were assembled around eight tables of about ten feet. Laird Campbell lounged in front of her at the end of the long hall with a look of guarded amusement dancing across his face. Silence thundered through the great hall. Another table rested to the Laird's left and behind it, two men clambered to their feet when her gaze lit upon them.

"Uncle Hugh? Calum?" Elaina took three running steps in their direction before being snatched off her feet by that overgrown oaf. "Damn you!" Elaina kicked and fought. "Release me at once!"

"Ye are not my master," Ruske growled in her ear. "If ye want yer husband to live, ye will shut yer bloody mouth and be still."

Elaina stopped her fight, and Ruske righted her on her feet. Her gaze returned to her family. Twenty MacGregors in total sat within the enemy's stronghold as guests, it seemed. Calum's face was haggard and drawn as if he'd not slept in ages.

Uncle Hugh studied Elaina from head to toe, his gaze alighting on hers. "Ye are well, lass?" he asked.

"As fair as can be."

"They have nay harmed ye?" Calum said.

"They have not."

"Caitir?"

"She is safe," Hugh answered, and relief washed over Elaina in a flood.

"See, all is as I said." The laird waved a hand through the air before snapping his fingers.

Ruske led her down the aisle between the tables of Campbell men who all rose as she passed like she were the queen and not a prisoner. Instead of leading her to her husband and clan, Ruske rounded the long head table from the opposite end and deposited Elaina between Laird Campbell and Robert. Her gaze held her husband's as she took her seat, followed by the entire room.

Calum's hazel eyes questioned her for the truth, and she hoped that her own told him she truly was in good health, but he needed to get her bloody well out of here.

"Now," Laird Campbell interrupted the silent exchange between them. "On with the negotiations. My demands are as I have said, the carved box containing the jewels given to Thamas and Mairi at their wedding, the land, and Laird Beinnmaree's son. You. Not Aron." Laird Campbell glared at Calum. "In exchange for the girl."

"No," Elaina said, the calmness of her voice surprising her.

"No?" The laird turned an amused look to her.

"You cannot negotiate with these men. I am the only child of Laird MacGregor. All that you demand belongs to me by right, and I say no to each one of your demands."

Laird Campbell's hand shot out and wrapped itself around her throat, choking off her airway. Calum was across the table and half-way to her before three of the Campbell guards descended upon him. His palm smashed into one's face, taking him to his knees as blood poured from his broken nose. He ducked a wild swing from another and landed him in the gut with a precise jab of his own. Five other Campbell men rushed in to help as black spots danced through Elaina's vision and her lungs seized in her chest.

"Enough," Laird Campbell's bored voice came to her through a fog as he loosened his grip just enough that she could suck in a small fragment of air. He pulled her face close to his, the image of pure evil dancing in his eyes. "You have no say in the matter, dear. I do not give one damn who you think you are. You hold no stake in the Highlands, having been given to the British but months after your birth." He yanked her closer, his breath hot upon her face. "A woman will not make demands of me nor deny me my due right. Is it understood?"

Elaina clawed at his hand, trying to loosen his grip.

He squeezed tighter. "Blink if we have an understanding."

She did, and he shoved her away with an annoyed sigh. She gasped for air, tears streaming down her cheeks. A disheveled Calum stood before them, blood dripping down his face from a cut on his forehead as he too huffed for breath, born up by Campbell men on either side. The MacGregors were on their feet, held at sword point. None of the visitors carried weapons. Laird Campbell was no fool.

"Now. Where were we? Oh yes. Jewels, land, and the lady's love. Seems like a fitting payment for all the MacGregors stole from me years ago. Hugh, make it happen or you will not like the repercussions to the lass nor your people. I hold the British army in my hand, and between them and my brood, I can erase your entire clan from existence. I am finished with these men. Escort them out."

"No, wait! Calum!" Elaina watched her life being dragged away, bloodied and battered. "Please!"

He stared at her over his shoulder. "I will come for you. I swear it," he called as they yanked him through the open doorway.

Only when the last of her allies were forcibly removed from the great hall at sword point did Elaina realize that tears flowed down her cheeks and dripped onto her heaving bosom. She dropped to her chair and buried her face in her hands and wept. She didn't care if they thought her weak. Hopelessness overtook her, and she lay her head on the table before her. The sounds of men feasting and drinking filled the air around her like the fog of a nightmare that only made her tears flow freer.

"Ye intend to hand her over to the Grahams?" Rabbie asked over Elaina's bowed head.

Her sobs had eased, but she hadn't the strength to look at her captors.

"Of course not. What kind of fool do you think I am? She will stay," his father answered.

"So ye can avenge Alex's death?"

"She will remain as my mistress."

Elaina's head snapped up at the announcement. "I am a married woman."

"Not for long." The laird forked a bite of venison into his mouth.

"She killed your son," Rabbie argued.

"She looks so much like Mairi." Laird Campbell cast Elaina a look of adoration. "'Twill be the next best thing. If I couldnae have her, I will have their daughter. What better revenge on the dead?" With a chuckle, he turned back to his meal.

"The dead are just that," Elaina said. "Dead. They feel no vengeance. You only bring darkness upon yourself, your clan, and your remaining son."

"And did you not set out to do the same?" Robert asked, drawing Elaina's attention to him. "To seek retribution for your parents' deaths?"

"Yes, and you can see where it got me. Here, in this humble abode, at the mercy of two imbecilic barbarians who have no respect for the sanctity of life nor marriage."

"You do flatter me, Elaina." Laird Campbell gave her a wry smile before raising his cup to his lips.

"All this talk of Mairi and none of Robert's mother?" Elaina turned a questioning stare on the Laird. "I do not understand. Are not the MacGregors your enemies? Yet, I have heard my mother's name several times while not once have you spoken Robert's mother's name aloud in this keep. I would wonder if she even existed if her portrait did not hang over the hearth in the small hall. She seemed a lovely girl, albeit a bit meek for the pompous, evil laird. Perhaps she was also a captive and not a willing participant in her own marriage?"

"Dinna speak of my mother," Rabbie hissed, his breath hot on her ear, making her shiver.

"And why not?" Rabbie's father asked. "Let us talk of Ailis, for such a sweet lass she was. Weak as a kitten, not the fiery temptress that Mairi had been. I loved your mother," the laird said. "Sweet, sweet Mairi. Her lips like wine, her spirit burning as fierce as whiskey."

The words slammed into Elaina, and she knew her mouth fell open but her brain could not close it.

"As a lad, I played with Thamas MacGregor. We were inseparable. A truce had been called between the two clans. I truly grew to respect your father over the years. A fine warrior. An idiot blinded by love," Laird Campbell spit out, his last words a sharp contrast to the ones previously spoken with admiration. "I loved Mairi long before your father did. I kissed her sweet lips before his ever touched hers. I wanted her, but your father betrayed me. My father betrayed me. Robert MacKinnon betrayed me... Laird Beinnmaree—Calum's grandfather. The day Thamas and Mairi wed, my father and Calum's grandfather gave them a wedding gift. A small carved box with a handful of precious stones. It should have been mine. She should have been *my* wife. Her dowry should lie in *my* coffers."

Elaina could do nothing but stare at the laird, his words chilling to her soul.

He had been in love with her mother. Everything was coming into focus. A man betrayed, sickened by jealousy and hatred.

He continued, his voice calm and his tone almost affectionate. "I vowed to kill your father that day. Our friendship was forever severed by his betrayal," he growled leaning closer to her, his face inches away. "He took her from me. He buried his cock into my sweet Mairi, and he sired a daughter with her."

She wanted to strike him, but fear held her hands in place. His gaze made her skin crawl, and the wine she had drank seeped like a burning river into her throat.

"I killed him. I let her watch me kill her beloved Thamas. She was to come with me, but the bitch…the filthy whore," he bellowed like a starving bear woken early from a winter's slumber. "She poisoned herself in front of me. I held her as she died. My face was the last she saw as she left this earth. I searched for the babe and tore that castle apart looking for this stone." He pointed a finger to the brooch he wore on the drape of his plaid. "My clan's jewel forever ruined by the MacGregors and their bloody, fucking pine trees." He growled. "I sought the box of jewels but found none of what I searched for. The only thing I accomplished that day was taking the life of your bastard father. But now…" His laugh chilled her to her core. "Now I have the stone, and I have Mairi's lovely daughter." He took her chin in his hand, and it was then she learned how badly she trembled. "And soon I will have the jewels and the land that came with them. I have nay doubt that Hugh Graham and Calum MacKinnon will give me what I want and they will kneel before me. I will have their allegiance or I will have their heads, my dear."

"And my mother." Robert's voice was but a choked whisper behind her. "What of her? Ye havenae spoken her name since her death. You hid our portrait that once hung in her chambers."

The laird released Elaina and leaned back in his chair, raising his glass to his lips before speaking.

"She doted on you far too much, I am afraid. She created an impudent lackey not fit for anything but the simplest of tasks."

Elaina chanced a glance at Robert over her shoulder. Hatred burned in his gaze as he stared at his father. Why would Robert stay and do the bidding of a man who thought so little of him? If he hated his father so much, could he not cut ties and move on with his life. Perhaps he was as greedy as his father and waited for his inheritance.

"My mother was an exemplary woman." Robert's fist clenched the knife in his hand.

"Aye. She was useful for some things, but tending a child was not one of them. If I hadnae spent years chasin' down those damned outlaw MacGregors, you might be better reared as Alex was."

"Your protege got himself killed by a woman," Rabbie sneered.

"Yes. A woman you were to have disposed of long before then."

Elaina turned her attention to Rabbie. She thought he had been under an alias only to spy on her. He was meant to take her life all along, even before she killed Alex?

"'Twas no my fault she and her brother didna travel to Edinburgh with their parents. We could have killed them all at that time."

"Why would you want to kill all of us? Was it not my mother who sent the funds you were after? How would you have gotten your dirty little hands on the money?" Elaina asked the laird.

"I have certain friends in England with special ties. But, 'tis no matter because you are here and soon your husband and your brother will be dead and I will have the daughter of my enemy, the money, the jewels, and the land."

"Now is where you give a sinister laugh at your cleverness." Elaina wiped her tears away with her handkerchief. That was enough of the blubbering. Turning to Robert, she studied his face, still twisted with anger at his father.

"What?" he growled, picking up his cup and draining it before slamming it down on the table. He snapped his fingers at a servant to refill it.

"Why did you not kill me...us...straight away?"

"Perhaps, I enjoy playin' with my prey before the slaughter." He didn't look at her.

"Mayhap the poor lad fell in love?" the laird goaded.

"Mayhap ye shut yer mouth."

Laird Campbell was across Elaina and on Robert in an instant. His hand twisted in his son's queue and yanked his head back. The point of his dirk nicked his son's throat, and Elaina watched the slow trickle of blood slide down Rabbie's taut skin.

"You will not talk to me in that manner in front of my men, nor ever. If I didna not need an heir so bloody bad, I would kill you now. But we shall see what the lady has to offer before I do myself the favor." He shoved his son's head back toward the table. "I knew I should have killed you when I killed yer ma."

"What?" Robert said in a ragged whisper. "My mother?" His hand inched toward his dirk.

"Oh, dinna think for a moment that you could get to me before my men slit your throat." The laird motioned over his shoulder at two henchmen standing guard inches from the horrid conversation taking place.

"Ma died in childbirth."

"Your mother was a means to an end, and when she birthed my second son, the heir to the Campbell legacy, she had completed her duty. Unlike her idiot first-born, I leave no task unfinished. I couldnae allow her to raise another worthless brat. If I had raised you, you would not have failed in your mission to erase the Spencer family from existence."

In an uncharacteristic show of defeat, Robert turned back to the food in front of him. "If I had succeeded, you would not have your enemy's daughter in hand," he mumbled before shoving himself away from the table.

The henchmen sprung forward, but Rabbie waved them off and stormed from the dining hall. Words had the ability to shape and form young minds, and to destroy them.

Elaina loathed the man next to her for the monster his son had become. What type of man would he be if his father had died in battle? The laird showed himself to be far more demented than she could have imagined and now he planned to breed her like a bloody horse. And damned if she would supply him with an heir. She would die first. Calum would come for her, but would it be soon enough?

"May I return to my room? Though the entertainment has been lovely this eve, I've had quite enough." Elaina glanced at the laird.

He didn't look up from his meal but snapped at Doireann, who came to stand behind Elaina.

Her legs felt as if they would not hold her up, but she walked across the floor and out of the hall without collapsing. She hesitated but a moment when her gaze met Erroll's. Turning from him, she spied Ruske sitting at the end of the long table by the massive double doors.

He looked from Elaina to Erroll and the men surrounding him and back to her.

Elaina tried to wipe all emotion from her face. She held her chin high as she followed Doireann out of the warmth of the great hall and into the chilly damp air of the castle halls. Away from the eyes of the men, her head dropped with the weight of the day. Gray stones passed by under her feet, and her gaze traced the cracks and joints between them. They were like a spider's web, trailing and twisting, coming to a stop in one place only to pick up in another. Laird Campbell had killed Robert's mother, and the man had not known all these years. His reaction to the news was not what she would expect coming from the half-crazed Scot. Where would his trail lead? The laird's led to Calum, revenge, and all that his greed entailed. Would Robert's end the same? Revenge...greed...murder?

Chapter Twenty-Two

ELAINA HAD FALLEN ASLEEP ON the rug in front of the hearth, fully dressed having refused Doireann entrance to her room once again. Solitude had called to her like a lonesome song, and she mourned the loss of her husband. She hadn't even gotten to touch him. But he was coming. He'd promised.

Her chamber door creaked open, awaking her from a fitful dream. Doireann entered with her breakfast tray and sat it on the table, leaving without a word. Where was Robert? Had the news of his mother's demise been too much for him to bear, causing him to seek the seclusion that Elaina craved?

With a groan, she pushed herself up from the floor and stirred the dying fire, adding more peat. She retrieved the food-laden tray and lay it upon the settee by the fire. Not sure she could eat, she poured herself a cup of tea and collapsed into the chair. In some ways everything had changed, but then again, here she remained in the grips of Laird Campbell. Only now, she knew he meant to keep her and betray his word to her uncle. He would kill Calum.

"Good morning."

Elaina jumped, sloshing her tea onto her lap. So lost in her thoughts and the crackling of the fire, she didn't hear the laird enter.

"My dear, did I frighten you? Here let me." He moved to dab the tea from Elaina's lap, but she snatched the cloth from his hand. "You look a frightful mess," he said undaunted. "You must let Doireann and the girls ready you for a little outing. Can you do that without a fight, or must I stand and watch over you?"

"What kind of outing?" Elaina leaned forward, returning the teacup to the silver serving tray.

"I thought we might go for a jaunt. Let you breathe some fresh air, if you like?"

"Beyond castle walls?"

"Aye, a ride. Unless you are too—"

"No. I will ride." Elaina stood, shaking out her damp skirt.

"I thought you might. Now, ready yourself. No woman of mine shall leave the keep lookin' like a frump." The laird quit the room, replaced by Doireann and a team of servants toting a copper washtub and buckets of steaming water.

———— ✦❖✦ ————

Dressed in a refined eggplant-colored riding habit, Elaina sat astride one of the Arabian stallions as it pranced its way down the bridge, exiting the castle walls and out into freedom. Freedom, except for the fact that twenty or more Campbell men accompanied her and the laird on their little outing. But, the choice of her thoughts was her own, and she ignored the guards. Instead, she admired the vast gray sky and the braes in the distance. It had been ages, it seemed, since she'd rested upon a horse, and what a fine steed this was.

Laird Campbell kicked his stallion into a cantor, then a gallop, and Elaina's followed suit, and the group flew across the field, circling the castle. The tree line passed in a blur, but Elaina kept her eyes open for signs of her clan. Twice she thought she saw a glint of steel or a flash of tartan. They were there, watching and waiting. The thought comforted her even if she was still in the laird's possession. Highlanders were resourceful. They would save her from this mess.

The laird's actions puzzled her, however. Why would he bring her out here in the open, taking a chance that the MacKinnons and MacGregors might attack and save her? It was as if he taunted them, held her before them as a prize on a string. But why? They slowed to a trot and eventually the pair rode side by side, Elaina's horse nearly as unruly as Laoch had been. They moved in a giant circle around the keep, and as they passed by a particular area of the woods, Elaina looked again to see if what she thought she saw was real. It was. Could she? Dare she? Lucky for her, she sat sidesaddle with her legs opposite Laird Campbell. She kicked her restless stallion into action while yelling at it to stop. She yanked the reins, spinning him toward the woods, and gave him a good kick again. He sped across the field and into the wood. She jerked on his harness, causing him to rear at just the right moment, and she dove from his back, pretending to be thrown. She hit the ground with a bone-jarring thud but scrambled to the bush she had spied from the clearing. Breaking a few twigs from the plant, she shoved them in her pocket as the Campbell riders approached. With a groan, she rolled onto her back and stared up into the face of an irate laird.

"I thought you could ride. That's what Robert said."

"'Tis not my fault you put me on an unruly horse," she grumbled as Erroll and another man helped her to her feet.

Rupert trudged through the forest, leading the runaway stallion back to its owner.

"Do you think you can control him on our return to the castle or shall you ride with me?" The laird raised his brow in question.

Elaina dusted the snow from her person, making sure her prize was well hidden. "We will be fine."

"You better," the laird growled, and she was once again hoisted upon the stallion and they turned toward the castle.

Her gaze locked with Erroll's. He would have to help her. She could not poison the laird and his son on her own. They would have to figure a way to get the Dwale into their food or drink. She knew Erroll could. If he could sneak a piece of paper into her bread, surely he could slip a little "spice" into the laird's meal.

Chapter Twenty-Three

FOR THE NEXT SEVERAL NIGHTS, Elaina slept little. Instead, she sat at the table in her room with a small stone she had found in the garden and ground and scraped on her twigs of poison until they were a tiny mound of wet mush. She didn't dare try to keep a spoon, much less a knife, with which to prepare her concoction. Knowing the laird, he had each piece of china and eating utensil she used counted before every meal and accounted for afterward.

She scooped the squashed twigs onto one of her handkerchiefs. How much poison it would take to kill two people was beyond her scope of knowledge, but surely this would do the trick. She twisted the handkerchief closed and crossed the room to the hearth where she had been hiding the Dwale in an earthen pot decorating the mantle. Her thoughts centering on how to get the bundle to Erroll on the morrow, she caught her toe on the edge of the rug and tumbled headfirst toward the fire, catching herself on the stone façade inches from the flames. Her heart pounded so at the near loss of her prize that she didn't hear the click of the stone as she pushed herself upright, but she felt it and where the gray stone of the hearth met the edge of the tapestry hanging beside it, a thin black line appeared. Elaina's hair fluttered in a frigid breeze.

Reaching a tentative hand toward the shadowy gap, she slid her fingers through it, feeling nothing but air. She rose to her feet and placed her palm against the tapestry and pushed, stifling a startled squeak when it moved inward. Blood rushed through her ears, deafening her thoughts. She scrambled to retrieve a taper and lit it in the fire. With a hand protecting the candle's flame and a deep breath, she advanced on the opening and eased through. She stood in a narrow passage, her candlelight illuminating the darkness a few feet in front of her until the corridor made a turn.

She inched forward, trying to will her heart to slow so that she might hear anything or anyone advancing on her. The hallway continued, and her jitters ebbed as she wiped cobwebs from her path. The passageway had not been used in some time. Her feet moved faster, but she remained vigilant in her watch for would be attackers. Up a set of stairs, around a curve, then down a flight to a landing, and on to another set of steps trailing downward, the corridor wound and twisted until she reached a wall across her path. She placed her shoulder against it and with a deep breath heaved.

Nothing.

Her fingers trailed the stone, searching, pushing. Stepping back, she held her candle aloft and moved its light slowly over the barrier, studying. *There!* She stood on her toes and stretched just far enough to slip her fingers into a slight gap, her frozen digits searched the opening.

Click.

Elaina held her breath. Hearing nothing, she put her shoulder to the stone wall and shoved it open about a foot. Again, she waited. A soft glow of light drifted through the opening. It was someone's chamber. When yet again no noise reached her ears, she slid her head through the gap, pushed aside the tapestry, and peeked out from behind it. It was not a bed chamber as she had thought. The room stood empty except for a small table against the far wall. Numerous candles burned at all stages of use, and there above them as if part of a shrine, hung the portrait of her mother.

Before Elaina could step around the tapestry to garner a better look. The door to the room swung open and Doireann slid through, peeking behind her before easing it closed.

Extinguishing her taper, Elaina darted back into the hidden corridor and held her breath, expecting at any moment for Doireann to tear back the wall hanging and find her hidden in the dark. Instead, the mournful sound of a woman talking to herself reached Elaina's ears, and she ventured a peek out from behind the cloth once more.

Rivers of silver hair woven with shadows of dark tumbled down Doireann's back. With her hair hung loose, her stature seemed more fragile than severe. The woman's normally board straight shoulders slumped forward, her palms resting on the edge of the table of candles.

"You are dead."

For a moment, Elaina thought the maid directed her statement at her hiding quivering behind the tapestry. That is until Doireann's head lifted, and she spat upon the portrait of her mother.

Elaina's hand flew to her mouth.

The maid's next words were a string of rapid Gaelic. Though Elaina had not a clue what she said, the tone of her voice clarified that she had no use for the woman in the portrait.

"He is mine."

The return to English speak took Elaina off guard, and she almost didn't catch what the woman had said.

"Your daughter will rue the day that she ever dared step foot in Scotland." And Doireann stormed from the room, never casting a glance toward Elaina's hiding spot.

The coldness of the stone wall cut through her nightclothes like frigid waters as Elaina sagged against it. Doireann the Evil was in love with Laird Campbell and posed more of a threat to her safety than she had imagined. She thought her only cold and heartless. Now she knew her to be cold, heartless, and jealous. Not a good combination for a woman. Especially a woman who had more control over Elaina's life and livelihood than Elaina had. She would have to tread extra carefully around the chatelaine.

Elaina pushed herself from the wall and snuck out from behind the tapestry to relight her taper from the candles upon the table. With the sleeve of her gown, she wiped Doireann's disdain from her mother's portrait. Though she had no memory of the woman, she thought she felt her presence all around her. She bowed her head to her mother in gratitude for the strength she had passed through her blood line, then fled back to her chambers, careful to re-seal the passageway behind her.

Chapter Twenty-Four

OVER AND OVER HER EYES traced the square canopy above her head. Sleep had eluded her most of the night. Her thoughts this morning were of her husband and uncle and the orders Laird Campbell had placed upon them. Jewels, land, and Calum. At the time, she'd been too distracted by the presence of her family inside the lair of the enemy to think about what those demands meant. The jewels were easy enough. But what land, and why would the laird want her husband? If he wanted him so badly, why let him go when his henchmen had him restrained in the great hall?

Sliding from the warmth of her bed, Elaina stared out the window at the heavy gray sky. The flags of Clan Campbell whipped furiously in the bitter wind. The same wind lashed through her soul. After discovering the portrait of her mother, she felt the reality of her situation burrowing into her skin and freezing her spirit as if the gale whipping outside were present in the room. Was it luck or fate that had kept her alive and intact this long in the hands of her family's enemies? Her plight became more dire as her safety dwindled away by the day.

Doireann and her entourage came to dress her, then disappeared once again. Elaina watched the stern maid with a new wariness and something that felt oddly like pity. To be in love with someone and they be oblivious to the matters of the heart seemed a sad state to be in.

When the women had vacated the room, Elaina hurried to the clay pot that held her key to freedom. Slipping it into her pocket, she hurried from her chambers and toward the stable, grateful that she was once again free to roam the keep.

She wandered down the aisle of stalls, whispering in Latin to each of the horses. After several minutes of searching, she came across Erroll, who unfortunately was in a stall with Ruske attempting to tend a large gash on the hindquarters of an agitated mare.

"Can ye lend a hand?" Erroll grunted, trying to restrain the mare who seemed intent on pawing the two men to death.

Elaina entered the stall and approached the wild-eyed horse.

"Watch the hooves, man!" Ruske growled, rounding the front of the mare and coming within inches of getting pummeled.

"I'm tryin', ye giant oaf. Just hurry and apply the poultice." Erroll's face shown red with the exertion of trying to control the horse.

"Stop for a moment and let her calm down. You are making it worse than it has to be."

Ruske cut her an annoyed glare but stepped away from the horse.

"I cannae release her or she'll surely try to kill us all," Erroll said, nearly jerked off his feet with the swing of the mare's head.

"Well, just stand there, but give her some slack. She's foaming at the bit. And lower your voice." Elaina did not approach the mare but whispered in French from her place by the stall entrance, her language of choice for an agitated horse because it seemed to be the most soothing of the languages she spoke.

After several minutes of the horse pawing and snorting, she calmed and stopped jerking Erroll around like he weighed nothing.

Elaina approached the horse and laid a firm hand on her withers, continuing her French whispers. "Now," she said to Ruske.

The giant crept up beside Elaina and, more gently than she imagined he could be, applied the poultice to the horse's wound.

The mare's brown hide shivered and jerked as if trying to shoo a biting midge.

"Shh," Ruske's soothing noise seemed odd coming from his massive frame. His touch calmed the injured horse. With the task accomplished, Ruske stepped back and admired his handiwork.

"How did this happen?" Elaina whispered as they all backed away from the mare who shook her head and snorted at her newfound freedom.

"Yes, how *did* it happen," Ruske raised his brow at Erroll.

"A wee stramash with the Duncans," Erroll answered, scooping mash into a feedbag.

"The Duncans, eh? I didna ken the Duncans were in the area. That is a fight

I would have loved to be a part of." Ruske fiddled with the items scattered across a small table in a corner of the stall.

"Aye, they set upon us on the way back in. We were lucky to have gotten away with our lives and our goods."

Ruske grunted in response before casting a hesitant glance at Erroll and Elaina both before he quit the stall and stalked down the corridor.

Elaina watched him until he turned the corner, then she hurried to Erroll's side. "Here," she whispered and grabbed his hand, forcing the handkerchief with the mashed Dwale into his fist.

"What is this?" he hissed, glancing over his shoulder at the empty hallway.

"Poison."

"Poison?" Erroll tried to shove it back at Elaina.

"No. You must take it. Your contact in the kitchen? Can they help us? We need to slip it into Robert and the laird's food."

"Where did you get this?" Erroll studied the handkerchief in his hand.

"Our little outing the other day when my horse broke into the woods. I had spied it and broke away and retrieved a few twigs. Hopefully it is enough. I have never poisoned anyone before. I don't know how much it takes."

"Have ye addled yer brain? What if they find us out? This is a great risk, lass."

"It is the only way to gain our freedom. We must kill them. Can your friend help us?"

"My friend?"

The one who helps you sneak messages to me in my bread?"

Erroll studied Elaina's face. "Aye. Ye have figured it out then?" He slid the handkerchief wrapped poison into his pocket.

"It wasn't difficult. You are the only friend I have in the castle."

"Indeed," Erroll muttered under his breath. "I will see that this gets to its destination. It may take time."

"That is something we have little of, I'm afraid."

"I think the time for chatterin' is over," Ruske growled at them from the other side of the stall door, sending Elaina and Erroll stumbling away from each other. "Didna mean to scare ye." Ruske cast them a wicked grin. "All this whisperin' 'round in the stables could cause a person to believe that ye are up to no good."

"We were discussing the mare's ongoing care is all." How Elaina managed to create an intelligible sentence was beyond her. She could hardly draw breath, her heart pounded so in her chest.

"Mmmm." The noise rumbled in Ruske's throat. "Ye are done here, Erroll."

"Good day to ye, mistress." The man hurried from the stall with his gaze cast down at his feet, looking quite the guilty party.

Elaina returned Ruske's suspicious stare as she left the stable to return to her room. She needed time alone to think. God help them if they were discovered.

Chapter Twenty-Five

D
AYS PASSED WITH NO SIGN of illness from either father or son. After asking around the stables, Elaina learned that Erroll had gone out on a raid. How she wished that she had kept the poison. She would have accomplished the task herself. Curiosity haunted her. How could she broach the subject of the Dwale and ask Bridgette if she had it in her possession? After all, she might be wrong about the source of the notes in her meals, but who else could it have been?

Overwhelmed with the boredom of pacing the castle halls, Elaina wandered outside and found a secluded bench where she sat and imagined her husband sitting beside her, his warm hand encapsulating hers. The ache of his absence tore at her until she thought it would rip her heart in two. There alone in the defunct winter garden, she let her emotions take over. Pulling her feet up on the seat, she buried her face in her knees to muffle her wrenching sobs and keep her tears from freezing to her cheeks. Her cries of grief had turned into hiccupping sniffles when she heard what could have only been Aron on the other side of the dormant brush. Laird Campbell's voice froze her halfway to her feet.

"I told Hugh the terms. What did he not understand? I want the land, the jewels, and Calum."

"All I can offer are the gems, Campbell," Aron answered. "Calum disappeared within two days of us leaving your castle."

Aron had been present? Why had he not been in the dining hall with the Mac-Gregors and his brother?

"I suppose his love for the lass was not as strong as his fear for his own life. How selfish of the lad. I always thought him a coward like your father." The laird chuckled.

She covered her mouth to stifle the sob that threatened to break forth at the news of Calum's disappearance.

"Just because Laird Beinnmaree willnae bow to your posturin' does not make him a coward. It makes him wise. Why start a war with the clan that celebrates its relationship with the British? And as for my brother, his love for the lass will never be in question. What he gave up to marry her should stand as evidence of such."

"Proof is in action, my dear Aron, and Calum's actions were to flee. No Calum. No girl. My terms were clear. What of the land?"

"Ye ken well enough that I dinna have the power to hand over the estate at Balquhidder. Ye demand the impossible."

"Nothin' is impossible, my dear man."

"And what of Hugh's family if the council gives ye the land? Where will they go?"

"I do not give one bloody damn where they go as long as they no longer reside within the halls of Balquhidder Castle. It is mine. Stolen from my family by Laird MacGregor many years ago. Hugh and the council can make it happen, of that I have nay doubt. Now, find the boy and hand over my land. I do thank you for these."

Elaina heard a muffled rattle that could only be the jewels.

"But if Hugh cannot meet my demands, I will not be responsible for the consequences of his inaction."

"Why not keep the girl and the jewels and leave everyone be?"

Elaina's mouth gaped open at Aron's suggestion and it was all she could do to keep from scrambling across the brush to strangle him to death.

"Dinna fash yourself, Aron. I will keep the girl and the jewels, and I will have my demands met one way or the other. The truth of Calum's involvement with the Rising will come to light."

"I'm sure I dinna ken what ye mean," Aron responded. "The lad kens nothin' about anythin'. Keep me instead."

Aron would trade his life for his brother's. His only redeeming quality.

"I ken well enough he has information that I need. He was in Paris, after all. Oh, you didna ken that? That is why I must have the boy and not you. Your laird places more trust in the runt than he does his oldest son. What a pity." The laird's statement dripped with disdain.

"I want nothin' to do with the Risin'. It is a doomed cause, so yer snide comments do not ruffle my feathers."

"Then come to my side. Spy for me. Gather intelligence from your laird and bring it to me."

"What's in it for me?" Aron had the audacity to ask.

Elaina once again thought to strangle the man. *The selfish turncoat bastard.*

"Perhaps a portion of these." The jewels rattled again.

"Hmm. Temptin'. I'll find Calum. He can't have run far."

"The two of you are a regular Cain and Abel." The laird chuckled at his own horrid statement and their voices faded away down the path.

Elaina sat in stunned silence. Calum was gone. Had he left her to fend for herself? Did he think the task too great? No. She would never believe that he had abandoned her in her time of need.

But doubt niggled in the recesses of her mind. Damn her giving the poison to Erroll. The odds of her being able to acquire more were slim to none. She was once again on her own.

That blasted bastard Aron! Wait until I get my hands on him. She would gut him. She stomped her foot. When that did not ease her anger, she kicked at a dry bush. She wanted to throw something…to scream. Instead, she clenched her teeth and her fists and stalked into the kitchen determined to talk to Bridgette.

Chapter Twenty-Six

WHEN SHE FELT CERTAIN THAT the castle had gone to slumber, Elaina crept from her bed and slid her feet into her slippers. She grabbed a taper and opened the secret passage, worming inside. Having had no luck finding Bridgette after her eavesdropping episode with Laird Campbell and Aron, she decided she would have to take care of things herself. Gripping the candlestick in one hand and the jagged piece of wood that she had broken free of the trellis in the defunct winter garden in the other, she made her way through the corridor and into the forbidden west tower. She cast a glance at her mother's portrait and, for a moment, had second thoughts as her mother seemed to scold her from her place on the wall. Was this truly the person she had become? A cold-blooded murderess?

"It's called self-preservation, mother," she whispered to the image. "Something you should know well."

Glancing up and down the shadows of the meagerly lit hallway of the west tower, Elaina extinguished her taper and took a chance on which direction she should go. Turning right, she set off to explore and hopefully find her way to revenge that would lead her one step closer to freedom. Her path led her down a hallway that turned into a spiraling stone staircase. There would be no shadows to fall back in if anyone headed up while she ventured down. Was she brave or a fool? Were they one and the same?

The staircase ended and another hallway continued, this one wider with shadows that might hide a trespasser. The sound of voices reached her moments before she turned a corner in the corridor. Flattening herself against the wall, she peeked around the corner in time to see Laird Campbell's silver queue disappear through a doorway and the ominous shadow of an unusually tall man dwindle away into the inky black of the unlit hallway. She couldn't tell if it had been Ruske or Aron.

She inched her way toward the entrance that the laird had passed through. The unmistakable thud of impact and the sound of air leaving a man's lungs brought her up short.

"I will ask ye again. Who is the Highland contact for Prince Charles Edward Stewart?" Laird Campbell growled.

Silence.

"Again," the laird commanded, and once again, the gut-wrenching noise reached her ears, only this time it came with a grunt that was unmistakably Calum's.

Elaina ran to the closed door. A cut out stood just at the top of her head with wide iron bars built into it. Holding her breath, she raised onto the tips of her toes and peered inside the room.

Calum's curled locks hung in a disheveled array like snakes swirled upon his head. Blood dripped from his hidden face to the floor. Laird Campbell wrenched his head up by his hair, and Elaina stifled her cry behind her palm.

Gaunt and drawn, they had starved and imprisoned Calum for longer than a day. Bruises of varying degrees of healing dotted his face and torso. She could easily count his ribs. The horror dawned on her that the laird had been responsible for Calum's disappearance two days following their feast weeks ago.

"I have spoken to your idiot brother. He has offered to let me keep your wife for a portion of the jewels. He also intends to become a spy for me, so eventually I will ken your secrets, Calum MacKinnon. You and your laird cannae hide behind the flouncy breeches of your prince."

"Aron would never betray me or my wife," Calum whispered, his voice raspy like weeds raking against a board.

How long has he been without water?

"It is surprising how little it took to bring him over to my side. Two rubies and an opal. That is the price placed on your head and your wife's virtue."

"Touch Elaina and I will slit you from throat to cock, I swear it!"

"Your threats mean nothing, MacKinnon, for here you are and there she is, minutes away within the same stone walls and there is not a damned thing you can do about it. I might have pity on one of you if you reveal your secrets, but not both. Give him a drink. I dinna want the bastard leavin' this world yet."

Elaina turned and ran. She dared not breathe until she had entered the shrine to her mother and closed the door behind her, leaning against it with her head buried in her hands. *That evil, lying, conniving, demon of a man! Laird Campbell had lied to everyone.* Elaina wondered if Hugh even knew Calum was missing. If he did, they would never find him trapped in the bowels of this horrible place.

She slid down the door and sat with her head buried in her knees, knowing she should return to her room, but she couldn't—not with Calum being beaten down the hall. She waited a long while until she thought the laird may have left before she wiped her tears and rose to her feet. She couldn't go back until she had spoken to Calum and let him know he was not alone.

Inching from her hiding spot, she listened for voices before she hurried down the hall and rounded the corner. Creeping to the door, she peeked inside. "Calum?"

There was no movement from the prone figure in the corner.

She tried again only slightly louder. "Calum, it's me. Please speak to me."

The shadow moaned and shifted his position.

He was alive. That's all that mattered. At least that's what she thought until he rolled into the dim light from the torch on the wall, its dancing flame exposing his bloody and battered face. The wounds to his body covered him from head to waist.

"What have they done to you?" Her voice cracked with the strain of holding back her tears.

"Elaina?"

"It's me. I'm here." She tried to hide her fear.

"Ye shouldna be here. It's too dangerous." The words came out strangled, and she strained to hear them.

"How long have you been here?" she asked.

"I-I dinna ken." Calum's head collapsed against the stone floor, his strength gone.

"Calum? Calum, dammit, talk to me. Don't you dare die and leave me here in this horrid place!" she hissed louder than she should have, her knuckles white as she gripped the iron bars trying to stay up high enough that she could see him. Her calves burned. "I would never forgive you," she whispered through her tears.

Calum grunted. "Nay, I ken ye wadna, *mo chridhe*." He seemed to fight for the strength to even speak. "Din-dinna fash. They will come."

"Who? Who is coming? Uncle Hugh? When? Calum? Calum!"

Her husband didn't move. He lay on the floor, his face half concealed in the shadows.

Elaina watched his chest. She thought it moved with breath, but she stared so hard she couldn't be sure if her eyes were playing tricks on her. She called his name several more times to no avail.

Voices trickled down the hall.

If she were to be of any future help, she must get back to her room undetected. "I love you," she whispered through the bars before turning and fleeing toward the hidden corridor. She gasped for air but didn't tarry long enough to light her candle. She slipped behind the tapestry and groped her way through a hallway as black as pitch, to her room where she collapsed onto the rug, sobs wrenching from her gut.

That bloody oaf gave her and his own brother over for two rubies and an opal. Damn him. She would kill him. Elaina had no doubts that as soon as the laird had the information he wanted, her husband's life was over, if he didn't die from starvation and the beatings first. She pounded the floor with her fists and buried her screams into the rug. It wasn't until she awoke the next morning, her throat raw and eyes swollen, that she realized she had lost her weapon somewhere along the way.

Chapter Twenty-Seven

"AND JUST WHAT IS THE matter with ye?" Doireann stood at her bedside with her arms crossed.

"I'm not well. Leave me be."

"Still? Ye have been in this bed for two days."

"And I will remain here for a third. Go away."

Doireann huffed but snapped her fingers at her girls and they deposited a tray of food upon the table before leaving.

Elaina needed to see Calum, but too many men had walked the hallways leading to Calum's cell the past two evenings for her to venture to it. During the days, she couldn't garner enough mettle to rise from her bed. No one had yet stormed into her room to demand an explanation for why she had defied orders to stay out of the west tower, but Elaina had no clue where she had dropped the stake. *Bloody coward.* She buried her face in her pillow, trying to drown out her own ridicule.

"Mistress Doireann informs me ye are once again refusin' her services. What is it this time? Ye are no a prisoner yet ye havenae moved from the bed in two days?"

Elaina pulled her pillow over her head, ignoring Robert's comments. She stiffened as she felt the mattress give under his weight.

He placed one arm on the other side of her body and leaned close enough she could feel his breath on the back of her neck. "I've never known ye to hide from the world, Elaina. What has happened? Have ye been harmed in some way?"

"Have I been harmed in some way?" She flung the pillow off her head and shoved him away from her. "I have been trapped in this keep for longer than I can remember," she roared. "I am a prisoner, or have you forgotten? My mind is a bloody mess and I miss my husband," she added in a choked whisper, her thoughts traveling back to his emaciated body. It was all her fault. She let Erroll and Aron talk her into that stupid bloody plan. If she hadn't felt the need to save her brother from the hangman's noose or she hadn't been set on revenge, none of this would have happened. If only she had let Calum take her home…

"It will all be well soon, my love." Robert brushed the hair from her face, and she slapped his hand away.

"Do not touch me and do not call me that. I am not your love. I am not your father's love. I belong to Calum MacKinnon."

Robert stared at a spot above her head, his jaw working. "I hate to inform ye, but I have it on good authority that the MacKinnon is dead. Set upon by bandits."

"Liar!" she screamed at him.

"I am sorry, but he is gone. Ye are a widow."

"If he is dead, it is because of you. You killed him. I don't believe you." A part of her wondered if his words were true. Had Calum died alone in that awful cell, starved and beaten to death or was Robert merely trying to scare her—to manipulate her to his will? "Get away from me," she hissed through her teeth.

Robert sat straight up on the edge of the bed but did not rise.

"Leave me be."

"Very well, but starvin' yerself willnae bring MacKinnon back."

"Maybe I mean to join him if what you say is true."

"Starvin' is a cruel and drawn out death, Elaina. I ken ye are stubborn to a fault, but there are quicker ways to go."

"I am sure you and your father can come up with something. Now leave."

Robert shrugged as he rose and headed toward the door. "Suit yerself, love, but life in the keep may no be as bad as ye believe it to be."

Elaina grabbed the brush from her bedside table and hurtled at the man's retreating back, missing him by inches.

Robert never flinched nor turned around but continued out of the door and down the hallway.

His words had decided for her. Until now, fear of being found out kept her from the secret passage and the west tower. No more. Tonight, she would venture into forbidden territory once more. After all what was there to be afraid of? If Calum was dead, and they found her out, it wouldn't make one damn bit of difference whether she lived or died for without her husband, she could not go on.

Chapter Twenty-Eight

THE DAY PASSED ABYSMALLY SLOW. Elaina rose from the bed after several more hours of moping and refused the services of Doireann and the girls. Instead, she washed in the basin as well as she could and picked at the food they had delivered. She wasn't brave enough to swipe a piece of cutlery for the coming night's jaunt. Mayhap she would find the stake in the hidden corridor. She hid some of her meal in case Calum was still alive. Somehow, she would get it to him through the iron bars.

After the lock clicked into place once again, confining Elaina to her room for the night, she waited until she thought most of the keep slept, then taking up her trusty taper, she set off through the corridor. As she crept cautiously along, she searched for her lost weapon—nothing. She leaned her head against the secret door into the west tower. Ever so gently, she pushed it open and peered out from behind the tapestry, once again finding the room empty. She crossed it in a daze and stood frozen to the spot. Her heart pounded against the wall of her chest. She had to go for Calum. Touching the pocket with the food she had brought for him, she closed her eyes and pushed the lever down with a soft click.

She peeked out of the crack in the doorway and when no one ran to accost her, she stepped out into the hall and gently clicked the door shut behind her. The tower seemed darker and colder than she remembered. Her stomach clenched in knots, and a cold sweat ran down her back. She inched down the hall, pausing at the stop of the spiral stairs and listening for voices. A part of her didn't want to know. If she remained ignorant, she could retain hope.

She leaned her face against the stones and whispered a quick prayer before she looked to see if anyone was near and listened for voices.

Silence.

Edging around the corner, she stalked toward Calum's cell and stood in front of the door for several minutes, trying to garner the courage to look inside. With a deep breath, she raised onto her tiptoes and peered into the cell.

The room was empty.

Her toes remained frozen to the floor, her hands clenched on the bars. In a panic, she glanced around her, hoping against hope that she had the wrong room, but she knew it was the right one. There were no other rooms.

Falling to her knees, Elaina held in her wail of grief. Her throat felt as if it would explode with the force of it. She didn't know how long she lay on the icy stones before she heard voices and had to gather all the strength in her body to force herself to her feet. She made a stumbling dash back to the room with the hidden door and pushed the lever.

Nothing.

She rattled it and shoved on it with all her might, to no avail. She had never closed the bloody thing all the way before. It must have locked itself and could only be opened with a key or from the inside. She turned and ran up the hall, away from the voices, with no idea where she was going and no way to escape the tower. In and out of the shadows she darted until a blinding flash passed across her eyes as something slammed into the back of her head.

<hr />

"Get up. No arguments," Doireann snapped, yanking the covers from Elaina's body. "The laird wants to see ye."

The snide look upon Doireann's face gave Elaina pause as did the pounding in her head. She obeyed, letting the women clean and dress her while she stood with her eyes closed against the light. "What time is it?" she groaned. Today of all days, the sun had to show its glory.

"Nigh on noon, ye lazy twit. Now let's get goin'." Doireann placed a hand upon her back and shoved her out of the room.

The hallway passed in waves of gray as Elaina kept her eyes trained on the floor. What would her punishment be for venturing into the forbidden tower? The image of the empty cell made her want to cast up her accounts. But who had knocked her in the head and who had placed her back in her room, in her own bed?

Doireann rapped on a closed door, and the laird's voice bid them to enter.

Elaina followed her escort, staring at the back of her skirt as she clenched her hands in front of her to stop the trembling.

"Good day, Mistress MacKinnon," the laird addressed her more formally than usual.

That didn't bode well for her situation. She bobbed a small curtsy, not raising her eyes from the floor.

"You are bein' rude to our guests, my dear," Laird Campbell admonished.

"Elaina, have they harmed you?" said a familiar voice.

Her gaze darted up, and she flung herself at her brother. "William!" She wrapped her arms around him and all but collapsed in his embrace.

"Pour the lass a dram," Laird Campbell ordered someone.

William's hand smoothed over Elaina's head like a father soothing his child, pausing at the knot on the back of it.

"I-I slipped and fell last night in my room. It's nothing," she whispered into his chest. "You have come for me?" The pleading tone of her voice sounded like a childish girl to her ears, but she couldn't help it. She needed to get away from the laird before she ended up dead like her husband, or worse, with child. Her tears clung to her eyelashes before tumbling down her cheeks as she pushed herself away from the comfort of his arms. "You have come for me." The realization dawned on her that her situation was no better—the British military had arrived to collect their prisoner.

"It's not quite that simple. Sit and let's visit a bit." Laird Campbell motioned to a seat.

It was then she noticed the other occupant of the room. "Your grace." Elaina gave the Duke of Newcastle a curtsy before embracing him as well.

"Yes, yes, yes. You love everyone," the laird said. "This may be the most civilized I have seen you behave since you became my guest."

Elaina cast him a withering glance. "Guest is an odd word for the situation," she said, taking her seat and the tumbler of whiskey Robert offered.

"Mere technicalities. Now, let's get down to the heart of the matter. I am a busy man." Laird Campbell leaned back in his chair, lacing his fingers together. "You can see she is alive and no worse for the wear."

"What is the price?" William asked, his cold blue gaze settled on the laird.

The Duke of Newcastle kept his attention focused on Elaina, his eyes seemed to question if she were truly alright.

Elaina glared at the laird. "I am not some piece of property to auction off to the highest bidder."

"There's my fiery lass." The laird beamed with pride, and Elaina wanted to knock the smirk from his face.

"Elaina," William whispered.

She snapped her glare on her brother like a vice. "What?"

His hand held out a handkerchief while his eyes glimmered with amusement.

She might skelp him as well. Wiping her eyes and nose, she cast a glance around at the four men sitting in the room. "How do you come to be here?" she asked the duke.

"He brought me word of where you were," William answered.

"And how did *you* know? Is it common knowledge throughout the country that I am a prisoner and no one sees fit to help a damsel in distress?"

"Dinna be so dramatic, Elaina," Robert said. "We have nay harmed ye."

Elaina turned on him. "Being held against one's will and locked in a frigid room is not the most pleasant of situations, Robert."

"No man has touched ye," he replied. "Yet."

"And no one shall, or the deal is off." The Duke of Newcastle's bulging eyes darted from Robert, to the laird, and back.

"No one will or I will slit their throat and feed them their bollocks as they lay dying."

Robert winked at her threat, sending her blood boiling.

"Enough," the laird interrupted. "The only thing I request in exchange for the criminal is the land belonging to the Grahams at Balquhidder. The castle and the lands that are rightfully mine."

Elaina sprang to her feet. "They are no more yours than they are the Duke of Newcastle's. How dare you try to lay claim?"

"I am a Campbell. They are MacGregors."

"They are Grahams."

"It's all the same dear, and by assaulting members of the British army, by rights, they may confiscate the land and give it to me."

"Assault? When have they assaulted anyone?"

"Why, the day that you killed Captain Cummings."

"I didn't kill him. Your son did. We were set upon and only defended ourselves."

"To raise arms against the British holds consequences, and Hugh knew that but let his men retaliate. And Hugh Graham has reverted his name back to MacGregor. That means he forfeits the land. It is no question whether or not he will lose the land. The dispute is to whom shall it be given. And by right, it should be mine."

"Uncle Hugh would never—"

"But he has, see. Two paltry words scratched at the end of this document. 'Hugh McGregor.'"

Elaina stared at the parchment, unbelieving. "You are a liar. I'm sure that is not his signature, William. Even if Uncle Hugh returned to the MacGregor name, would not the land and castle revert to his next of kin—me?"

"That is not how things work in the Highlands, my dear." Laird Campbell laid the sheet of parchment on his desk and folded his hands.

"He wouldn't. He couldn't," she replied.

"And why not? What would stop him?"

Elaina searched for a plausible answer, one that would not reveal the demands she overhead him make of Calum days ago. The thought of him lodged a wedge in her throat, and she fought back the tears. "His pride and his family," her voice wavered, and she bit the inside of her cheek to keep the grief at bay. "He would never do that to his people."

"Perhaps you dinna ken yer uncle as well as ye think," Robert said, chuckling under his breath.

"Maybe I ken you and your father all *too* well," she replied. "Did he tell you, William?" Elaina turned to her brother. "Laird Campbell has offered me to my uncle in exchange for the very land he is asking you for, a handful of precious jewels, and the life of my husband? He is a liar who has no intention of handing me to anyone. He means to make me his mistress so I might produce him an heir of his choosing rather than the worthless son standing before you."

Robert lunged at her, but William jumped to his feet and placed himself between the two.

"Then I must meet his demands first. If they do not relinquish you to me, they will answer to Cumberland himself."

"I have Cumberland in my pocket, dear lad." The laird sneered at William.

"Why would the British army care so much about a murderess that they would intervene in a clan war?" Elaina asked William.

"You have killed three British soldiers, Elaina. We cannot let you go."

"One," Elaina replied to her brother. "I killed *one* soldier. Robert and Captain Cummings hung the other, have you forgotten? Robert shot Cummings between the eyes. I killed one lousy soldier who deserved worse."

"You were still my prisoner, and if I would like to keep my neck from a noose, I will return you to face your punishment."

"This is all about saving your own hide and has nothing to do with releasing me from the clutches of this mad man?" she snapped at her brother.

"You do flatter me, dear," the laird said with a mocking grin.

"You may go to the devil." She cast him a withering glance. *Damn William. He is no better than the rest.*

William ignored her statement, instead turning toward Laird Campbell. "When I return, you will relinquish the prisoner or answer to the powers that be."

"Your idle threats mean nothin' to me. Bring me the deed to the land and the castle and we shall call it an even trade. Now, if you will, I have other matters to attend to." The laird rose and motioned the two men to the door.

"Do not give him what he wants, William. I beg you." She turned, imploring the duke, taking his arm. "Please do not give him my family's lands."

"I cannot leave you here, Elaina." William removed the duke's arm from her clutches.

"You can. You must. Please. There is nothing for me out there. Calum is dead." The sob ripped from her throat, and she collapsed against her brother.

"What do you mean, Calum is dead?" William tensed even as he wrapped his arms around his grieving sister.

"Th-they killed him. Th-they killed my husband."

Williams sturdy arms kept her from collapsing to the floor. "Who killed him?"

"Bandits," Robert answered. "Now, if ye are quite finished. Ye must be on yer way. We'll take excellent care of her."

Robert opened the door where Ruske and another man waited on the other side. "Escort them out," he instructed.

Ruske nodded, catching Elaina's eye as Robert peeled her from her brother's person.

"I will return for you," William uttered, just as Calum had.

"Do not give them what they want, William. I beg of you. No one else needs to be harmed. Where would Hugh and his family go? Please don't come back."

William cast her a forlorn glance before he and the Duke of Newcastle disappeared.

Elaina wrenched herself from Robert's grasp and collapsed into a chair, weeping. Not for William's return as she had Calum, but in prayer that he and the duke would not accomplish their mission.

—◦◦◦—

Robert entered her chamber ahead of her, and Elaina's eyes darted to the entrance to the secret passage. Whoever had accosted her in the West Tower and returned her to her room had closed the door that she had most assuredly left ajar. She studied Robert for any signs he knew where she had been. His gaze never lit upon the secret door. Instead, he stood at the window she often stared out of dreaming of her husband riding across the open field to rescue her.

"Ye ken there is no escape?"

It was as if he'd read her thoughts. "Escape?"

"From here. From me." He turned to her, pinning her with his hard-green gaze. You are mine now, Elaina, whether you think I am worthy or not."

"That's funny. I thought I was your father's. The two of you need to make up your minds. This little back-and-forth muddles the brain."

"Dear ol' Da is agin' a bit." Robert leaned against the sill of the window and studied her.

She tried not to squirm under his scrutiny.

"It wouldn't surprise me if one day he went to sleep, never to wake again."

The silence following his statement roared in her ears. Her pulse raced, and she wondered if he had learned of her and Erroll's plot against the two of them. She chose her next words with careful consideration. "He has always seemed quite spry to me, for a man of his advanced age, that is. He doesn't seem weak nor ill. Why would you ever think he might die in his sleep? Have you plans to quicken his demise?" She took a step toward him, eyeing him with caution.

"Have you?"

His answer stopped her. "How could I kill him in his sleep when I am locked in this room each evening?" She prayed her voice did not disclose the trepidation she felt.

"There are ways around everythin', love." He pushed himself away from the window and advanced on her.

It took every ounce of her being to not flee to the other side of the room.

"William and the Duke are safely out of the keep. I suppose ye are free to roam. Remember the rules?" He cocked his head in question.

"How can I forget? You and your father take every opportunity to remind me. Guards are on duty all hours of the day. It makes you wonder what manner of evil deeds occur within the walls of the West Tower."

"The truth might surprise you," he said as he brushed by her on his way out of the room. "Then again, it might not."

Her knees threatened to buckle beneath her as his blond head disappeared around the corner. He whistled a sinister tune while his retreating footsteps echoed down the hall.

Chapter Twenty-Nine

To walk amongst living foliage, even if they were dormant for winter, brought Elaina a certain sense of normality. The dismal stone fortress towered around her like a slumbering giant. Her gaze followed the wall above her, counting the guards as her hand trailed the tops of the sleeping plants and knocked their snow caps loose.

"May I walk with ye?" Bridgette's question startled Elaina out of her pondering state.

"Of course." She gave the lass a half-smile.

She enjoyed another woman's company, although she dearly missed Caitir, who had found her way to Elaina's uncle Hugh. Not that there seemed much he could do to free her besides surrender the family lands, and that could not be allowed to happen. The Campbell's had accomplished the other two parts of their plan. The laird had the jewels and had murdered her husband. Only one stipulation remained, but it could lead her to a hangman's noose. Which did she prefer—staying alive in a castle and being someone's whore or leaving the keep only to die? Perhaps begging William not to return had not been her brightest moment, but she could not put her family out of their home. They had sacrificed so much for her—the least she could do was to fight for their right to remain on their land.

"I ken we have known each other but a short time and have had little interaction, but I read people well and ye look like a woman workin' on a plan."

Elaina stopped and faced the cook's assistant. "That easy to tell is it?" No point denying it.

"Aye, when ye've made the same lap around the keep three times, staring at the guards on the wall, 'tis evident."

Elaina sighed, clasping her hands behind her. She returned to her stroll through the kitchen garden.

"I cannae blame ye. 'Twould be hard to be away from one's husband."

Elaina stopped short. "He is dead."

"Dead? What makes ye think that?"

How much could Elaina trust her with? Should she mention him being beaten in the west tower and how frightfully awful he looked? She wasn't certain, so instead, she answered, "Because Robert told me."

"I see," the girl said, her gaze studying the brown foliage.

"Not knowing what the laird has planned for me makes it even harder. I never know what each moment might bring. I fear for my virtue and my life. Robert is just as evil as his father, if not more so. You said you came to the keep when you were but one and four? How old are you now, if I may be so bold?" Elaina cast a sideways glance at Bridgette.

"Two and four," she answered without hesitation. "I've been at the keep nigh on ten years."

"So, you arrived when Robert was still a young man?"

Bridgette chuckled. "I'm no sure the Campbell had the chance to be a young man. His father is ruthless. He may have allowed me to live here, but I have never mistaken his behavior as anythin' other than a means to an end. He needed another hand in the kitchen, and I was it. There is no love lost between father and son, as I'm sure ye can tell."

Elaina gave a small huff of acknowledgment.

Bridgette picked the dormant head off a flower and pushed it into the dirt with her finger. "Hatred and anger are like this seed," she said. "When planted and tended to, its roots will grow deep and the stalk of it will rise tall and flower, spreading its seed to anythin' nearby. It invades the hearts of those 'round it. From the talk about the keep, Robert had not a chance of anythin' but bein' a monster."

"I do feel for him. I'm sure he had a horrid childhood and upbringing after his mother passed, but do you not believe that after a certain amount of time, a person is responsible for their own actions? He is an adult and chooses to continue his father's legacy of murder and destruction. He crushes all those around him. Greed and pride are the devil's handiwork. I'm not sure what his motivation was for killing my father and beating my mother to death. Money is the only reason I have discovered."

"The laird gave the order. He wants the names of the Highlanders leadin' the rebellion. He thinks it will gain him favor with the king, and no matter what Robert says, he wants the approval of his father."

"How do you know that?" Elaina asked, her brow raised in suspicion.

"Castle gossip. Ye would be surprised what I ken of things that go on in the keep."

"So what if his father gave the order? He did not have to follow through with it. You talk as if he is an innocent in the matter and that I should pity him for his upbringing?" Elaina crossed her arms and studied Bridgette.

"Not pity. A man has to answer for his own deeds, and I believe that Robert Campbell will answer, but what I am sayin' to ye is that ye are a good woman, Elaina MacKinnon, but the longer ye remain in the keep, the more yer heart will be infected with the poison of Laird Campbell. I ask that ye fight hard against it. Do not let the deeds of the father taint ye and turn ye into the beast that Robert Campbell is."

"Meaning?"

"Meanin' what I said. Ye are no a monster, mistress. Guard yer heart. Now, I must go." Bridgette gave Elaina's arm a squeeze before she hurried off, leaving her staring at the indention in the raised bed where Bridgette's finger had pushed down the head of the flower.

Her mind drifted to the Dwale she had given to Erroll. She had no other recourse, and she had set out on this mission to exact her revenge on Robert Campbell. Glancing over her shoulder at the raven-haired lass hurrying back to the kitchens, Elaina brushed the woman's words aside. Avenging her parents' deaths did not make her a monster. The act would set her free. She would no longer have to look over her shoulder at every turn, wondering when the cat would pounce. Robert had beat her, laid her back open with a whip, broken her nose, and damn near broke her spirit. No, revenge would be hers, and it would be oh so sweet.

Chapter Thirty

THE MUSKY AROMA OF THE horses mixed with the fresh scent of new-fallen snow permeated the air, and Elaina breathed it all in savoring the atmosphere as she wandered her way down through the stable's corridors searching for Erroll. The raiding party had returned days ago, but she had yet to run into the elusive man. She wondered if he was avoiding her—if he hadn't the nerve to distribute the poison and if such, she would demand its return. She had to break free of the laird's grasp to ensure that the Grahams kept their land.

A nicker from one of the horses drew her attention. It was the injured mare they had doctored weeks earlier.

Elaina slipped into the stall and inspected the horse's injury. "You are looking well," she whispered, running a hand across her back and inspecting the wound that had scabbed over and closed well. The mare would have a scar, but what was a little scar, after all? She took up a brush and smoothed it over the horse's coat in long, gentle strokes.

The mare turned and bumped Elaina's shoulder with her head.

"You are welcome, my dear," Elaina said with a laugh.

She lost herself in the soothing motions of grooming. Minutes passed before she realized that tears ran down her face. The brush fell to the floor, and Elaina wrapped her arms around the neck of the mare and wept. How could she go on without Calum? If she escaped the keep where would she go? She didn't want to put the Grahams in harm's way. She could return to the Royal Colonies. The family still had friends there. Surely, the British army would not search for her all the way across the ocean.

Wiping tears from her cheeks, Elaina picked up the brush, returning it to its home. "Thank you," she whispered to the mare, running her knuckles across its jaw.

She turned to leave, but what she saw huddled in a discreet corner of the stables brought her to a halt with her hand on the stall latch. She ducked to the other side of the horse and peered from under its neck at the couple who were trying to hide from sight.

When Bridgette reached up a hand and cupped Ruske's cheek, Elaina thought she might fall out in a dead faint. *Bloody hell?* Ruske pulled the kitchen maid close, and her pebbled laugh trickled into the stall with Elaina and the mare. When Ruske leaned down and kissed Bridgette with such gentle affection that Elaina felt sure she was dreaming, she sank down into the corner of the stall. Her hands trembled, and she grabbed fistfuls of hay hoping to stop them, but it only sent the tremors up her arms. How close she had been to asking Bridgette about the poison and in effect nailing her own casket closed. She had duped her into a false sense of security and companionship. All this time, Bridgette had been a spy for the enemy. Elaina swallowed down the bile that rose in her throat. This explained Bridgette's odd reaction to Elaina's announcement that her husband was dead. God help her, the woman already knew. She knew that they had killed Calum, and she didn't tell her. She knew that he was being held in the west tower.

How naïve am I? Why would I think that a woman who had been part of the Campbell clan for ten years would befriend their prisoner?

Footsteps sounded beside the stall, and Elaina held her breath as the couple whispered to each other in Gaelic before their footsteps continued in different directions.

Minutes may have passed, or it could have been hours that Elaina sat frozen in place. Of all the men in the keep, Bridgette had chosen the roughest, dirtiest, and unruliest imbecile. The stomping of the mare eventually brought her out of her stupor and coaxed her into motion. Stumbling to her feet, she glanced up and down the corridor before exiting the horse's stall.

Hurrying from the stables with her skirts in her hands, Elaina ran across the courtyard wondering what on earth she would say to the girl when their paths crossed again. Should she warn her that the man was an attempted rapist? Who knew if he had assaulted any other women besides Caitir? Mayhap Bridgette knew all that and did not care. She was not the sweet innocent woman that she had portrayed.

Chapter Thirty-One

A SOFT SNOW DRIFTED ONCE AGAIN from the gray sky. It was hard to tell where the stone walls ended and the sky began from her vantage point at her usual table in the kitchen. Days ago, this had been her favorite place in the keep. The stables were not as comfortable as she would like. She would spend more time there if not for Ruske's presence. For now, her position at the table helped her keep an eye on Bridgette, and Elaina debated on confronting the lass but wasn't yet sure how she wanted to broach the subject.

The lack of a howling Highland wind was both calming and unnerving. A windless day in the Highlands could mean the fiercest of rages to follow. Much like things inside the keep. A storm had been brewing within her bones for days. She felt certain that robert knew she had been in the west tower, but she hadn't a clue who had knocked her unconscious and delivered her to her room. If it had been him, why hide it—unless to make her suffer with the worry of it all? If that was his plan, it had worked splendidly.

"Ye are thinkin' so loudly I cannae hear myself over the din in yer head." Bridgette slid onto the bench across from her.

Elaina jumped, sloshing mulled cider from the cup she held clasped tight on the table in front of her. "*Merde*," she hissed, flinging the stinging liquid from her hands.

Bridgette giggled and passed her a kitchen rag. "Ye are jumpy as a toad. Is there a reason?"

Elaina wiped away the cider as she eyed the lass with wariness. How much did she know?

While Elaina contemplated her answer, Bridgette turned to gaze out of the window. "A storm is comin'," she whispered, her gaze lifted toward the sky.

"Is there?"

"Aye." The lass turned her doe-eyed gaze back to Elaina. "'Twill be intense. Will ye be ready?"

"Pardon?" Elaina asked, a chill creeping across her skin.

"Have ye enough peat in yer room? Blankets? I ken well enough ye dwell in the draftiest room in the keep."

Elaina couldn't shake the feeling that the woman's original statement held a different meaning altogether. "Yes. I wonder why that is? It seems solid enough."

"'Tis odd. As far as I can tell it is unlike any other room in the keep. Except perhaps the drawing room in the west tower. It is a bit drafty as well, and it havin' no windows 't all."

Elaina stared at her. "You've been in the west tower?"

"Aye."

"And what is there? What is so secret?" Her knuckles turned white on the cup in front of her, and she had to force herself to relax and attempt to act ignorant.

"Well now, I've not seen *all* the tower. I've only delivered meals to the chamber of himself and his son."

So, that was where the laird and Robert slept. She suspected as much.

"As for secrets," Bridgette continued. "'Tis no secret the trouble one might find oneself in if ever caught where they are forbidden to go."

She knew.

"The general help of the keep may not venture down the stairwell, only up. What takes place below would be no business of mine if I valued my life."

Does she not know? Elaina's head spun in confusion. "And what floor would the drafty drawing room be on?" she asked, turning her gaze into the kitchen and watching the help add the finishing preparations to the afternoon meal, hoping the question sounded casual enough.

"The ground floor—two floors below Robert's chamber and four below the Laird's...if ye must ken. Now, I best hurry. I'm sure my bread is ready. Until next time, mistress."

Elaina watched Bridgette slide off the end of the bench and scurry to the ovens with a towel in her hands.

With new information tumbling in her mind, Elaina left the kitchen and wandered down the winding hallway. Robert slept on the second floor and the Laird on the fourth. If she could procure a weapon of some sort and find Robert's chamber, she could catch him unawares and kill him and his father in their sleep and be done with it all.

A rough hand grabbed her and pulled her into the shadows of a recession in the hall. She stifled a squeal and swung a fist at her attacker.

He caught it before it collided with his face and pinned her arms to her sides. "It's me," Erroll hissed into her ear.

"What the devil? You scared me half to death," Elaina said, still reeling from her wild heartbeat under the strength of his grasp.

"I called yer name twice. I didna think it safe to do it a third. What are ye thinkin' that ye cannae hear a thing?"

"They killed Calum."

Erroll stilled, his grip tightening on her arms. "Why do ye say that?"

"Robert told me."

"And just why would ye believe him?"

"I saw Calum. They had him as a prisoner in the keep. They starved him, and they beat him." Elaina's voice cracked, and she fought to bring her emotions under control.

"Where did they have him?" Erroll growled.

"In the west tower."

"Ye've been in the west tower? What in the bloody hell are ye thinkin'? How did ye get in?"

"There is a secret passage from my chambers to a drawing room on the ground floor. It empties into a kind of shrine erected to my mother." She shivered at the thought of it.

"Ye don't say?"

"Yes. Calum was in a cell. After Robert told me he was killed by bandits, I went back to the tower and it was empty. He looked so horrible when I saw him that I don't doubt he died." Elaina forced down a sob. "That's what I'm thinking about. I'm trying to work out a plan of attack. We need Robert and the laird dead."

"That's what I need to talk to ye about, lass. Tonight is the night. I have given the Dwale to an associate."

"Who?" Her mind flitted to Bridgette.

"Never ye mind that. It is in expert hands."

Elated, Elaina brushed aside her fears. Thank God for Erroll. She shook her arms loose from his grip and wrapped them around his neck. "Could we truly be free by tomorrow?"

"I'm no sayin' that. How will ye get out of the keep?"

Elaina buried her head on his shoulder. "I don't know," she whispered into the rough fibers of his coat. He smelled of snow and horses.

"Dinna fash about it." He patted her on the back. "Everything comes to fruition in its own time. I must go before someone sees us. Tonight." He pushed her away and scurried down the hall as Ruske and another man turned the corner.

Ruske glared at her, suspicion registering in his beady little eyes.

She held his gaze while he stared at her over his shoulder as he passed her and continued his trek toward the kitchens, she presumed. When he finally broke their glare, she collapsed against the wall.

"Tonight," she whispered and wiped a grateful tear from her cheek.

Chapter Thirty-Two

E LAINA TOOK HER MEAL IN her room that evening, needing the peace to help her think. There had to be a way out of the keep. God, she hoped there was enough poison to take care of father and son. Part of her felt guilty and almost dirty for even thinking such thoughts, but they had killed her husband. An eye for an eye.

Elaina lifted the teapot to fill her cup but stopped short at the folded note revealed underneath it rather than in the bread as usual. She stared at it for several seconds before bringing herself to pick it up.

"Calum is alive."

She read it again. And again.

How? Did they only move him to a different cell? Did they find out that she had seen him? I did lose that stake somewhere. He is alive!

She flew to her feet and would have squealed with delight if Robert hadn't chosen that moment to enter her room. She shoved the slip of paper into her pocket. "You could knock. That would be the proper thing to do," she said, trying to hide her excitement.

"Yes, I could...if I wanted to. Sit," he ordered. He deposited himself in a chair.

Elaina took the one across from him. She couldn't help but stare at him and think that in a few hours he would be dead. The act of looking him in the eye made it difficult to contemplate the deed. It was hard to look an unarmed man in the face and then kill him. But she wouldn't have to stand before him, for it was Erroll who would deliver the poison. That thought did little to ease her conscious since she'd given the poison to Erroll in the first place.

Silence filled the room. A usually talkative Robert stared out the window while Elaina picked at a slice of cake dotted with berries. Something new from the kitchens.

"Tea?" He turned to her, his green eyes darker than usual.

"Yes. Please," she answered.

He poured her a cup, doctoring it just right, and then one for himself, but instead of taking a drink, he fingered the handle of the fine china and gazed once more out of the window.

Gray smoke blurred her vision of the sullen man sitting before her as she raised her tea to her lips. "What of it?" she asked, curious where his brooding came from.

"Your clan will surrender their lands in three days' time." His voice held an eerie monotone quality. He turned to her, his eyes showing the same lifeless sensation. "Father means to have ye before then."

"Have me? I've been in his ke—" The meaning tore through her gut, and she felt the piece of cake she had eaten lodge itself like a rock in her throat. She washed it down with another gulp of tea.

Robert watched her while she tried to pull herself together.

Could she overpower the laird? Could she fight him off?

"Whallas… hecranta…" Her tongue. She moved to touch its tip with her finger, but her hand stopped in front of her face and she studied it, wiggling her fingers and watching them wave like ripples on the water of a burn.

Robert was at her side. "Come, love. Let me help you."

Her limp body fell against his chest as he scooped her from her chair. Trying to protest, she found that no words could make it past her mind to her mouth. She closed her eyes against the spinning room.

A muddy puddle of familiar voices sloshed in her ears as they entered the coldness of the hall. Her body floated on air. Unable to hold her head up any longer, it fell back, and she stared at the yawning gray ceiling as it rippled by like a stream.

"Did ye kill her?"

"Nay, she's still breathin'."

Silence.

She couldn't swallow. Her tongue was too big. She tried to wipe at her eyes, but her hand was stuck. She pulled and yanked at it. *What the hell is wrong with the bloody thing?*

"Shh." The sound swooshed against her ear, meaning to comfort her, but she fought harder and her lungs seized, searching without success for air.

"Elaina. Look at me. Breathe."

Prying her eyelids open, she peered into Robert's green eyes inches from her face. "That's it, love. There you are. Thirsty?"

Elaina forced a nod, and Robert's face drifted away only to return seconds later, holding a cup to her lips. She gulped it down before the bitterness of it reached her tongue. Confused, she stared at him and his loose blond hair encircling his head like a halo, spilling over his bare shoulders in small rivulets. His chest…the muscles taut and straining…his hands that trembled as they brushed the damp hair from her face.

"He can't have you," Robert whispered, sliding down next to her. Against her. Skin burning hers. His fingers traced a path between her breasts and down her stomach.

She tried to struggle, to scream, but her mouth wouldn't work. The room faded in and out of a darkness that she fought to hold at bay.

"I shall leave ye then. Looks like ye have it under control." A voice floated to her on a dream and she turned toward it.

His face was out of focus, but his stature familiar. The sound…haunting yet…

"Best of luck to ye, mistress." He laughed as he twisted to go, his silhouette coming into focus.

A dagger pierced her heart as the door clicked closed behind him and she began her descent into darkness. *Erroll.*

The first thing she was aware of was a heaviness against her belly and the horrible ache in her shoulders. Forcing her eyes open, she struggled to clear them and take in her surroundings. Burgundy drapes encircled her, nesting her in a cocoon of blood red shadows. They hung closed from canopy rails of the bed. She tilted her chin down and took in the sight of her near-naked breasts rising above Robert's blond head that nestled itself in the concave of her stomach. She wore nothing but her shift, her bare legs stretching out as if extending from his face. She blinked and shook her head. Her attempt to move and ease the pain in her shoulders led to the discovery that he had tied her arms to a post at the head of the bed. She pulled against the ropes. The rough hemp grated against her wrists, but Elaina yanked harder, panic cutting off her airway. Her movement stirred her captor, and he raised his bloodshot gaze to hers. Puffy eyelids flickered at her. Had he been crying?

"Elaina, my sweet." He smelled like a whiskey bottle. His hand caressed her cheek, and she tried to jerk away.

He gave her a wan smile and rose from the bed, pushing back the veil of curtains. His blond hair hung loose just past his bare shoulders. Wearing nothing but a pair of breeks, he weaved his way across the room and attempted to pour liquid from a silver pitcher into a cup, sloshing it on the tabletop. His form was so unlike her husband's. Where Calum was broad and lengthy of thick muscled legs, Robert had a long narrowly chiseled torso and shorter legs.

Her stomach sickened at the comparison. She closed her eyes, trying to clear her mind as she continued her attack on the ropes holding her wrists. Her thoughts remained jumbled and cloudy.

"Elaina. Stop. There is no escape, and ye are makin' a mess of yerself."

Exhaustion took over, and Elaina sank against the pillows as Robert planted himself beside her on the bed.

Bits of moments returned to her as she sniffed the liquid in the cup with caution when he held to her lips.

"'Tis only water," he whispered, his voice thick and choked.

She glanced at him as she gulped it down. Had he raped her? Did he ruin her?

"Ye look at me as if I'm a monster. I am only a man." He crossed the room again and wet a rag in the wash basin. When he returned, he dabbed at the blood running down Elaina's arms from her raw wrists.

She opened her mouth to reply to his statement but couldn't find her speech.

"Ye needn't say anythin', Elaina. Yer eyes tell it all. I am accustomed to bein' looked at in that manner, but it especially hurts comin' from ye. That is the look that has darkened my father's eyes every day of my life. I'm sorry for all the pain I have caused ye, love. I mean to make it up to ye." He leaned down, his hair falling around her face like a silken curtain. "Ye belong to me and no one else. Not my father...and not the MacKinnon," he added after a long pause. His lips brushed across hers, and she struggled to move away.

Robert continued his whiskey binge while Elaina tried to break out of her stupor. Tears slid down her cheeks at the realization of Erroll's betrayal. He had given the poison to Robert. When had he crossed over to the Campbell side? It was his suggestion to hand her over to the British to be rescued. He talked her and Aron into the plan, and in turn, they convinced Calum. The entire thing had been a setup to get her into the hands of Robert Campbell.

Robert offered her a drink of whiskey.

"I would love one," she said, "but my shoulders are bloody killing me. Could you please untie me?"

"How do I ken ye will behave yerself?" Robert's words slurred together.

"You have my word. Please."

Robert sat for several moments, and she had decided the answer was no when a *sgian-dubh* appeared from somewhere unseen and he cut the ties binding her wrists. The knife clattered to the tabletop by the bed.

Groaning at the act of moving her arms from over her head, Elaina touched the raw and bloodied skin around her wrists and wondered just how long she had been there.

"Here, sit up." Robert slid an arm under her shoulders and scooped her up into a sitting position.

Elaina grabbed the blanket, covering herself, and accepted the tumbler of whiskey he offered her.

In an unnerving show of familiarity, he slid onto the bed beside her and laid his head upon her lap. Her gaze darted to the knife on the table.

"Do it, Elaina," Robert whispered.

She swallowed hard. "Do…" she croaked and cleared her throat. "Do what?"

"Take up the blade and slit my miserable throat, or do ye no have the courage?"

Elaina stared down at him. *The poor drunk fool.*

"He has taken everything from me." His words became choked as through tears. "He killed my mother. He trained Alex to follow in his footsteps and forced him to join the Black Watch. He has taken everything that I held dear." His words grew slower, drowsy. "He killed my soul. And now he wants the one thing that I have left in this world. I cannae stand by and let it happen. I…"

Elaina waited for him to continue, but the heavy sounds of sleep came instead. She sat there with a cup of whiskey in her hand, a knife on the table, and a drunk, broken man unconscious on her lap. Her gaze traveled from the *sgian-*

dubh, to Robert, and back. Lifting her hand, she inched it toward the knife, leaning, her fingers stretched upon the surface of the table.

Robert stirred and reached for her arm, drawing her hand toward him. He laid a gentle kiss upon her palm. "I love ye," he whispered, his breath warm against her hand.

And so she sat with tears dripping into her tumbler as she finished her whiskey. Tossing the glass aside, she laid a hand upon Robert's head while he still clung to the other. Now was her chance. She hated him. He'd killed her parents, imprisoned her husband, tortured her, and possibly raped her. Why could she not bring herself to pick up the knife and exact her revenge?

Self-loathing suffocated her like a blanket, and she brushed Robert's blond locks behind his ear. The shadow of a beard showed along his jaw. Her other hand lay cupped in both of his. He clung to it like a small boy would cling to his mother.

Coward. He asked you to do it. Pick up the knife and kill him.

Bridgette's words returned to her. *"Do not let the deeds of the father taint ye and turn ye into the monster that Robert Campbell is."*

Perhaps the perfect punishment for Robert's crimes was having to live with the thought of them and with all the pain his father had inflicted upon him. Death was too good for the man. She laid her head back against the headboard of the bed and contemplated Erroll's involvement. He had given Robert the poison intended for his ingestion. He was supposed to set her free, but instead he'd handed her to her enemy like a sacrificial virgin. When had Erroll turned? This morning? A sennight ago? One and twenty years ago?

The effects of the poison combined with the tumbler of whiskey she had guzzled kept her head spinning in a maddening swirl. The angels carved into the ornate bedframe looked more like writhing demons, and she closed her eyes against them.

Chapter Thirty-Three

ELAINA WOKE TO FIND HERSELF curled in the crook of Robert's arm. Her head rested against his chest, his hand stroking her hair. Scrambling off the other side of the bed, she stared at him, her body shivering with the sudden change in temperature.

Robert rose, naked, on the opposite side. His eyes remained puffy, but his mordant smile had returned. "Ye are beautiful standing there with yer hair amuss…your nipples like ripe berries." His eyes roved over her body, and she snatched up the edge of the blanket, covering herself with it. "No need to be bashful now, love."

"What did you do?" The words did not want to leave her lips.

A look of melancholy crossed his face as his gaze dropped to the bed and back to her. It was gone as quickly as it came. He reached over to his *sgian-dubh* lying beside the pillows. "I recall that I asked ye to kill me." He tossed the knife to a spot in front of her, its silver blade a stark contrast to the blood red cover on the bed. "If you do not, I will have to consider it an act of devotion." His brow rose, questioning.

Elaina snatched up the knife, her other hand still holding the edge of the cover over her body.

Robert began a slow trek around the bed, his fingers trailing a path across the ornate frame. "'Twas my mother's bed," he whispered.

Elaina's eyes remained upon his hand.

"'Twas my mother's chambers. My father took that which was mine, and I will possess what is his."

The tip of the blade pressed against his bare chest and trembled in her grip, her knuckles white. "I belong to neither of you. I am the wife of Calum MacKinnon," she whispered, unable to look at him.

"No. You are the *widow* of Calum MacKinnon."

Her gaze darted to his green eyes, searching for the truth. "But the note... the note said he was alive."

"What note?"

When she didn't answer, he grabbed her wrist and wrenched her arm behind her. The knife clanged against the floor, its sound like the tolling of a bell. Robert shoved her face onto the bed with all his weight pressed against her. His heat burned through her thin shift. "What note?" He wrenched her arm higher until she cried out.

"In my meal. The note hidden on my tray." She grunted.

"Who wrote it?"

She couldn't breathe.

"Elaina, do ye wish for me to break yer lovely bones?"

"I don't know. I swear it!" she replied as he twisted her wrist, bringing tears to her eyes. She truly believed he would snap her arm in two.

He pushed himself off her and snatched up the knife. "You should have killed me while you had the chance." He stalked across the room and grabbed his breeks from their resting spot on the back of a chair. "I knew all along that ye wadna be able to," he said as he drew his tunic over his head. "Given the choice between my father and myself, I believe ye have chosen wisely."

Elaina slid to the floor, dragging the blanket with her. Blood rushed in her ears like a thunderous river.

"I will find your little friend if I have to torture everyone in the keep. Then I shall return and finish what we started." He squatted in front of her, his hands cradling her face.

She could shove him back and snatch the dirk that now hung from his waist, but she sat immobile while he kissed her, forcing his tongue between her frozen lips and his hand blazing against her skin as it slid down the rounded neck of her shift, cupping her breast.

After a moment, he pulled away and chucked his fist under her chin. "Ye are going to have to put in a tad more effort next time. Now dinna go anywhere. We've business to attend to when I return." He rose and left her.

The lock clicked behind him.

Chapter Thirty-Four

TIME TICKED BY WHILE ELAINA stared at her bare feet on the stones before her. She sat frozen, awaiting Robert's return. She had squandered the one opportunity she'd had to kill the man. Sympathy for the child in the portrait had tainted her heart to the wretched man that the child had become, and now she sat branded as a coward incapable of saving her own life. She had no problem sentencing others to death, however. The blood of yet another person would be on her hands when Robert found the owner of the hand that had penned the notes.

The sound of a clock chiming brought her out of her stupor, and she realized tears streamed down her cheeks and her body trembled so that her teeth clanked together. The chime was the same as the one that had graced her father's study in the colonies. The sounding of the hour scolded her for her weakness in the face of the enemy. Her father raised soldiers, not victims. She could hear his speech echoing on the waves of the clock bell.

The final toll of the hour sent her scrambling to her feet, and she yanked the cover from the bed, scouring every inch of it and the sheets for signs of Robert's seed. She inspected her shift. Finding nothing brought a small glimmer of hope that he had not committed the unthinkable. She scrubbed her body with the frigid water from the urn until it was almost the same color as the curtains, trying to erase the feel of him from her soul. Afterward, she turned to the hearth, pushing on every rock, tapping her knuckles across the panels beside it. She moved every pot, every vase. Making her way methodically down the wall, she searched for an entrance to a secret passage. The farther she went, the more frantic her actions became.

Please! There must be one.

The rattling of keys outside her door brought her up short, and she gripped a silver candlestick protectively in front of her.

Doireann entered, closing the door behind her and turning her key in the lock.

Elaina returned her weapon to the tabletop. "Working alone today, are you?" she asked the severe woman still standing beside the heavy oak door. Elaina walked back to the hearth and stared into the fire. "You didn't want to alert anyone as to where I am, is that it? So, Robert can do to me whatever he wishes, and no one will be the wiser?"

When Doireann didn't respond, Elaina turned to discover the woman barreling toward her. She ducked as Doireann swung her chatelaine. The large ring of keys skimmed the top of her head.

"You whore," Doireann roared, advancing on Elaina again.

Elaina's hand sought any weapon she could find, never taking her eyes off the woman whose gaze burned with hatred.

"I have done nothing." Elaina hurled a vase at Doireann.

The woman brought her arm up in time to keep the vase from smashing against her face, then lunged at Elaina, snagging her by her hair and yanking her backward. The two women tumbled to the stone floor. She clawed at Elaina's face, and Elaina administered a swift elbow to her ribs, gaining her a chance to roll over and grab the fire poker, but not enough time to secure an advantage.

Doireann tackled her from behind, sending the poker flying. "You bloody filthy whore." Doireann's knee was in her back, crushing her. "I will kill you before I stand by and watch ye destroy what is left of his life. Ye are a curse, just as yer mother," she spat into Elaina's face.

The woman was in love with Robert, not the laird. The realization stunned Elaina so, that for a moment she stopped struggling, which worked in her favor as Doireann eased her hold just enough that she swung her forearm around and knocked the witch from her back.

"I don't want him," she panted, going for the ring of keys she spied by the post of the bed. "Let me go. Get me out of here and you can have him." She had the keys in her hand when Doireann pounced again, yanking Elaina to her back, her hands encircling her throat.

"As long as ye walk the earth, he will never be free. Do ye no see that? Look at his father. He is bewitched. The only thing to stop it is your death. I have raised that boy since birth, and I'll not let ye destroy him." Each syllable was accentuated by Elaina's head hitting the floor, buffered only by the rug on which the two women had landed.

Darkness ensued, and Doireann's image and words swam in and out of Elaina's consciousness. The witch was not in love with Robert. In her eyes, he was her son. Elaina's heartbeat pounded in her ears like a boot heel against a door. The woman's grip increased, and Elaina swung the chatelaine in her hand with all her might, knocking Doireann from on top of her. She lay gasping, knowing she should move, that she should try to get away again, but she hadn't enough air in her body to do so. She gasped for it like a trout out of water, expecting the woman to pounce on her yet again, but when she did not, she garnered enough strength to turn her head and look. Doireann lay on her back, her eyes open and unseeing, fixated on the ceiling. A dirk protruded from the woman's chest. An enormous hand wrenched the knife free, and Elaina looked up into the sneering face of Ruske.

His hulking frame towered over her. His gaze traveled over the scene before he lunged at her.

She scrambled to her knees, but he dove on top of her, smashing her face to the floor and knocking the breath out of her yet again.

"Quit fightin' if ye ken what's good for ye." He snatched her up as if she weighed nothing and dragged her from the room with her kicking and flailing and still trying to catch her breath. He clamped his filthy hand over her mouth just as her air came back to her, blocking the scream she had inhaled to let forth.

Elaina wanted to wretch at the thought of what was to come, his warnings haunting her. Down through the winding stairs of the west tower. Past the cell where her husband had been held captive. They traversed two more flights, sinking even farther into the bowels of the castle. The air turned colder and musty, wet almost. The small, darkened hallway they had spiraled down came to a dead end and Ruske crouched down, struggling to open a hatched door in the floor. He had to release her mouth to pry at it, and she squirmed and fought, slipping out of his arms for a split second, but he snatched her back by her bare foot. A scream ripped from her throat, and he once again slapped his hand over her mouth, but not before she managed to sink her teeth into it.

He grunted a low growl. "Dammit, woman. I warned ye." As he wrenched his hand free from her teeth, she glimpsed the black water of the moat through the now open door and Bridgette's face peering up at her. She opened her mouth to scream again but something slammed into her head.

Chapter Thirty-Five

A SEARING PAIN POUNDED IN HER brain, and she raised her hands to press it into submission, her fingers finding the large knot on her temple. "Oh God," she groaned, holding the sides of her head while struggling to open her eyes.

A hand grabbed at her, and she scrambled away, falling off whatever she laid upon and rolling across the floor. A wooden floor! Wood planks ran smooth under her knees instead of the cold gray stone of the keep. She forced her eyes open and took in her surroundings. A room with a bed and a roaring fire.

Caitir!

A pair of black boots appeared in front of her, blocking the view of her friend. Her gaze followed them up the long legs of their owner and into the face of...

"You bastard!" Elaina lunged at the man's knees, but he side-stepped her, then scooped her off the floor and held her with her legs flailing as she tried to turn around to gouge his eyes out.

"Now calm down," Aron said, pinning Elaina's arms to her sides.

She got a few good kicks to his shins before he collapsed onto a chair, wrapping his legs around hers.

"Let me go," Elaina growled between clenched teeth, the back of her head connecting with his chest and not his nose like she'd intended. *The tall bastard.*

"Quit yer heetherin', and I will. I willnae let ye go until I explain."

"I don't want to hear anything you have to say to me, you treacherous... evil... You snake!"

"That's a good deal better than what I thought ye would call me." Aron chuckled.

Elaina wanted to cut his tongue out.

The memory of him standing before William with his fist twisted in her hair and that devilish sneer across his face and then his words traveling over the dead brush at the keep. He'd sold her out for two rubies and an opal. The memories lit a fire in Elaina's belly. How dare he tell her to calm down. She would cut his oily heart out and eat it for breakfast—Calum's brother or no.

Someone else appeared, and Elaina's fighting became a frantic scramble to climb out of Aron's grasp and over his shoulder, away from the man.

"Now, dammit, Elaina," Aron grunted, trying to gain control of his struggling victim.

"The lass is a she-devil," Ruske chuckled and was caught off guard when Elaina turned and lunged, her fingernails raking down the side of his face.

"Calm down, lass." Auld Ruadh's words brought her to an abrupt halt.

"Wh-what are you doing here? What in the bloody hell is going on?"

"Quit fightin', and we'll tell ye." Auld Ruadh's brown eyes sparkled with humor while he laid a calming hand upon the top of her head.

Elaina could kiss him if she could get to him. She was so happy to see his red-headed self. She would kill Aron, however—and Ruske. *Ruske.* In a panic, she glanced at the man holding a rag to his bloody scratches. He had plopped himself down on a stool beside Caitir, who sat as if this were a perfectly normal situation. Two women trapped in a cabin with a would-be rapist and an evil backstabbing oaf, and Auld Ruadh. She stared at the old man. Had he turned into an enemy as well? No. The way he looked at her, he had not. She stilled for Auld Ruadh—and in hopes that Aron would release her so she could bloody throttle him.

He did not loosen his hold.

"Where are we?" Elaina asked, looking around the small cabin.

Caitir grinned at her from her place in front of the fire, and Elaina thought about throttling her too for acting so calm about the entire thing.

"The house of a friend," Auld Ruadh answered, pulling up a chair in front of her and Aron.

"I'm sorry I knocked ye on the head," Ruske growled his apology while studying the bloody handkerchief before reapplying it to his face.

She opened her mouth, but no words made their way from her throat.

"Well, ye bloody bit me."

"I would have castrated you if I'd had a knife."

"Now, is that anyway for ye to talk to a friend?" Aron said.

She twisted her head around and glared up at Aron. "Why the devil am I not surprised that you are a traitor to your family."

"It's not what ye think," Aron replied, grinning at her. "When I gave ye up to the English—"

"I know who you gave me up to," Elaina spat out at him. She wanted nothing more than to wipe that smile off his face. "You don't have to remind me."

Aron chuckled, his broad chest vibrating against her. "When I gave ye up, I had to make it look genuine. If I had told ye the plan ahead of time, I'm no sure ye could have faked it well enough for them not to be suspicious. I am sorry if ye felt betrayed."

"Damned right I felt betrayed, you traitor! You did it for the money. You took the reward. Did you tell Auld Ruadh about that little detail or did you keep that to yourself?"

She heard the metallic rattle of coins and turned to face Auld Ruadh. He sat holding the bag William had handed Aron in payment for his prisoner. "This money?" he asked. "Fifteen pounds, was it not? That is a hefty price for a lady."

"She is a murderess, remember?" Aron said.

"Wait until you let me go. I'll show you a murderess. Did you tell him about the jewels? You sold me to the devil."

"How do ye ken about the jewels?" Aron raised his brow in question.

"I heard you. I was behind the bushes when you and Laird Campbell were having your little exchange. You wait until I'm free. I will gut you—"

"Now, now. I tracked ye for days, even through a blazin' blizzard, then lied my way into a Campbell stronghold and executed this nice little plan to rescue ye."

"Tracked? Rescued?"

"I followed ye the whole time. I sent Calum back to gather men with Auld Ruadh because I didna ken whether he could keep his head if they did ye any injustice along the way. I told him I would keep watch. So, I followed yer brother and the British, and then Uncle here caught up with me and told me what the Campbells had done and that they had Caitir. I saw them when they took ye from yer brother. Now, Red and I here are two valiant and mighty warriors, if I do say so myself, but we are none so good as to take on a gang of Campbell men alone, so we followed ye. We sat out in that damn snowstorm waiting for an opportunity to save ye or to watch for where they took ye next."

Elaina sat in stunned silence. She turned to Caitir who had kept her distance through all the fighting and explanation.

"Oh, Elaina." She fell on her knees in front of her, cupping Elaina's face in her hands. "I thought we would never get ye back." Caitir's sky-blue eyes brimmed with tears. "Did they…did they harm you?"

The fact that Elaina could not answer her friend one way or the other lodged a lump in her throat. She decided to change the subject instead. "What is he doing here? How can you sit there so calm?"

Caitir turned to look at the giant of a man who had tried to rape her. "He is a spy for the MacGregors."

"He is a *what*? But…but…"

"He has apologized a hundred times over. 'Twas a way to keep me safe from Robert and the Campbells. If he lay claim to me, he could *almost* guarantee my virtue would remain intact."

"You… He…"

Ruske gave her a sheepish shrug.

"Did you have to wallop me in the head?" she asked for lack of anything else to say.

"That's it? Not a thank ye or nothin'? Even after I saved ye from that witch? Yes, I had to knock ye out. Ye fight like a damn wildcat, and ye bloody bit me."

"I thought you would rape me! Why didn't you just tell me what you were doing instead of attacking me and dragging me around like an overgrown ape?"

"Would ye have listened?" Ruske cast her a questioning glare.

"No," she said after a moment's pause. "Thank you?" The words had to fight themselves across her lips.

"Would ye call a truce so ye can eat somethin'?" Caitir asked.

Elaina sat still for a moment before she gave a slight nod of her head.

"I can let ye go?" Aron asked.

Elaina nodded again.

With hesitation, he eased his hold on her.

She turned and punched him in the chest before she threw her arms about his neck. "Thank you. Truly." She kissed his cheek and then turned on Auld Ruadh, giving him the same treatment. Still unsure of whether or not she could trust him, Ruske received a nod of appreciation.

"Now, let's get some food in ye," Auld Ruadh said.

"First things first," Elaina answered. "Is Calum alive?"

Aron and Auld Ruadh exchanged a look between themselves.

"Is he?" Elaina repeated, her heart in her throat. "I received a note saying he lived."

"Honestly? He was in a bad way. Hugh took him. Last I knew, they were at an Inn at Callander. Hugh sent out a message to all the MacGregor sympathizers in the area. He is gatherin' an army, but we dinna ken for certain where he is or how many he will bring. We must move on the morrow so the Campbells cannae find us, but dinna fash yerself. Calum is a robust man. I'm sure he has recovered well," Aron said. "Tomorrow we shall set out to find him and Hugh and tell them the splendid news of yer rescue. 'Twill be quite the surprise."

"Hugh doesn't even know where you are? He doesn't know that I am out of the keep? What if he attacks the castle looking for me? What if…" Elaina collapsed to her knees. When she would lie awake at night thinking about her rescue, it was always by her fearsome husband and not by his arrogant brother and never by Ruske.

Auld Ruadh slipped his hands under her arms, lifting her to her feet and depositing her on a stool by the fire. Caitir wrapped a blanket around her shivering shoulders. It was then she realized she still wore only the thin shift.

The door to the cabin burst open and a cloaked figure stumbled through followed by a howling wind and swirling snow. "A storm has come, and it's a good thing too. The castle is all abuzz searchin' for our missin' lass. Oh, you're awake." Bridgette had flung her hood from her head and glanced around the room. "Ah, looks like ye reacted as expected," she laughed, taking in Ruske's scratches.

"She bit me too." He held up his war wound.

"Are you a man or a wee babe in the cradle? I can't tell." Elaina rolled her eyes. "I am to guess that you are in on this little conspiracy as well?" she asked Bridgette.

"Aye, mistress, and we got ye out none too soon. I brought ye some clothes. When I saw what ye were wearing when they tossed ye into the boat, I scrambled for what I could find. Why don't ye men step outside for a moment and let her have a bit of privacy?"

"Aye, let's check the horses," Auld Ruadh said, and the other men rose without a grumble and pulled the tails of their kilts over their heads to protect them from the wind.

"Now," Bridgette turned to Elaina. "I have no stays or petticoats, but I have an arisaid, boots, and a belt. I am sorry that I couldnae get more. By the time I had snatched these, the alarm was being sounded at your absence. Thank the heavens above that the storm came up, so I wasn't spotted crossing the moat."

"Why would you help me? Why would you turn your back on the Campbells after all they've done for you?" Elaina's situation was growing more confusing by the minute.

"Because ye didna deserve to be a prisoner. No woman should be held against their will." Bridgette draped the arisaid around Elaina's shoulders and belted it at her waist. "Besides. Ruske stole my heart, and he fights for the MacGregors."

"Ruske? Stole your heart?" Elaina stared at Bridgette, the scene that played out between the two of them in the stables flashing through her memory.

"I ken well enough ye dinna like him nor trust him, but he is a good man. A good man in need of a clean shave and a bath," she said with a laugh. "He has lived in that disguise long enough."

"Here." Caitir shoved a bowl of parritch into her hands. "Warm yer middle while yer mind works out the details. It's hard enough on a full stomach, I cannae imagine it on an empty."

A knock sounded at the door, and Bridgette ushered the men in out of the raging black night. How long had she been unconscious? Moments before she had been starving, but now she sat and stared at the bowl in her hands. Aron said they would move again in the morning. How far were they from the keep? The Campbell men could be out searching now with their torches. They could easily follow them.

"Maybe we should leave tonight?" she said, eyeing the three men and two women. Her fear must have been written on her face.

Auld Ruadh crouched in front of her. "Dinna fash, lass. They will no find us tonight. But we must leave at first light."

"How do you know they won't find us tonight?" Elaina's chest squeezed tight. She stood, her knuckles white on the bowl still in her hands.

Auld Ruadh laid a soft hand upon her arm. "We have covered our tracks. I swear to ye that they willnae find us. Sit. Eat. Then ye will sleep. Dawn will come in a few hours." He squeezed her arm in reassurance.

When Elaina resigned herself to her stool by the fire and spooned a bite of parritch into her mouth, Auld Ruadh said, "What I want to know, is how did they ken ye were the missin' MacGregor babe in the first place?"

"My pendant came out of my shirt when Robert dragged me across the ground. Laird Campbell recognized it and looked for my birthmark."

"He looked for yer… Oh…ooohhh."

Elaina felt her face flush at Auld Ruadh's realization of what must have taken place.

"How did he ken of the birthmark? There were but a few who knew it existed." A grim look passed across Auld Ruadh's face as he turned to Aron.

Aron's expression turned equally grim. "There was a rat in the hen house. That is how Laird Campbell knew when to strike. He knew when Thamas and Mairi would be most vulnerable."

"But aren't you too young to remember?" Elaina asked Aron.

"Aye, but it is a tale that I heard recounted a hundred times over the years. All the allies of Clan MacGregor ken the story well."

"Erroll," Elaina whispered.

"What?" the three men said in unison.

"Erroll gave Robert the poison that was meant for him. They used it on me instead. You are a spy for the MacGregors. Erroll is the Campbell's spy." Elaina stared at Ruske, whose head bobbed agreement.

"He has been there since the beginning and has been the messenger each time Laird Campbell sent word of wanting to meet. In fact, I saw him the day Calum disappeared. The rat bastard." Auld Ruadh slammed his fist down on the table. "We have been waitin' for twenty years to exact revenge for Thamas and Mairi's deaths. I have nay doubt that Laird Campbell will chase us, and when he leaves his stronghold, we will do just that. Sleep now. We leave as soon as there is enough light, and we must find the MacGregors before the Campbells find us. Sleep, ladies, for tomorrow there may be war."

Chapter Thirty-Six

THE SNOWSTORM HAD EBBED, AND the sun reflected off the snow in blinding rays. Calum held her tight, and she rested her head against his chest, eyes closed, listening to his heartbeat and inhaling his scent. "Never leave me again," she whispered.

"Never." The sound of his answer rumbled against her ear.

Gripping him tighter, she looked up into his ever-changing hazel eyes—today more gold than any other color. "Kiss me?" she asked.

"Aye," he whispered, his voice thick with emotion. Taking her chin in his hand, he tilted her face toward his. The warmth of his breath held her in anticipation of the moment their lips would touch—that moment never came for Aron rudely interrupted them, shaking her until her teeth rattled.

"Wake up! We must go. Now!" He yanked her from the warm confines of the bed.

Auld Ruadh grabbed Caitir, and the men threw blankets around the women.

"What's going on?" Elaina hissed in a whisper, not knowing why except that everyone else was whispering.

"We must go," Aron repeated as he forced her out the door and into the still raging snowstorm.

Dawn was close at hand. The black of night had brightened into an ominous shade of gray. Elaina glanced over her shoulder as Aron and Auld Ruadh pushed them around the corner, and she glimpsed what had the men in an uproar. Flashes of red shown in the distance, barely visible through the drab light and the blinding snow. The British had arrived.

Aron threw Caitir up into the saddle in front of him as Ruadh hoisted

Elaina up. They headed in the opposite direction of the redcoat soldiers and disappeared into the storm, hopefully before being detected.

Elaina wanted to ask about Bridgette and Ruske, but she would have to yell over the biting gales and was not that daft. She ducked her head against the bitter winds and the stinging sleet. How in God's name would the MacGregors be able to find anything or anyone in this nonsense? It did serve to hide them from the British and the Campbells. If it was possible, she believed the storm was intensifying as the day got lighter, the sun hidden behind a curtain of churning ice and snow.

One minute she was riding, head down, in front of Auld Ruadh, and the next she lay stunned on the ground.

"Hide!" he hissed and dropped a dirk at her feet.

Caitir landed beside her a moment later with a knife of her own in hand, and the two women scrambled without question into the middle of the nearest mass of gorse bushes, the brambles and twigs scratching and pulling at their blankets. They watched as the men disappeared behind a curtain of white. The screech of metal on metal and the unmistakable cry of *"Cruachan!"* sent chills down her spine. The Campbells had announced their arrival.

Elaina and Caitir huddled for several moments, Elaina gripping the handle of her dirk so hard she thought it might break off in her hand. Even amid a raging blizzard, she began to sweat. Horses and men raced around them at an alarming rate and an incredible amount, as if they had manifested from the storm itself. Elaina caught a glimpse of tartan from under a thick coat of fur as it flew by. Her heart leaped into her throat. Could it be? Then, the most beautiful sound she had ever heard echoed through the frozen air.

"Àrd-Choille!"

She and Caitir embraced each other in relief, but their relief disintegrated as the world came crashing down on them. Men struck from the other direction. A sea of Campbells gushed through the storm. A horse fell with an earth shuddering thud and slid into the gorse bush, nearly crushing the two women. They dove out of the other side and ran toward a small grove of trees nearby. Elaina slipped on the ice, and Caitir wrenched her up as if she weighed nothing. They made it behind a tree just as a blur of red streamed by them.

"Mary, mother of Joseph." Caitir's hand went to her mouth.

Elaina crossed herself. *Hail Mary, full of grace...* The battle had turned into a free for all. They heard more than they could see. Glimpses of silver off the swords flashed, and bits of reds and browns danced in and out of the snow as the three groups fought each other. The stramash moved closer to the hidden observers. The groups were backing up...or moving forward, depending on which side you were on. A fierce hand to hand battle raged between a redcoat and a Highlander in Campbell colors. Elaina could only catch glimpses here and there, but they seemed to be moving closer toward their hiding spot. She looked at Caitir, silently questioning whether they should evacuate to the next set of trees. There was no time for an answer before the redcoat was cut down and his severed head rolled into view, his unseeing gaze resting on the women.

They took each other by the hand and ran toward a small clump of bushes that turned out to be fallen bodies instead of foliage. The women dove behind them anyway as the clanging of swords sounded close to them. Elaina tried not to look at the corpses, not wanting to know what clan they were from, but she could not escape the metallic smell of blood emanating from the fallen bodies. Ice water ran through her veins as they huddled behind the dead. They had abandoned their blankets somewhere in the storm. The wind roared in Elaina's ears along with her blood, and she squeezed Caitir's hand as another man fell. A MacGregor. Bile rose in her throat. She clamped a hand over her mouth to suppress a scream as a Campbell fell on top of the bodies they hid behind.

He rolled over, raising himself, and Erroll stared into the terrified eyes of the two women. Grinning, he lunged at Elaina and yanked her from behind the pile of dead men. The first sounds of his exuberant announcement of the women's whereabouts were cut short by Caitir's dirk slamming hilt deep into his eye. He never screamed, but Elaina could feel hers rising in her throat and pressed her hand even harder to her mouth. Caitir had to put her hand on the man's face to wrench the blade free from his skull.

Elaina stood frozen just as she had in Robert's chambers, unable to defend herself. She turned her terrified eyes away, and they came to rest on a highlander and a redcoat, their swords flashing through the snow and connecting with small sparks. There was something about the soldier that drew her attention, his stature familiar even through the swirling blizzard that would temporarily block her view of the melee. The next glimpse she caught of them she knew. Without his hat, William's black hair stood stark against the whiteness surrounding him. Her heart leapt with joy before it plummeted with sorrow. *William.* He still hunted her, and now he was embroiled in the middle of a clan war. *Damn him!* She caught Caitir's attention as the men's struggle raged closer to them. *Should they run again?*

Caitir cut her eyes away and gasped.

Elaina turned and followed her startled gaze. William had fallen. The Highlander stood over him with a foot on his chest, his sword poised to drive into the heart of her brother.

Elaina stumbled forward, her action grabbing the attention of the Highlander, and Robert's smirking face turned toward her.

"What are ye goin' to do, little mouse?" Robert applied more pressure to his sword.

Elaina's running steps stuttered to a halt. "William!" she screamed, but his eyes remained closed, his head lolled to the side. She looked from the prone figure of her brother back to Robert.

"Yer heart longs for me, lass. There is nothin' ye can do."

The unfortunate truth of the matter was that Robert was right. Elaina stood unable to move except for the trembling in her body. She gripped the hilt of the dirk harder, afraid she might drop it.

"Ye had yer chance and now it is gone." Robert turned back to William, both hands gripping the hilt of his sword.

The sound of the MacGregor war cry shredding her throat startled her as much as it surprised Robert. He froze, his sword touching William's chest and his eyes wide as he turned toward the woman in a Campbell arisaid flying at him, dirk brandished in her hand. An amused smirk spread across his face as he started to press down on the hilt of his sword only to have his legs kicked out from under him.

William rolled onto his hands and knees as Elaina landed on Robert Campbell's back, driving her dirk deep under his ribs and up as her father had taught her. She had no time to check if he was dead or if William was injured before she was wrenched from Robert's back by her hair and the icy touch of steel pressed against her throat. She looked up into the leering face of Laird Campbell.

"Hello again," he said as he yanked her backward, putting more distance between her and the now upright figure of her brother.

"Give her to me." William held out a hand toward his sister. "She is wanted for murder." His gaze rested on her, not relaying any emotion. Even after she'd saved his life, he would still arrest her.

"Have you brought the deed to my land?" Laird Campbell asked while continuing to back away.

William moved two steps forward. "She is my prisoner," he said instead of answering the question.

"Nay. She is mine. What should it matter to the British if she were dead? I will take care of your murderess. It is my right as she has killed both of my sons."

Elaina's gazed flickered to Robert's form lying face down in the snow, her dirk protruding from his back. Tears stung her eyes as the laird pulled her head farther back and pressed his knife harder against her throat. He was going to kill her right here and there was nothing William could do about it.

William's gaze moved to Laird Campbell's. "It is my duty as a British officer to bring her in. Alive." He pulled a broadsheet from the inside of his coat and held it up for Laird Campbell to see.

"You can take that broadsheet and shove it up your pretty little arse. The woman is mine, and I will gut her like a hog if you come any closer."

"Let her go." William pulled a pistol from his belt and leveled the barrel at the laird's head.

Elaina glanced up into the laird's face.

The man never flinched. "She will be dead before you can pull that trigger." His voice never faltered, and he grinned down into Elaina's face. "Are you ready then, to meet your maker and burn in hell with your father?"

Elaina heard the click of the pistol, but William's gun didn't fire. She felt the blade of the dirk penetrate her skin as the terrifying grin on the laird's face froze. The cold steel sliced across her throat, and she fell face down in the snow with the laird's body crushing her.

She drew freezing air into her lungs as best she could and swallowed—the pain of it bringing tears to her eyes. A pool of crimson spread through the blanket of white in front of her face like dye on fabric. She watched in fascination as the edges turned pink, then a brighter shade of red. Her fingers found their way to her throat, and she could feel the warmth of her life's blood as it left her body. Yet she lived. She could breathe. The crushing weight lifted from her and a pair of hands tenderly turned her over.

The horror filled gaze of her husband looked down on her.

"Calum," she whispered, choking back a sob. She squeezed her eyes closed against the pain of speaking and her overwhelming gratitude to God above that her husband lived.

"Dinna talk, *mo chridhe*," he said as he tore a piece of his kilt and pressed it against her throat. Then his lips were on hers with a burning fierceness that stole her breath. "I was afraid I would never see ye again." He swallowed hard as he held the cloth to her throat, fear and worry written all over his face.

"You look terrible." She managed a slight laugh as she studied his bruised face and sallow complexion. "But you are alive." Her tears began to well. "Are you truly? Or am I dead?"

"No, *mo chridhe*. I am as alive as are you."

"How bad is it?" she croaked out against the pressure of his hand.

"Nay that bad." His eyes betrayed his words.

"The laird?" She tried to rise, her mind snapping back to their present situation.

"Lay still," Calum ordered, forcing her shoulders back down. "He is dead." Her husband turned her so she could see the empty stare of her enemy, the handle of Calum's knife protruding from his neck.

She stared unbelieving. Was she truly free of the Campbells? Could it be that simple? Father and son gone within minutes and the doors to her parents' murders closed forever, twenty years separating their deaths. "Thank you," she whispered.

"No other deed has brought me more satisfaction." He kissed her forehead.

"William?"

"I am here." Her brother took her hand.

"Thank God." She looked into his brilliant blue gaze and saw the first emotions he had exhibited in a long time. Love and fear.

He lifted Calum's hand and the piece of kilt. His gaze dipped down to her neck.

She thought she saw a little color drain from his face. "I'm fine," she whispered, trying to sit up, but the hands of her husband and her brother pushed her back into the snow.

"Dinna bloody move," Calum chastised her again. He looked at William, questioning.

William studied him for a heartbeat and then Calum's head flew back as William landed a punch to his jaw. "That is for marrying my sister without my permission."

Calum shook his head and rubbed his chin with his free hand. A tense moment of glaring passed between the two men, and Elaina wondered if Calum meant to return the deed. A slow grin spread across his face before he dipped his head at William. "I'll give ye that one. With all sincerity, I beg yer forgiveness."

"Granted. And as for you…" William turned his gaze to Elaina, his eyes searching hers before looking off into the distance where the sound of fighting could still be heard. He closed his eyes and sighed. When he opened them again, they were filled with tears and pain and she knew that his duty called to him. Ever the honorable soldier.

She would go with him and take her punishment. Her attention turned to her husband whom she had not touched in months. "I do love you so," she whispered as she caressed his bruised cheek. Her tears spilled down her temples, freezing into her hair. "Never forget that. I have loved you like no other, Calum MacKinnon, and I will love you into eternity. I will see you again."

The realization of the meaning of her words did not readily appear on Calum's countenance, but when it did horror, filled his eyes before he wiped his face free of any emotion except love. He fought to produce even a modicum of a smile as he leaned down and softly planted his lips against her own.

She felt him choking down his emotions.

He pulled back. "I will love ye into eternity," he whispered, then he turned his pained eyes to William. He nodded and took William's hand, replacing his on the cloth he held against Elaina's throat.

William looked away, the muscles in his jaw clenched tight.

For several moments, the howling wind and the distant sound of a battle still raging filled her ears. She watched her brother struggle with his obligations.

"What kind of monster do you think I am, Elaina?" he said, turning an accusing eye on her.

"You are no monster, William. They are dead. I know that your duty calls to you. I understand who you are and what you stand for, and I will face my punishment as the courts see fit."

William closed his eyes and sighed. "I did not conspire with Hugh Graham to break you free from that bloody castle only to drag you to the gallows, you foolish child. Go as far as you can," he commanded Calum as if he were a member of his regiment. "Keep her safe and love her well. As for you, Elaina Spencer MacGregor MacKinnon," he whispered and pressed his cold lips upon her forehead. "I will also love you into eternity." He held her gaze for but a moment before he rose and laid a hand on Calum's shoulder.

Elaina could see him squeeze it and then he disappeared into the storm, yelling orders to his men.

Calum wasted no time scooping Elaina into his arms and fleeing in the opposite direction.

Chapter Thirty Seven

THE MOTLEY-LOOKING CREW ARRIVED AT the crofter's cottage late in the day, starved and half-frozen.

Auld Ruadh stepped onto the porch, avoiding a rotten spot in the boards, and rapped lightly on the door. After a moment that seemed like a century, it creaked open a hair's breadth and a pair of suspicious whiskey-colored eyes peered out at them.

Auld Ruadh stood with his hat in his hand. "Mistress. We mean ye nay harm. We are only in need of a place to rest our weary bones. If ye would be so kind as to let us bunk up in yer barn for the evenin', the men and myself could patch this old porch up if'n yer husband has the supplies to do it." He looked down at the weathered hole where the boards had rotted away from neglect.

The silver-haired woman eyed them warily for a long moment, and Elaina all but gave up hope, slumping against Calum's leg, her head spinning.

"Whut's wrong wi' that one?" she finally said, hitching her chin at Elaina.

"She is tired is all—"

"And injured," Auld Ruadh blurted out, cutting Calum off.

"Whut happened?"

"She was hurt in battle. We were all fightin'," Auld Ruadh continued speaking for the group.

"Nearby?" The door creaked open wider, and the woman's wide eyes darted around the surrounding landscape.

"Nay. At least half a day's ride."

"We can pay you," Elaina added, tired of standing in one spot. The lady of the house needed to make her decision so she could either lay down or they could be on their way to the next house, if there was a next house.

The woman's eyes lit up at the promise of payment, and a smile spread across her wrinkled face. "Well, why didna ye say so. Come right in." She opened the door wide.

The group hesitated but a moment before filing inside. They filled the tiny room near to overflowing. It's incredible what the offer of money will do to a hostess. She didn't even ask how much they would pay her, but set about stoking the fire, prattling on about feeding them and how her husband had died the winter before and her only son not long after.

Calum planted Elaina on a stool close to the hearth, and she watched their host, spry for her years, flit about the room and talk nonstop. Apparently, guests were few in these parts. The woman, who introduced herself as Essie, stood willowy and tall with her hair pulled tight in a bun at her neck.

"Now," she paused for breath, hands on her hips. "If ye're true on what ye said about the porch, my husband's tools be in the shed and I believe ye may find some boards if ye look hard enough. I just haven't had the strength about me since he died." She turned to stare into the fire, wiping at a stray tear with the corner of her apron.

"We'll get right on it," Aron said. He and Auld Ruadh lit out for the barn in search of supplies.

"Why don't ye join them? It may take all of ye to accomplish the task." Essie addressed Calum. "Me and the lasses will handle matters in the house."

Calum cast a worried glance at Elaina as if unsure whether to leave the three women alone.

Elaina nodded at him to go. She would be fine.

With reluctance, he joined the others outside.

"Next things next." Essie turned a burning gaze to Elaina and Caitir. "Are ye prisoner? Have the men kidnapped ye, then, and…" She dipped her chin to Elaina's lap.

"What? No!" Elaina exclaimed. "Calum is my husband."

"Does he beat ye, then?" Essie hissed in a whisper as she studied Elaina's battered face. "And ye." She shot a pointed look to Caitir. "Are ye married to one of them too? The big one that looks like a simpleton?"

Elaina couldn't hide her snicker but clamped a hand to her throat, the sound irritating her wound.

"Nay! He's my cousin."

"We can poison them, if ye wish. Leslie used to beat me somethin' terrible, but no more." Essie rummaged through several little glass jars in her cupboard.

"Nay, no poison!" Caitir grabbed her arm. "They are our family."

"Sometimes family or no, ye just cannae take the nonsense any longer."

Elaina cast her eyes to the soup that had filled the room with its enticing aroma and wondered if it was safe to eat. She hadn't witnessed her putting anything strange in there, but then again, she hadn't known the woman was tetched either, or she would have watched closer.

"Settle yerself, Essie," Caitir said. "These men are honorable. They saved us. They didna do this. Campbell men are responsible." She gently touched the bandage on Elaina's neck.

"Campbell?" Essie looked at Elaina, questioning.

"Aye."

"My husband was a Campbell."

Elaina's heart dropped to her feet. They sat in the home of the enemy.

The woman spit into the fire. Her pale brown eyes burned with hate when she turned back to her guests. "To hell wi' the Campbells. I put up with Leslie's whorin' and beatin's for many a year until it became clear he had twisted my son against me and taught him his evil ways, God rest their souls." She crossed herself.

"What happened to them?" Caitir asked, her eyes darting to Elaina and back to the woman.

"They got their comeuppance."

Did that mean she had killed her husband *and* her son? Elaina swooned a little on the stool.

"Well, then let me look at yer injury, my dear," Essie's voice took on a sweet, motherly tone.

Elaina cut her eyes at Caitir, who looked equally disturbed but shrugged. They were women, and not Campbell women, so Elaina prayed they had nothing to fear.

Essie's ministrations were gentle as they untied the wrapping from around Elaina's neck, giving a small gasp when she caught sight of the wound.

"Oh, *mo phàiste.* That willnae do at all. Here. Drink." She shoved a jug into Elaina's hands.

Elaina sniffed it suspiciously.

"'Tis only whiskey. Drink it, or ye'll regret it when I sew ye up," Essie barked as she strolled into the other room.

"What in God's name?" Elaina whispered to Caitir as she peered into the jug.

"I dinna ken what the hell we have gotten ourselves into, but I think as long as we are no men, we are safe. Mayhap she thinks us kindred spirits with the beatin's and such. I have never been happier to no have a pair of bollocks between my legs in my life."

"I'll second that," Elaina said and turned the bottle up, taking the tiniest sip. It tasted like whiskey.

"Drink it." Essie returned to the room and tipped the jug against Elaina's lips, dribbling some down her chin.

By the time the men had finished hammering on the porch, Elaina herself was quite drunk and sewn up thanks to Essie, the poison master. She had a gentle touch, and Caitir inspected the woman's handy work when completed, nodding in appreciation.

"Does it look like a"—*hiccup*—"necklace?" Elaina asked, touching the fine stitching.

"Keep yer fingers off it!" Essie barked.

Elaina jerked her hand away, nearly falling off the stool.

The men came through the door, kicking snow off their boots before entering.

"Look, darlin'," Elaina slurred to Calum as she pointed to her neck. "New as good."

"Christ, how much have ye had to drink?" Calum asked, catching Elaina as she wobbled again.

"Enough to get the job done," Essie said. "Let's eat. Maybe that'll sober her up a little."

Calum held Elaina's arm as he moved her to the bench on one side of the table. Essie, Caitir, Calum, and Elaina sat at the table. Auld Ruadh and Aron found spots on the floor close to the hearth.

Essie pushed a bowl of soup in front of Elaina and Calum both. When she turned back to the fire, Elaina leaned close to Calum, "Dinna worry, love."

Calum cut his eyes at her odd attempt at a Scottish accent.

"I dinna think it's poisoned, but I would let the old lady take the first bite."

"I've seen ye drunk, but I dinna think I've ever seen ye this drunk. For Christ's sa—"

Elaina cupped his manhood, before patting it roughly.

Calum grabbed her hand, freezing like a stone. "What the hell is wrong with ye?" he whispered out of the corner of his mouth.

"I am so glad that I dinna have one of those on my person," Elaina slurred. "But it's quite nice on you." She cast him a wink before turning her attention back to her soup. She dipped up a spoonful and sniffed it, glancing at Essie, who slid a spoonful into her mouth. Elaina shrugged and did the same.

Calum stared at her before glancing at his bowl, then at Essie, who chuckled at him across the table. "I dinna ken what the hell took place while I was outside, but it's makin' me a wee bit uncomfortable," he whispered to Elaina.

"Ye are safe, *mo Choille*," she slurred.

"*Mo Choille*?"

"My love...right?"

"*Mo chridhe*? My heart. Eat yer soup." Calum cut his eyes to Caitir, who snickered in-between mouthfuls.

The meal finished with little incident. Caitir helped Essie clean up, and Calum helped his drunk wife out to the barn.

"We dinna have to sleep in the loft," Calum said, holding Elaina by the waist as she attempted to climb the ladder, her foot slipping off the rung.

"But I want to," she pouted.

Calum huffed a sigh and stuck his shoulder under her rear, supporting most of her weight as she perilously made her way up.

"Ah." Elaina flopped down on the hay, her arms outstretched. The roof of the barn swirled in circles above her.

"What in the hell went on while we were outside?" Calum asked, plopping himself down next to her.

"She fixed me up. Do ye want to see my pretty little necklace?" Elaina started to untie the new wrapping Essie had secured over her handiwork.

"Nay, I've seen it, remember. Dinna take that off." Calum placed a hand on hers.

The warmth of his touch on her cold skin, the nicker of the horses below, and the sweet smell of fresh hay, not hay sullied by prisoners and rats, lulled Elaina into a drowsy, seductive trance.

"Come here," she whispered, reaching for her husband.

"Shh."

"What? I've missed you." Her hands were on the ties of his breeks.

"Elaina."

"I don't know how you wear these blasted things all the time. You were right. I should have worn a kilt. A cock would come in handy when you have to take a piss in the freezing cold while wearing a pair of breeks, 'cause I will tell you, it is no fun when you're a woman having to squat and your bum is hanging out in the wind freezing. Well, if your cock is out in the wind, is it freezing too or is it always that warm?" She grabbed his crotch again.

"Jesus Christ," Calum muttered over the muffled laughter coming from the barn below.

"Ye got it under control up there, brother? Ye need Auld Ruadh here to come lend a hand?"

"I'm not going up there," Auld Ruadh sputtered.

"I have everything well in hand," Elaina called out.

"Aye, I bet ye do, lass," Aron replied.

Calum slid a hand down his face, shaking his head.

"Well, I do," Elaina said.

"Elain—"

"We have before. While they were all around the fire, remember. You didn't care."

"Aye...er...that was a little different. They were no directly below us, and I really wadna care to reenact our wedding night."

This time, Caitir's laughter floated up through the boards, and Calum fell flat on his back, shaking his head.

Elaina crawled on her hands and knees to the edge of the loft and peered over at the group below.

Calum grabbed her ankles to keep her from toppling over the side.

"If you could, give us but a minute of privacy," she announced much to the entertainment of those below.

"That's all it'll take is a minute," Auld Ruadh called up.

"Well, maybe a tad longer, but someone is a little performance shy at the momen—"

"Dammit, Elaina," Calum growled, hauling her back from the edge.

Hysterical laughter ensued. "Aye, we'll give a minute, but no more. Make it snappy. I'm tired, and I want to sleep," Caitir called up between choked gasps for air. The sounds of shuffling reached the loft, and the laughter dwindled as the party below moved out of the barn.

"Now." Elaina turned on Calum. "You have no excuse. Off with them." She tugged at his breeks.

"What has gotten into you?"

"Well, I wish for it to be you, but seeing as how you are stalling, 'tis only whiskey." Elaina undid the belt holding her arisaid around her and let it fall to the hay floor of the loft. Her fingers fumbled, trying to find the end of the strings in the neck of her shift.

"Dear God," Calum whispered, staring at her in the moonlight. The cloud cover had lifted, and the full moon cast its glow through the interior of their nest.

"Well, thank you, but it's nothing you haven't seen before."

"What have they done to ye?" He took her wrists, his fingers skimming the surface of the raw skin encircling them.

"It's…" she shook her head.

The moonlight cutting through the window of the loft cast a hazy glow upon the straw on the floor and her gaze focused on that instead of Calum's worried eyes. She shivered as he grabbed the hem of her shift and, gentle as a spring breeze, slid it over her head.

"Who did this to ye?" he whispered, touching a bruise on her shoulder before tracing the pale pink scar across her belly and up under her breast.

"They…I mean…they are only battle scars."

His fingers traced the scratches down her face. He found all the bruised and scraped places that peppered the landscape of Elaina's body. "Battle scars?" he said with a hardness to his voice.

"I received this one when Robert dragged me back to the horse after I tried to run." Elaina's chin touched her chest as she scoured her body, seeing her injuries for the first time as well. Her eyes followed Calum's searching fingers and had to admit that his concern and gentle touch made heat travel to certain parts of her body, though her skin prickled with the cold.

"These on my face are when Doireann the Evil attacked me when Robert had me hidden in his mother's chambers."

"Why were you hidden in his chambers?" Calum's fingers paused their exploration.

Elaina cleared her throat. "He was hiding me from Laird Campbell."

"Why would Robert care to hide you from his father?"

"Laird Campbell meant to have me before Hugh handed over the land at Balquhidder." Her lip trembled, and she drew her knees up, burying her face in them.

"Elaina. Look at me," Calum whispered.

She shook her head.

"*Mo Chridhe.*" His firm hand found her chin and lifted her head until he forced her to meet his gaze. "What did he do to ye?"

The tears she fought so hard to hold back fell. "That's just it, Calum. I don't know what he did or didn't do. He drugged me, and when I awoke, I was in nothing but my shift and tied to his bed. He…he was drunk and said he could not let his father have what was his. He told me he loved me. He asked me to kill him." Elaina's words came in hiccupping sobs. "I could have killed him twice, Calum, but I hadn't the courage."

A tense silence thundered through the loft, and Elaina collapsed onto the hay. Her sobs filled the night air, joined only by the nickering of the horses below.

"Elaina? What did he do to you?" Calum's question came out in a low growl.

She knew that she disgusted him. She was unclean, ruined by a mad man.

"Elaina?" He grabbed her by the shoulders and snatched her up, forcing her to look at him. "Answer me. What happened?" Calum shook her, his eyes dark as pitch.

She could hear his teeth grinding in his effort not to strike her. "Just do it," she whispered through her tears.

"Do what?"

"Hit me. Beat me. Punish me for my crimes." Her words came between choked sobs.

"What crimes have ye committed, Elaina?" His fierce growls dropped to a whisper.

"I… He… I don't know if he…"

"Ye dinna ken if he *what*? If he raped ye?"

She nodded her response, unable to speak.

Calum roared, his voice echoing off the rafters. He released her only to pick up a discarded hammer and hurl it against the wall. He kicked beams and slammed his fists into the walls until his knuckles bled. Anything he laid his hands on he threw.

Elaina cowered where he'd left her, terrified to move or make a sound. She had never witnessed this side of him. She clenched her trembling knees tighter to her chest and waited for him to attack. When he finally turned on her, she curled herself into a ball on the hay, anticipating the first blow.

His ragged breaths sounded close to her ear, and she tensed, determined not to cry out. She would take her punishment in silence. Instead, Calum's body curved around her own and he embraced her, his lips gentle upon her head.

"Why," his voice shook as he whispered in her ear. "Why would ye ever think I would strike out at ye for anythin' such as that? Have I ever laid a hand to ye before?"

Elaina shook her head. She couldn't look at him.

"*Mo chridhe—*"

"I am soiled, Calum. I understand if you do not want me any longer. I can return to the colonies. My father has friends there."

"Look at me," he said, forcing her to face him with one trembling hand. "Ye are not soiled. Ye dinna ken if he even… And I wadna give one damn if he did. I am no angry with you. I am furious at that devil and at myself for not protecting you, for letting all of this happen in the first place. I never should have let you go. I love ye. I want to be with ye always, if you will have me. When I spoke my vows, I meant them. I will never leave ye until death takes me."

"If I will have you? I don't blame you for anything, Calum. The guilt rests on my shoulders. My stubbornness, once again, is my downfall." Elaina buried her head in his chest and released all her fears, all her sorrow and guilt, into his loving embrace. She didn't deserve this man and his enduring understanding, but she needed him and if he would have her, she would keep him.

Calum wrapped her in his arms, the heat of his body engulfing her. He lay her back onto the hay, the pieces of straw rough and poking her skin, but she didn't care. She required him—all of him—and she fumbled madly with his clothes.

"Ye dinna have to, *mo chridhe*," he whispered into her hair.

"I need to. If he… If—"

Calum silenced her fumbling words with a kiss. "I understand. Dinna say it."

She nodded, tears coming to her eyes once again. As always, Calum read her thoughts. They must couple in case Robert *had* raped her. If she were with child… She choked on her sobs.

"Dinna cry, hen."

He tried to be gentle with her, but Elaina would have none of it. She rolled him to his back so that she could have control and give herself what she needed—a full release—an escape from the nightmare of the last several weeks. Now was not the time for gentle. She required the madness and the fury to be driven from her body, her soul, and her mind. To hell with the others she could hear talking outside the barn.

Calum clamped a hand over her mouth, and she bit his finger.

He raised an eyebrow at her, his teeth clenched. "It's like that, is it?" he growled.

She nodded.

Flipping her to her back, he pinned her arms above her head with one hand, the other still firmly over her mouth. "I'm tryin' to play nice," he whispered in her ear.

Elaina wrapped her legs around his back, locking her ankles and squeezing him to her.

"Ye dinna want me to play nice?" The side of his mouth crooked up, and she caught the briefest glimpse of the fear he harbored before he veiled it behind his teasing smile. The sympathy and devotion churning in his eyes threatened to melt her through the floor of the loft.

She shook her head at his question, biting his finger again and pulling him tighter to her. She lost herself in the bruising and desperate joining as Calum gave her everything she needed and more, releasing all the anxiety and fear consuming her. His hand muffled her cries as he buried his own in her hair.

As she lay gasping for breath beside her husband, the soft rumble of the voices below made their way into the loft and she wondered through the mist of coming sleep just when the crew had given up and returned to the barn.

As the sweat that drenched their naked bodies cooled in the frigid night air, Elaina began shivering, but her body heavy with sleep and gratification refused to move from the crook of her husband's arm to cover herself.

Calum pulled their plaids over the top of them and wrapped his arms around her, pulling her closer.

She smiled for the first time in days. She was home. Wherever her husband was, that was her home, and she rejoiced at being safe in his arms again.

"Elaina?" he whispered into the night.

"Mmmm?"

"What was all of that about in the house? With the soup?"

"Oh. It's nothing," Elaina mumbled against his chest. "She's a Campbell. She poisoned her husband and her son, but it's fine. She ate it first."

Chapter Thirty-Eight

"WHAT IS IT?" ELAINA MUMBLED, her brain foggy with sleep and a pounding headache.

"Get yer clothes on. We're headin' out," Calum said in a harsh whisper.

With great effort, she peeled an eyelid open to a squint. "It's not even daylight yet." She rolled over and covered her head.

"There's moonlight. Come on." He snatched the plaid from her naked form, and she broke out in gooseflesh, which did nothing to help the boulders bouncing around inside her head.

"Stop it. Give it back." She reached for the plaid, but he pulled it out of her reach. "Why are you acting like an arse?"

"I havenae slept a wink all night thinkin' that witch is goin' to sneak out here and curse us all. My wame is in a knot, and I dinna ken if it's from worry or her poison soup. We are leavin' before she wakes up and tries to feed us anythin' else." Calum dressed Elaina like a child throughout his rant.

Elaina snickered, shooting blinding flashes of light through her head. "I don't know how you expect me to ride on the back of a horse with my head feeling like a smashed...a smashed... Well, feeling smashed."

"Ye shouldna have drank so much. Let's go."

"But I promised her money," Elaina argued as Calum pulled her toward the ladder leading out of the loft. She looked down and squeezed her eyes shut against the spinning world.

"Send her down. I'll catch her," Aron hissed from below.

"I don't need you to catch me."

"Are ye sure of that?" Calum asked, gripping the back of her arisaid as she wobbled precariously over the edge of the loft.

"No," she grumbled.

With her feet safely on the floor, the group led the horses as quietly as possible from the barn. Auld Ruadh sprinted from the direction of the porch, his knees nearly colliding with his chin and him moving faster than Elaina had ever seen him move before. "I left her clink by the door, but I swear I heard her up movin' around, mumblin' to herself. I'm sure she was talkin' to the Diabhal himself."

"Oh, haud yer wheest. Ye're not scaring anyone with that nonsense," Aron said, but his eyes darted toward the house.

"Sit here if ye want and have the hex put on ye. I'm getting' out of here." Auld Ruadh threw himself onto his horse as if he were but a youth and lit out, leaving them all staring after him.

They mounted their horses and set off after him, not nearly as fast, however. Not until the surrounding snow glowed a faint yellow in the cast of a lamplight being held high, and a woman's voice called out something in Gaelic that Elaina couldn't understand. She didn't know if it was the fact that the woman was awake and caught them leaving or if it was whatever she said that lit a fire under the menfolk, but it didn't take long to catch up with Auld Ruadh.

"Doubt me again when I tell ye a witch is at yer back," he said, "and ye'll all be frogs in her fryin' pan by nightfall."

"No one said she was a witch." Elaina rolled her eyes. "She poisoned her husband and her son, is all."

"Ye better sleep with one eye open, *mo bhràthair*," Aron said. "Poison is all," he mocked Elaina.

"Well, I'm just saying you don't have to worry about being turned into a frog, although it would be a nice improvement from the horse's arse that you currently are."

"Aye, that's the truth of it," Caitir said as the group did nothing to hide their mirth at the little exchange.

"Aren't ye the witty one, miss ruttin' in the hayloft?" Aron tugged at a strand of Elaina's hair, sending a shot of pain like an arrow through her head.

Calum punched him in the arm.

"What's that for? I'm only teasin'?" Aron rubbed his arm, casting Calum a withering glance.

"Now's not the time for teasin'," Calum answered with a glare. "Now is the time for ridin'."

Aron cast Elaina a puzzled look before he kicked his horse on ahead of her and Calum.

"Can we leave him behind?" Elaina asked, leanin' back into Calum's chest.

He kissed her on top of her head. "I'm afraid ye're stuck with him, *mo chridhe*. He is family, after all."

"We should have let her turn him into a toad," Elaina grumbled, closing her eyes and trying to block out the sniffles and snorts of those around her.

Chapter Thirty-Nine

C ALUM SAT HER UPON THE rock jutting out from the face of the mountain and reached up, untying the wrapping from around her throat. "It looks good. I think it will heal nicely."

She nodded, looking back at the mountains they had traversed, thinking of the valley that lay on the other side where so much blood had been shed all because of a girl orphaned in a foreign land. The thought of it weighed heavily upon her heart. The last of her family was gone. She would probably never see William again. Something came to rest on her back, and Elaina looked over her shoulder at the top of Caitir's redhead. She reached around and patted her friend's head. Aron came riding over the hill followed by Auld Ruadh, and she sat up straight, taking her arms from Calum. Aron and Auld Ruadh had backtracked to be sure no redcoats or Campbells pursued the group.

"Is it over? Is it done, then?" she asked the men as they dismounted.

"Aye, seems as so," Aron answered.

A third horse and rider materialized out of the drifting snow. Elaina stared at the wavy-headed figure with incomprehension as he slid from the saddle and knelt before her, his head bowed. He held out a sheathed sword in a grave presentation. "I believe ye lost something, mistress," he said, raising his eyes to meet hers.

"Ainsley? But I thought—"

"I thought ye were dead?" Caitir finished Elaina's sentence for her, and the women threw their arms around the stunned young man weeping and laughing and smothering him with kisses.

"Ye should count yerself lucky, lad." Auld Ruadh chuckled while taking a seat on the large rock. "It's nay so often a man has two lassies fawnin' over him at the same time."

Ainsley turned crimson as he handed Angus's sword to Elaina.

"How?" she asked, staring at the object in her hand.

"I was…um…relieving myself when the Campbells attacked the camp. I fled to find Calum and yerselves." His gaze roamed to the other men present. "To get help to rescue Caitir."

"See," Elaina elbowed Calum, whispering, "Taking a piss can be fortuitous."

Shaking his head, Calum rolled his eyes. "I dare say that every time ye relieve yerself, ye get assaulted or kidnapped."

"Nay more pissin' in private for you," Aron said.

Elaina cast him a withering glare.

"By the time I caught sight of the redcoats," Ainsley continued, casting Aron a puzzled look, "ye had already stolen Elaina from them and the camp was in an uproar. I watched for a little while, tryin' see if they kenned in which direction ye had left, and spotted wee Angus's sword propped against a tree. I snuck in and retrieved it. I tried to follow the regiment as best I could, but the blasted storm overtook me and I became lost. Thought I would damn near freeze to death. I did find this, however." He placed her lost MacGregor broach in her hand. "Not too far from where I found that, I spied a piece of tartan I thought tore from yer kilt, making me think I was on the right path. Someone had carved the word *'trap'* into the root of a tree, which spooked me and I laid low. Then came the storm. I spent weeks huntin' and searchin', followin' every clue I could find, which were slim to none. I have been all over this damned countryside lookin' for ye. I returned to the Grahams only to learn from Letitia that Hugh had left weeks before and she had no inklin' where he was. So, I came back this way to search again."

"Did ye no think to ask around?" Aron said.

Ainsley glared at him. "Aye, I did. I'm no dolt, only I didna want to draw attention to the fact that ye had taken the mistress from the redcoats." He turned his attention back to Elaina. "I had given up and was climbing to higher ground to try to find anythin' that resembled a group of Highlanders on the run when I spied these two and tried to chase them down." Ainsley paused for breath and his eyes dropped to Elaina's bandaged throat. "What happened to yer neck, mistress? How do ye have Caitir? Why are all of ye bloody and battered?" It was as if he were truly seeing all of them for the first time. "What have I missed?"

"It's a long story, lad," Auld Ruadh said with a sigh. "We can fill ye in on the way home."

"I can never repay you. Any of you." Elaina studied her family. Love crashed over her in a drowning wave and she tried to choke down her emotions. Family. The word resonated through her being. She was not alone in this vast world. She looked with regret and sorrow at the valley below—the valley where her brother had given her freedom.

"I am sorry." Calum followed her gaze. He laid his head upon his wife's and, putting his arm around her, pulled her close. "I ken ye will miss him, but I will try to make ye as happy as I can."

"As will I." Caitir hugged Elaina from behind, laying her head on her cousin's back.

"And I." Auld Ruadh slid his arm around his niece's waist.

"Aye, and I suppose even I, but I cannae speak for Ma," Aron said with a chuckle, laying his large hand on top of his sister-in-law's head.

Ainsley stared at them, confused.

As much as Elaina missed her mother and father, and now William, she had found her place in the world. She belonged with these wild, fighting, loyal, sarcastic heathens. These were her people.

She turned to Calum, "Take me home?" she asked.

"Aye," he whispered, planting a kiss upon her lips.

"Is anyone going to tell me what happened?" Ainsley grumbled in frustration.

Elaina gave him another hug and a kiss on the cheek. "Aye," she said with a laugh., "But let's bloody get out of here while we can."

TO BE CONTINUED...

Thank You

A great big THANK YOU for giving up the most precious asset you own…your time. I hope you thoroughly enjoyed *Betrayal's Legacy*, and if so, I would love for you to share your experience with your friends and the world through avenues such as Facebook, Instagram, Twitter, Google, and/or Pinterest. I would love for you to leave an honest review on your favorite retailer's site. Reviews are one of the best gifts you can give an author!

To learn more about upcoming sequels (yes, that word ends in an 's'), you can swing on over to **http://www.reneegallant.com** and sign up for my newsletter to see what exciting things we have planned for the future. Emails are always welcome too. I love hearing from my readers!

You can also find me at:
https://www.facebook.com/thewriterenee
https://twitter.com/thewriterenee
https://instagram.com/thewriterenee
https://pinterest.com/thewriterenee

About The Author

Renée Gallant is an author, business owner, avid reader, Lyme Warrior, and lover of all things historical. Learning is a never-ending process she thoroughly enjoys. She is even learning to tolerate computers.

Residing with her husband in the great state of Texas, Renée is the mother of four and grandmother of six. She spends her free time gardening, hanging with dinosaurs, painting, coloring, or sitting with one or more little person on her lap and staring at weird YouTube videos.

Strap on your broadsword, grab up your targe, and prepare to do battle! You're invited to join Renée Gallant on the harrowing journey she refers to as her writing life. It's exciting, occasionally hilarious, and at times terrifying, but it is NEVER dull!

http://www.reneegallant.com/

CPSIA information can be obtained
at www.ICGtesting.com
Printed in the USA
FSHW021144130820
72935FS

9 781734 066630